Eden

JAMIE LISA FORBES

Pronghorn Press
pronghornpress.org

For my mother, Letty Coykendall

1

ROWEN FLEW UP the courthouse stairs two at a time, nearly smacking into the white double doors. No doubt about it, he was late. Damn. He'd look like a fool to anyone passing by, frozen there with his nose up against the hand grime on the paint. If he burst in, the judge might throw him out in front of the whole town. He pressed his ear against the door. No good. All he could hear was muffled drones. There wasn't any other way. If he wanted to watch Franklin White's murder trial, he'd have to go in.

He pushed the door open just enough to squeeze through and nearly shut it again at the tangy wave of human sweat that broke over him. Every bench in the courtroom was filled, and though the ceiling fan whirred overhead, only a dribble of air spiraled down. Throughout the benches, women's fans fluttered.

Rowen crouched to avoid the bailiff's scrutiny and scooted into one of the back rows. The judge frowned as the door shut, and Rowen ducked down even farther to avoid notice. Slowly, he eased himself into the seat and scanned the rows around him. It had been three months or more since he'd last seen any of this throng: the whole community of White Rock, Purdie County, North Carolina.

He was smashed next to Sanford Hollinger, who owned the Sears store, nearly suffocated by the large man's flesh and perspiration.

Hollinger whispered, "Rowen Hart, I ain't seen you since your daddy's funeral three months back. How ya been?"

The downside to Rowen's planning was staring him right in the face. This wasn't what he had come for, to be the object this crowd pecked over. He fixed his gaze straight ahead.

"All right."

Bowman, and all of them here—he resented them every bit as much as he had at the funeral. He should have figured that people would be curious and that if he showed up, he'd have to explain himself. He shouldn't have come and he wouldn't have, except that Franklin White had been such a fixture in his daddy's house, one of the men who had congregated on the wraparound porch, complimenting his mama on her lemon bars and smoking with his daddy, while they all speculated on tobacco prices next season.

Eden

Hard to believe the news that last Christmas, before Rowen's own fortunes had upturned, mild-mannered White had shot his brother-in-law. As much shame as Rowen felt, he was itching to see how much lower White would fall than he himself had. Heck, if White went to prison, that had to be worse than his own daddy killing himself faced with bills he couldn't pay.

After the funeral, he and his mama had lost the house in town. They'd had to move out to the country. Though it wasn't in the newspaper, like this murder trial, everyone here would have heard by now that his mama was ill. "Troubled in mind," that was the expression they'd murmur, soon as they spotted him, same as they'd murmured at his daddy's open grave.

Why hadn't he heeded the omen of those double doors and turned around?

"Why are you so late?" asked Hollinger.

Rowen pretended to be engrossed in the scene up front, but Hollinger elbowed him. Seems like the trial alone could have kept the fat fool occupied.

"Chores," Rowen answered.

"Chores? Didn't you get up early enough?"

Second time he'd heard something like that today. First time he'd heard it was when Adeline shoved a mound of laundry into his arms just as he reached the front door. Another hitch in his planning: He hadn't figured on laundry. Laundry had never come his way at the old house.

"I gotta get out of here," he'd pleaded. "The trial's about to start."

"What come out of your mouth just now, I can't even make it out. A goat bleatin'. That's what it sounded like."

JAMIE LISA FORBES

"May I please do the laundry when I get home?"

"Folks wanting to poke their noses in the town's mess is up before daylight getting their work done. Your mopin' don't do nothin' to me. Your mama dreams you're off to that university in the fall. I pray that it's so. But as you wile away your last days among us, you can start classes in the College of Life, where everybody's sheets, including your own, are washed and hung out."

Hollinger's frog eyes were fixed on him, waiting.

"I wouldn't think you'd have chores anyhow. Y'all still got that colored woman, don't you? Adeline?"

"Yes, sir."

Hollinger elbowed him in the ribs. "Let that be a lesson, all women'll do that to you sooner or later." He gestured toward the front. "The lawyers been arguin' over whether the little girl can testify. The judge is gonna let her. You ain't missed too much."

The district attorney boomed from the front of the courtroom. "Eden Whitney to the stand, Your Honor."

The courtroom rustled, like leaves rattled by a breeze, while the judge rapped his gavel. The rustling slowly pattered away. No one moved.

"Eden Whitney," the prosecutor said again.

A twig of a girl popped up in the second row. Her dress was splotched with sunflowers, a jarring image amid the rows of bleached-out shirts and overalls. Carrot red hair stuck out from under her straw hat.

Her mother, Coman Whitney, rose much more slowly, almost as if she was being forced to stand

against her will. Either Miz Whitney was playing to the courtroom decorum, or she dreaded this moment. Here it was nine months past Whitney's death and she was still stuffed in a black dress stretched tight across her straining bosom. She ought to have been panting from the heat, but her jowls were clamped shut. With the net from her hat over her face, no telling what ran through her mind. She turned away when the judge eyed her and looked down at the floor as she guided the girl through the row.

Rowen leaned over to watch them enter the aisle. The girl's white gloves were every bit as grimy as the white doors outside.

The girl hesitated at the gate the bailiff held open, looking for reassurance first from her mother, then from the bailiff.

"Go on," Miz Whitney said roughly and loud enough for the whole courtroom to hear. The girl reached for her mother's hand, but Miz Whitney stepped back and nodded toward the witness stand. The bailiff put his hand on the girl's shoulder and ushered her through. The gate swung, squeaky on its hinges with no one to stop it.

Once settled in the witness chair, the girl sought some sign from her mother, but she must not have found any comfort there because her gaze lifted and shot over all the heads in front of her toward the double doors. The ceiling fan stirred the fetid air.

The judge paused to allow his audience to feel the swell of impending justice. When he was satisfied with the silence of bated breath, he leaned toward the little girl.

"Miss Whitney."

She jumped as if she'd been caught daydreaming in school.

"Eden Whitney, isn't it? How old are you, girl?"

"Ten," she whispered.

"Speak up, girl. The court reporter here is trying to take down your testimony."

"Ten," she said again, loud and clear.

"The clerk will ask you to swear on the Bible. And to tell the truth, the whole truth and nothing but the truth. Do you know what that means, girl?"

"I have to tell what I seen and not make up stories."

"It means you're not to tell a lie. Have you ever told a lie before?"

"Yes, sir."

"What did you lie about?"

The girl's eyes drifted to her Uncle Franklin in the defendant's seat.

"I don't want to say."

The judge spoke sharply. "Girl, I'm speaking to you."

Her head whipped back around.

"The question is, have you ever lied, young lady?"

The judge tapped his reading glasses on the bench. She looked down at her lap and said, "Mama got me a new coat last winter and the sleeve tore off. When I come home, Mama was mad, and she asked me what happened. I thought she was going to whip me, so I said Booger Davis tore it. She went right up to his parents' house and he got in trouble. It wasn't him. I tore it going through the fence to pick apples off Mr. Sawyer's trees."

Eden

Damn. That was who Rowen was working for! He was supposed to be out there right now picking tobacco!

"And did you tell your mama what really happened?"

"No, sir, not before today," she said into her lap.

"I said, speak up, girl, the court reporter needs to hear you!"

"No, sir!" she shouted.

Mutters erupted throughout the courtroom.

"Why haven't you told the truth before today?"

"I did tell the truth. I just didn't tell Mama. After Booger got whipped, I told Daddy."

"And what did your daddy say?"

"I told him I felt bad that Booger had gotten in trouble when it was my fault and he said feeling low was punishment enough and he hoped I'd remember it the next time I thought about lying."

"Your daddy's dead now, isn't he?"

"Yes, sir."

The judge gestured out to the courtroom. "How do we know you're going to tell the truth before all these people here?"

She faced him head on. "Because I just did."

Rowen rubbed his sweaty palms on his pants. Good Lord, how much he longed to be up at the front to see her mama's face and her Uncle Franklin's! If it hadn't been for Adeline and that "college of life" business, he could have been closer, right up there. He leaned forward and rested his arm on the back of the bench. The woman in front of him turned and glared.

The judge nodded to the prosecutor. "Your witness."

The prosecutor's voice rapped like a hammer. "State your name and address for the record, please."

"Eden Whitney. Number 1, Live Oak Way, White Rock."

"Who are your parents, Eden?"

"Mama's sitting right there." Eden pointed to the second row. "Her name's Coman Whitney. My papa's Birch Whitney. He's dead."

"When did he die?"

"Last Christmas."

"How did he die?"

"Uncle Franklin shot him."

The judge shouted for order over the clamor. Franklin swiveled around, trying to catch some snippet that might be sympathetic to him. Rowen recollected that among his parents' friends, Franklin hadn't been the outgoing one. He wasn't one to tell jokes or stories or propose toasts. He'd always been invited because he'd grown up with Rowen's mama. And he had money. But mostly Franklin holed up in the shadows, chain-smoking.

Now sweat streamed down his pallid face.

"How do you know that?"

"I saw him."

"Tell the courtroom what you saw."

"Daddy and Uncle Franklin were in the kitchen. Daddy told him to get out. Uncle Franklin said he wasn't leaving. He said he'd bought and paid for that house hisself and he had the same right to be there as Grandma and Paw-paw, and if they were staying, so was he. Paw-paw told Daddy to sit down and said that Uncle Franklin done a lot for Daddy all the time even when Daddy didn't ever

pay him back and Daddy had better be grateful, 'specially as it was Christmas and all.

"Daddy said he couldn't take them all anymore and he was leaving. He went outside. Uncle Franklin followed him out and asked if he was going to drink with his nigger buddies. Daddy opened the car door and Uncle Franklin grabbed his arm. Daddy pushed him away. Then Uncle Franklin shot him."

"Where were you?"

"I was hiding behind the holly tree in front of the house."

"And you could see and hear everything from under that tree."

"Yes, sir."

"No further questions, Your Honor."

There was a collective sigh in the courtroom. Next to Rowen, Hollinger took out his handkerchief and mopped his face.

Was she lying? She couldn't make up a story that wild. Still it was hard to picture skinny-ol-Franklin pulling a gun on his brother-in-law. If Whitney had owed him money, seems like Franklin would never get it back if he shot him. But that girl's blue eyes never blinked, never wavered.

"Your witness," said the judge.

White's lawyer's voice was the opposite of the prosecutor's, slow as molasses as it pooled throughout the courtroom.

"Miss Whitney, you opened your Christmas presents that morning, didn't you?"

"Yes."

"Your Uncle Franklin here got you a big doll, didn't he?"

"Yes."

"The biggest doll in the toy store, right?"

"Yes."

"'Cause you told him you wanted it?"

"Yes."

"Now, Miss Eden, you loved your daddy very much, didn't you?"

Her voice quavered. "Yes, sir."

"And you miss him very much, don't you?"

She was going to bust out sobbing, any moment.

"Miss Eden, can you say 'yes' or 'no' for the court reporter, please?"

"Yes."

"But you've told us you're going to tell the truth today?"

"Yes."

"Your daddy was drinking nontax paid liquor that morning, wasn't he?"

"No, sir, he was drinking shine."

Titters popped throughout the courtroom.

"And he drank shine every day, didn't he?"

"Yes, sir."

"Let's go back to what happened when your Uncle Franklin went out with your daddy. You didn't follow them out, did you? You stayed inside by the window."

"No, sir."

"That holly bush you talked about is right in front of the window, isn't it?

"It's in front of the window, but I was outside."

"When your daddy opened the car door, he didn't get behind the driver's seat, did he?"

"No."

"May I approach your Honor?"

Eden

The judge nodded.

The lawyer walked to a table and picked up a pipe wrench. He held it up in front of her face. "This pipe wrench was on the front seat of your daddy's car, wasn't it?"

"Daddy had a pipe wrench, but I didn't see it that day."

"You didn't see it because you couldn't see it. You were inside."

"No, sir."

"The last words you heard your daddy say was, 'I'm coming after you, Franklin,' isn't that true?"

"No, sir."

The lawyer roared, "What did you hear him say, Miss Whitney?"

"He looked back and saw me and he said, 'Get in the house.' And he opened his mouth to say something else, but that's when the gun fired. He was looking at me when that gun went off."

The voices in the courtroom resumed like wind ruffling trees at the onset of a hurricane. The judge beat the gavel furiously and shouted, "I will clear this courtroom."

When the room quieted, the only sounds that remained were the hum of the ceiling fan and the girl gulping sobs. No one moved to comfort her. The judge wiped his glasses, then glared at the lawyers until they both murmured they had no further questions. The bailiff offered Eden Whitney his hand and he led her down to the gate.

Coman Whitney rose with an annoyed huff, not a tremor of maternal concern visible anywhere in her bulk. Without even looking at the child, she grabbed her wrist and towed her back up the aisle.

Rowen tried to peer through her face net as they passed, hoping to catch her eye so he could figure out where she stood. She'd lost her husband, her brother was accused, her daughter was torn up with grieving—whose side was she on? But her gaze shot rod-straight to the door, refusing to acknowledge anyone around her—all the friends, neighbors, acquaintances who'd known her all her life and who wanted to know the same thing. She wasn't giving anything of herself away, not to anyone, not even to her daughter.

The girl sagged limp in her grasp. All the pluck that had fired her ten minutes ago was snuffed out. Everyone shifted in their seats to follow the two of them, the girl's sobs subsiding to whimpers as they retreated. When Rowen turned back around, one of her gloves was at his feet. He turned to call out, but the door had closed.

"Noon recess," the judge grumbled. The men in the jury box rose and shuffled out. Then the judge left, and people stirred, stretching and rubbing their numbed limbs.

Hollinger turned to Rowen. "You and your mama doing all right?"

If Rowen didn't hustle, he'd face a throng likely to pin him down with the same questions. He thought back to how miserable he'd felt when the neighbors had gathered, like roosting buzzards, on the day he and his mama had left town.

Adeline hadn't paid attention. She'd been too busy shouting at the men loading the truck until she turned and saw the look on his face.

"What's wrong?" she asked.

"Why don't they go away?" he said under his breath.

"You sure are right about that. These boys are sorry, treating your mama's wedding china like it was bales of hay, but if you and I go to loading this truck ourselves, we'll be out here past dark."

"Not them." He nodded in the buzzards' direction. "Them."

Her eyes roved up the street and then back down to him. "We ought to get blinkers for you, Mr. Rowen, 'cause just like a mule you is more engrossed in what's going on a mile away than what's directly in front of your plodding feet. These folks you're all worried about don't have no good works to occupy themselves with, that's all. And I can assure you, they don't know nothin'. For all they know Rowen Hart is leavin' for the stars and beyond."

Stars and beyond. They were headed for a clapboard shack, but there was no sense in arguing with Adeline even to point out the obvious. Eighteen years of living and he'd never realized how flimsy their perch was here, how they could be blown away as easily as sparrows.

He turned back to Hollinger. "We're doing all right."

"You been by your old house lately? Dr. Stuart's wife, she put yella rose bushes out front and I mean to tell you it is something, shows off the whole street, even in this dry spell."

Rowen wished a hole would open up and swallow the house, Dr. Stuart, his wife, rose bushes and all.

"I don't have a reason to go over there."

"You ought to, you can run over there right now during the break."

"No, I gotta leave. I'm 'sposed to be picking tobacco for Mr. Sawyer."

"The same Sawyer's that got the apple trees that girl was talking about? Wonder he didn't fill her butt full of birdshot for doing that. He's an ornery type, ain't he?"

"The Sawyer I work for does have apple trees."

"Well, tell your mama to stop by. We already got next year's dryers in, the 1954 models. She hasn't been in the store for so long, I bet she don't even know that you can get an electric dryer nowadays."

As if they'd ever have money again to buy such a luxury.

"Gotta run," Rowen mumbled.

"Say hello to your mama."

Rowen said over his shoulder, "I sure will."

He threaded through the sweat-stained bodies spilling into the foyer and trailed them down the stairs. Outside, the August heat mashed down on him, heavy as the lid on a griddle. A few folks lingered in knots to peck at the morning's nuggets, but most hurried off, eager to get out of the sun and to their noon meals.

The dirt road, ground fine as chalk dust, was empty. Cicadas buzzed in waves, each wave waxing louder. In the cotton field next to the road, a lone oak shouldered the heat, its leaves singeing at the edges. The road stretched on before him, dust-choked weeds on either side. Moving through the heat felt like walking through sludge; there wasn't any progress to it.

When, at last, he reached his own yard, the hinge on the picket gate popped and the gate dropped in his hand. Ever since they'd moved here, one thing after another was busting, sagging, decaying. Nothing had ever worn out when his daddy was alive.

Eden

Adeline was boiling ham hocks in the kitchen, and the fan on the counter blasted the odor around him. She spoke without turning. "Since you been gone 'bout two hours, we can assume you seen all you needed to."

She wasn't going to give away the slightest sign even though she was dying to know what had happened. She was counting on him not being able to contain himself and spilling it all. That's what he'd always done when she'd acted uninterested because it was so damn frustrating. But even if he fooled with her a little and didn't breathe a word, she'd just keep on stirring pots and slamming lids. After all, she always found out everything anyway. An underground current plugged right into her, and most times she spilled the White Rock scandals long before they were whispered in church.

Then it came to him, how to cast out a hook.

"Nothing much happened. The only witness they put on this morning was the Whitney girl."

He held his breath and didn't say another word.

That did it! She looked over her shoulder.

"They put that baby on the stand? What did she say?"

"She said she saw Franklin shoot her daddy."

Adeline turned back to the stove. "Upsetting that orphan baby for nothin'. It'd been better if they'd left her alone."

"She's not an orphan! She's still got her mama."

"You got a mama like that, you's an orphan. I worked for the Whites before I come to work for your mama and daddy, and I've knowed Coman Whitney from before she dropped out of school. Low down mean as a sow. But that's not the point. Point is she knows her brother shot her man in cold blood and instead of standing up and telling it like it was, she throws her child to the dogs. She knows ain't no one going to listen to that child."

"But it happened outside the house. Sounds like the girl was the only one who saw it all."

Adeline turned to look at him as she took a pie out of the oven. "Uh-huh."

"If the girl's the only one that saw it and she says Franklin shot her daddy, how can they find him not guilty?"

"Think on what your Bible say. The race is not to the swift, nor the battle to the strong, but the man's that got a big bank account can cut 'em all down like standing grain. Mr. White, he's same as Jacob, and Mr. Whitney, he's the Esau, and all that little girl'll ever be is a lamb for the sacrifice."

As well he knew, there were two Bibles: the King James Bible and the Bible According to Adeline. "But Whitney's dead. And Jacob didn't kill Esau. That was Cain and Abel."

"No, you got it wrong. Cain, he was marked. Franklin White, he'll keep himself pure as the driven snow." She ladled some broth into a bowl. "Here, you take this to your mama now."

He shuffled to his mother's room slowly so as not to spill the soup and bumped the door open with his elbow. His mother's favorite scent, lavender, greeted him, but the scent underneath it, the human stench, nearly made him gag. He'd never smelled her body scent before at the old house. He didn't even realize she had one. He hated himself

for his revulsion. She was sick, after all. It wasn't her fault that she was here, it was his daddy's and his daddy had seen fit to put himself in a place where you couldn't even go shout at him. So far, Rowen hadn't managed to make things any better. What a sorry excuse of a son he was if he couldn't even bring her lunch without feeling sick and ashamed.

The dimmed room gave him an excuse to hesitate. What she would see as his eyes adjusting would cover his effort to master himself. She hadn't allowed an open shade here since they'd moved in. Her classical music station played in the background, piano chords softly rolling.

"Brahms, Rowen. Isn't it lovely?"

In addition to the odor, he hadn't gotten used to the sight of her lying in bed every day. Up until his daddy had died, he'd woken every morning to the rap of her heels crossing the bedroom floor. "The sun is waiting to greet your smile, Alexander Rowen Hart," she'd sing out as she snapped up the shades. He'd grown to hate that routine about the time he'd sprouted underarm hair. And then off she'd flown down the stairs, hollering for Adeline to help with whatever events she was heading up that week for the Daughters of the Cape Fear, or the Women's Missionary Union. Throughout the kitchen, there were full calendars and lists and invitations waiting to be mailed.

But after the funeral, the last event she'd planned, she'd gone to her bedroom and shut the door, ignoring the folks congregated downstairs. Toward evening, after the house had emptied, Adeline had rapped on her door. "Miz Rita, Miz Rita," she called.

Rowen had sat in the foyer, listening to

JAMIE LISA FORBES

Adeline's voice reverberate through the house. He loosened his tie, untied his shoes. For the first time in his life, no one switched on the lights and started supper. He didn't look up when Adeline went out to fetch the doctor, and he was still sitting in the dark when she returned. The doctor muttered words about "terrible shock" and "breakdown" and then said to him, "She's fortunate that you're grown now and can take care of her."

He looked over the doctor's shoulder at Adeline. Grown? Was eighteen years of age grown? He'd never taken care of himself, much less anyone else. Any moment now, Adeline would speak up and say so.

She hadn't said anything. She'd just stared back at him.

"Yes, Mama, Brahms sounds real nice."

On the night table, a fan cycled back and forth. His mother sat up. Tendrils of hair stuck to her forehead. "I heard that row with you and Adeline this morning. I know how much you wanted to be on time for Franklin's trial. I'm sorry, Rowen."

He gestured with the tray he clutched, "Adeline made you some broth."

"It's too hot to eat, but we must not hurt Adeline's feelings when she devotes herself so. I'm ready, you can set it down. No, you mustn't charge out the door, as if you are ashamed to spare a moment with me. I want to hear everything that happened this morning."

He perched at the edge of the bed.

"Were they all asking where I was? I know Claretta Ingersoll has been saying awful things about me, saying that I was too lavish and that was

the cause of your daddy's suicide. When he never talked to me about our finances, ever. I'm sure they're all repeating her lies all over town. I'm sure the courtroom was full of it."

"No one was talking about you, Mama."

"Are you sure? Did you see Claretta there?"

"I had to sit in the back because I was late. She mightta been there."

"I'm telling you she was there and saying horrible things about me."

"How do you know that?"

She paused, and her lower lip drooped. "I heard it, that's all."

"Who could you have heard it from? Not one of 'em has been here."

"Rowen, you're young, still a child practically. It's how people talk, that's all, how they've always talked. Especially since everyone loved your father and so they must have someone — his widow — to blame for his death. That's what makes it comprehensible. Now stop talking back to me and tell me what happened this morning."

"Miz Whitney's little girl testified."

"What did she say?"

"She said her pa and Franklin had been fussin' in the house, that her pa was drinking but that he left and went to the car and Franklin shot him."

It gratified him that a spark of interest lit in her eyes. The pillows rustled as she leaned forward. "Was she telling the truth?"

"I don't know. But Franklin's attorney said Whitney was coming after him with a pipe wrench."

"Where was Coman?"

JAMIE LISA FORBES

"Sitting behind Franklin. That girl was bawling like crazy and Miz Whitney wouldn't touch her, wouldn't hug her, wouldn't even wipe her face."

His mother picked up the spoon and sipped a thimbleful of broth. "The problem was Coman wasn't pretty as other girls in her milieu. Bless her heart, she could not shed her baby fat though they took her to doctor after doctor. She did have such a marvelous wit that she could make a stone laugh 'till it cried."

She set the spoon back down.

"Her birthday parties were well attended and not just because her family had money. She had friends. But she was the autumn baby, the autumn of her parents' lives that is, and that blunder always results in the most undisciplined children. At fifteen, she mortified her parents by carrying on so with that Whitney boy. They met at some Negro tavern, I heard. And then she ran away and married him. Of course, one must allow for the possibility that she had to get married.

"Whitney, mind you, was just a farm laborer's boy. He had no education or money. Poverty must have been a rude awakening to Coman—no more parties—and well, a young lady might sour.

"The last time I saw her was in the sewing shop, you know, The Stitch-in-Time. Eden was in a stroller. Such china blue eyes that child had with gorgeous red hair. 'Eden,' I said, 'what a lovely name,' although I had never heard of anyone naming their child after the place where the Devil brought Evil into the world. Pray that it isn't an omen.

"And all Coman said was, could she borrow a

little money to buy material for a baby dress. I gave her a dollar, but I tried to explain that the church consignment shop had such adorable clothes for babies. She acted as if I'd said something vile and whipped that stroller straight out the door. All the ladies at the counter noticed.

"And Franklin—he's never mentioned her once in all these years, neither her nor the child." She collapsed back against the pillows. "I believe that's all I'll have now, Rowen."

"You didn't hardly have none of it."

She closed her eyes."Tell Adeline, I'll eat it in the evening, when it's cooler."

Adeline had his lunch laid out when he returned to the kitchen: ham and collard greens and fresh sliced tomatoes. He set his mother's bowl by the sink.

"She wouldn't eat anything."

"Don't you worry. By fall, she'll be better. This heat ain't bringing her no relief, that's all."

"Daddy's been gone two months. And she's still in bed."

"You were there when the doctor was telling us that time was what was needed for her to heal. He didn't expect no kind of miracles."

"How's she ever going to get better just lying there?"

"I don't see how you goin' to get paid if you don't eat and get on over to Mr. Sawyer's. Did you tell him you was goin' to be late today?"

"No."

She picked up her wooden spoon and smacked his knuckles. "Mr. Sawyer took pity on you and give you that job when you ain't never been out in the fields before and now you do him like that. I swear you don't make no sense to me. The Rowen Hart I been around was raised better than that. You got something to say for yourself?"

"I didn't think he'd let me go. So I thought I'd tell him I was sick."

"Hm, hm. Spreading on the greasy lies to dress your sloth. Everyone lay a table before the eyes of the Lord, Mr. Rowen. What's He gonna think when he sees yours?" She snatched his plate away. "I ain't feeding no hobos here. You better be out the door to be finding out if you still got a job."

Outside, the heat had stifled the cicadas at last. All the sun-blistered yards he passed were emptied of children and old men. Everyone had fled indoors. He'd eaten most of his lunch, but what he knew he'd missed was whatever Adeline had made for dessert. What kind of pie had she baked — blueberry, lemon meringue? If she was still there when he came home, she'd let him have it. Only trouble was all the long hours to endure before he could sit down with it, whatever it was, among the fireflies on the porch.

Sawyer's house was the oldest in the neighborhood with towering yellow pines shading the yard. The house itself was a palace compared to the neighbors' — two stories high and whitewashed, not a smear of mold anywhere. Fresh-painted white rockers lined the front porch.

Behind the house, he crossed the footbridge over a ditch where insects swarmed in shrinking puddles of muddy water, and then rows and rows of chest-high leafy stalks pressed all around, nearly squeezing him to suffocation.

He pushed through into a row, and down

at the end, he could see a mule's ears twitch. He followed them and there was old man Sawyer on the skidder.

Sawyer addressed the mule. "Well, Hester Prynne, Mr. Hart has blessed us with his presence." He turned to Rowen. "I 'spose you're going to tell me you been layin' in bed sick."

Trouble with Adeline was, he could shrug off whatever it was she had to say only to find later that little barbs of it had pricked him.

"No, sir. I went to watch Franklin White's trial in town. Sorry I didn't say nothin'."

"Even the niggers do me better than that, boy. I guess it comes from growing up with a silver spoon in your mouth."

"I'm sorry, Mr. Sawyer. It won't happen again."

"That's right, it won't happen 'cause I won't pity your mama a second time."

Hester Prynne squirted a river of piss. In the mule's eyes, he saw *spoiled little city boy.*

"I'd have thought a boy whose daddy shamed him by stiffin' his bill collectors and then killin' hisself, leavin' that boy and his mama as begging paupers, would be more..." He glanced at Hester Prynne, as if she was going to finish the sentence, "...obliging."

The stench of piss filled the air. Flies bit his ears.

"Yes, sir, Mr. Sawyer, you're right. I'm grateful for the work, and I didn't mean any disrespect. It was just...Mr. White being who he is and all, I wanted to see what was going to happen."

No point in bringing up Sawyer's tangential role at the trial. Heck, maybe he didn't even know Eden Whitney was stealing his apples.

Sawyer nodded off to where the colored boy, Sammy, whisked leaves off the plants. "That boys worth two of you. He doesn't find the excitement in town to be so distracting."

"I understand, Mr. Sawyer, and I won't either no more."

Rowen snatched a sack off the skidder and started on the row next to Sammy's. He hadn't known Sammy until he started working there. If Sammy had gone to school at all, he would have been in the colored school. Sammy was his own age, but towered over him, with legs and arms moving so fast it seemed the leaves jumped off the plants.

As they met along the row, Sammy said, "You new here, boy? Don't believe I know you."

"Cut it out, I already took it from Sawyer."

"Oooo, bet you was worn out from a hot date," Sammy leered. Sammy's topics of conversation always jumped to sexual exploits that so far had eluded Rowen. Sammy's air of superior knowledge in such matters made Rowen jealous and he knew he couldn't hide it, which made Sammy taunt him even more.

"I was at Franklin White's trial. You shoulda been there. The rest of the town was there."

Sammy squatted to pluck some lugs and peered up at him through the leaves. "Weren't any Negroes there, right?"

"No, but the bank vice-president's on trial. I bet there are Negroes that owe him money, too. He could go to jail for the rest of his life. Or maybe even get the death penalty."

Sammy laughed as he scooted on past Rowen. "Boy goin' to the U-nee-ver-sity, but how he

gonna succeed when he's so weak in mind?" Rowen straightened to make a comeback, but Sammy kept on moving and now he was at a distance where Rowen would have to shout a response.

Adeline. That's who would have trumpeted the news about his university admission.

When the letter came a month ago, his mama and Adeline had whooped like guinea hens. Now he'd be a university student like Adeline's daughter, Chloe, who'd taken off for Howard University just last fall!

They didn't bother to consider for a moment that he wasn't anything like Chloe. Chloe could have had the face of the Queen of Sheba for all anyone knew, because her nose had never been out of her books. The times she'd come over with Adeline and sat at the kitchen table, she'd never been able to tear herself out of a page for more than an instant to say "Hey, Rowen," while all he had to do was crack open *World History*, or whatever fool tome that he'd had to lug home, and his mind shot straight out the window, daydreaming about that shiny Skylark down at the Buick lot that he'd be able to put a down payment on one day if he could just get out of school and start his real life, whatever it would be. He couldn't fathom what he might be doing but he was dang sure he would have money.

Without so much as asking him, his mama had sat up in her bed long enough to reply that, yes, he'd be attending the University of North Carolina. Back last fall he'd applied because that's what his parents had told him to do. That's what his daddy told him to do, the daddy who, it turned out, had steeped them all in a life of lies. Rowen hadn't defied him at the time. He had thought that it wasn't a matter of choice. For as long as he had lived, it was White Rock's tradition for the children of the prosperous to be packed off to the university, some never to return and some, like Franklin, to come home and be set up on pedestals.

Why should Adeline and his mama get to decree his fate now? Never mind where the money was going to come from. As miserable as things were, he had no urge to start from scratch among a throng he didn't know, just to attain some higher life too foggy to imagine. What was the hocus-pocus by which a boy turned into a man? Far as he could tell, it didn't have anything to do with how many degrees he got. All he'd ever be was the boy whose daddy picked suicide over bankruptcy. Hadn't Sawyer said as much?

And the Skylark, that dream was gone for good.

Yes, all right...he was living in a shack, but outside on that front porch, he could see a person coming from a mile off and know, white or colored, who they were and what they wanted. Everything within his range of vision was known, and if he had to be busted poor, he wanted life to stay right like it was where he could see everything coming.

And here came Sammy down the row again. Sammy glanced back at Sawyer who was picking himself and not watching them anymore.

"That 'trial' is just a big cover story for you, Mr. Rowen. You was there to chase you some pussy."

"The only girl I even seen was the one that testified. And she was ten years old."

"Whoa, you got to look at them that young?"

Eden

Rowen's wits were buckling in the heat. He couldn't utter more than a bleat. Sammy laughed and moved on, his hands flying so fast they were a blur, while Rowen dragged his sack down the row and emptied it on the skidder. He'd have to give up trying to keep up with Sammy. It was all he could do to focus on the next stalk.

There was no passing of time through the stifling afternoon, only a continuum of mule stench and leaves snapping off stalks and rows following one after another, thousands of them. And when Rowen gave up talking, Sammy whipped out his transistor radio and the buzz of it alternately magnified and receded as they passed one another. Seemed like the only sound Rowen could make out was Hollinger's advertisements for his Sears store, which contributed to the sense of infinite purgatory.

Once the sun dropped below the tree line and the blaring furnace heat abated, he could begin to anticipate the end of the day. Still more hours passed, as the tobacco stalks ahead faded into the dusk, before Sawyer hollered, "Quittin' time." Rowen barely glimpsed Sammy stand and stretch and then he was gone.

The steamy heat of the evening hadn't yet broken as Rowen dragged home. Yard lights snapped on one by one and children spilled out of screen doors. Lights burned from his own house, which surprised him because Adeline should have left by now. Instead, she was waiting for him at the porch door, arms crossed over her apron.

"Your Uncle Hugh was here," she said.

Hugh Grimes had been his daddy's partner in their auction business. Since moving out here,

Hugh had visited once a month. Adeline had never come out and claimed her opinion of him one way or another. Instead, after pouring him a cold drink, she'd scoot outside.

The ritual that had evolved was that Rowen would sit at the dining room table across from Uncle Hugh while he scrawled out a check. The check would be slid, dramatically, under Rowen's nose and Rowen would mumble an incantation of gratitude. All he really felt was shame, which was what he suspected that Uncle Hugh wanted, and savored.

Meanwhile, outside, Adeline would bang garden implements and bellow songs as loud as she could. "'My good Jerry is a Carolina mule, he been everywhere and he ain't no fool.'"

Uncle Hugh's lip curled. "She never caterwauled like that in town, did she?"

Was she acting that way because she thought Uncle Hugh should have given them more money? That's what Rowen guessed. Surely Uncle Hugh gave them all that he could. He was his mother's brother after all.

Now, as he met Adeline's stare, he wondered what the hell she expected of him. None of this was his fault.

"Does he want me to go over to his place?"

"I told him you'd be home anytime. He'll be back. I guess Mr. Sawyer took pity on you and kept you on."

"Yes, and I won't skip out again. Did Uncle Hugh talk to Mama?"

"He didn't talk to her, didn't even ask to see her."

Rowen took his plate of coleslaw and pintos

outside and sat on the stoop. Moonbeams poked through the trees, and the cicadas revved back up from their afternoon drowse. Down the road, children whooped and shrieked. The night pulsed with noise.

A car slowed and he recognized the rumble of his uncle's Cadillac. Uncle Hugh parked next to the fence, then took his time getting out. The car roof gleamed in the moonlight.

Rowen called out. "Hey, Uncle Hugh."

Uncle Hugh stood in the broken gate and pushed his straw hat back on his head. "Evenin', Rowen. Adeline says you're pickin' tubaka for Sawyer."

"Yes, sir."

"Good thing, you'll need that extra money when you start school."

"Mama says it'll cover my books while the money you give us will cover my tuition."

"That's what I come to talk about. Let's go inside."

Adeline sat at the kitchen table. Her sewing basket was on the floor and she appeared to be thoroughly absorbed in repairing one of Rowen's shirts. She didn't look up as they crossed to the dining room. "You all want some lemonade?"

Uncle Hugh's lips curled over his yellow teeth as he pulled out a chair. "You'd think that woman'd pick herself up and come in here to address working men."

He called back that he wanted some and Rowen shifted to watch her. Her hand trembled as she lifted the pitcher and poured. It shocked him, what could it mean? He blinked to wash it out of his vision.

She brought them their lemonade, backed two steps and then balked in the doorway.

"Adeline, I need to speak to the boy alone."

She blurted, "Ain't nothing you can say to him that you can't say to me. I been working for his folks all his life."

She looked solid as a granite slab, standing there. But Uncle Hugh hadn't seen her pour the lemonade.

"It's family business, Adeline, it ain't nothin' that concerns you."

"Then why ain't you talkin' to his mama?"

"Rita's sick, doesn't hardly know what's going on around her, you know that. The boy…well, he's not a boy anymore. He's a man. He oughta be taking on the family affairs."

Adeline didn't budge.

"Adeline, it ain't your place to be here."

"'Till Rowen tell me to leave, my place is right here."

Uncle Hugh ran his fingernail down the checkered pattern in the oilcloth. "Adeline, you know better than this. You're a sharp girl. You been around enough to know we live in strange times. You never can predict what'll happen from day to day. Them that are proud and vain, they're the ones God strikes down. Your preacher preaches that, don't he?"

"If it's all right with you, Uncle Hugh, I want Adeline to stay."

Uncle Hugh's eyebrows arched and then he gulped back his lemonade. He set the glass down heavily on the table. "You're half orphaned and you ain't getting the schooling a young man needs. You're lucky I come 'round as often as I do. But if

you don't watch yourself, it'll spread like wildfire all over this county that Virgil Hart's son is letting a Negra woman run his business. It'll tear you down in this community! God knows I'll hear of it. Now send her home!"

Rowen's pulse pounded in his ears. Whatever Adeline was made of — the material that held her upright in the face of his uncle's swelling rancor — there wasn't an ounce of it in him.

"Uncle Hugh says it's business, Adeline."

"You sure about that?" she blurted.

No, he wasn't. "Yes, ma'am."

Adeline turned away. He heard her gather her things, then the screen door spring squealed.

"'Night, Rowen."

Uncle Hugh's shoulders twitched at her failure to address him. "Your daddy's not been gone two months and that woman's lost all respect. People hear about this, my guess is no decent family in town will have her.

"Now what I've come to tell you..." he grimaced, as if the words gathering against his teeth pained him, but despite all his effort to hold them back, they were set on bolting out anyway.

"Your daddy died owing me money, too. Though killing himself — what a fool thing to do. No disrespect, he was your daddy, but as a man, son, he wasn't much more than a bowl of pudding. I been carrying him ever since he married my sister. And he didn't help hisself by drinking the way he did. I ain't blaming you. Though you've been coddled something shameful.

"Every couple a months he might re-pay me

a dollar or two, after I reminded him I had a crippled child to support. And you know good and well, I shouldn't have had to remind him. She was there at the door in his face every morning when he came into the office. Didn't seem to bother him. But his debt's never been repaid. It's built up and up. Even without the interest.

"What I come to tell you is this: the appraiser's done appraised the auction yard, and it ain't as good as we mighta thought. We thought your daddy's share would take care of his debts and be enough to support your mother. Best case, there'd be a little extra to put you through school.

"It didn't come out that way. If I take a good cut on what I'm owed, there's enough there for your mother to live on for a few years. If she watches her money. Lord knows she oughta be able to get help cheaper than what she pays Adeline. But there ain't enough for you both. Unless you want to take her share. I don't think that's what you want."

Uncle Hugh's eyes bugged out at him, demanding a response. "Did you hear me? I'm forgiving part of your daddy's debts, which, if you was any kind of son, you oughta pay, and I'm doing it so as to keep your mama up. You'd think I'd get thanked."

Rowen didn't know which angered him more, Uncle Hugh, or the sobs clogging up his throat. His voice squeaked loose. "She's sold all her jewelry, all her furniture, nearly everything in the house."

"I didn't charge her no fees for that auction, did I? Now that you've been brought to your rightful place by the hand of God Almighty, the place you would have been in years ago, but for

my sense of duty, let me tell you, nobody owes you nothin'. I don't owe you or your mama nothin'. I didn't tell your parents to live the way they did. That woman mewlin' in that bedroom, she ain't my mother. Now you're going to show me some manners, or I'm gonna walk out that door."

Where was the code of behavior that could prompt him on how to act, or what to say? How he wished Adeline had stayed, because then he could have looked to her, and she would know.

"Thank you, Uncle Hugh."

Uncle Hugh leaned back in his chair. "That's better. Now you kin prob'bly get a scholarship to go to that school. Or maybe you can work."

"Yes, sir."

"If I were you, I'd look into that tomarra."

"Yes, sir."

Uncle Hugh wrote the check and slid it across the table with a searing glare. The figure was less than half of the last month's check.

"Like I said, son, Rita's gotta learn to watch her money." The chair squeaked against the linoleum as Uncle Hugh pushed back. "You tell your mother I said hello. I'll send out a car with your cousin, Mabel, in a couple of days. She's lonesome for y'all, 'specially you, Rowen. With the office so busy, I haven't been able to spare her to travel all the way out here."

That's all they needed, a visit from Cousin Mabel. It would be more trouble than it was worth. He wasn't sure if her wheelchair would fit through the door. She'd protest about all the fuss—Cousin Mabel always protested about people fussing over her—and his mother would insist that she come in. He pictured her wheeling through the rooms, ignoring the squalor, while murmuring dainty compliments. She'd be so gracious in masking her pity, and she'd expect them to notice it.

It wasn't any mystery that his father had killed himself to escape this helplessness in the face of ruin. The mystery was that he'd cared so little for what would happen to them.

"Mama would like that. If Cousin Mabel came out."

He saw his uncle to the door. Insects, from mosquitoes to beetles the size of his palm, swarmed around the door light, and Uncle Hugh called back from the road, "You oughta fix this gate here, son."

Rowen went back to his mother's bedroom. The lights were off, and he listened from the doorway. He was about to turn away when he heard, "Rowen?"

"Yes, Mama."

"That was Hugh, wasn't it?"

"Yes, Mama."

"Come here."

He shuffled in and sat down. She squeezed his hand. "Did Hugh give you the tuition money?"

Even though he couldn't see her face, the air of expectancy swelled.

"Yes, Mama."

Eden

2

SAMMY PAWED THROUGH the toolbox that Rowen had hauled from his storage shed. "Boy, this is all you got for tools? Where's a drill and bits?"

Rowen shrugged. "I don't know." He was too embarrassed to add that he couldn't recall seeing a drill and bits in his whole life.

"How you 'spect to drill a hole in this gate post if you ain't got a drill?"

The sun hadn't snapped free of the tree line and already Rowen felt slammed by the heat. The new gate post jutted out of the hole at a forty-five-degree angle, every bit as accusatory as Sammy.

"You don't want to help out, just go on home. I'll figure it out by myself."

Sammy dropped the tools on the ground. "I'm trying to help you, but you ain't got the sense of a brick. I hope you find you some money again, Mr. Rowen, 'cause you ain't goin' to survive bein' poor. Ain't nothin' else to do now but get a drill in town, or walk back to my place for one."

Rowen kicked at the dirt around the post. That didn't fix the lean. "I'll go to town," he said.

"You gotta have money to get a drill with, you know that, don't cha?"

Rowen tried to ram Sammy with his shoulder. Sammy stepped aside and Rowen tripped and fell over the dirt mound.

When he rolled over on his back, Sammy's face loomed above. "What's gotten into you?"

"Nothing."

"Might as well leave you laying on the ground then. I don't have no more business here." He straightened, as if he'd heard something. "You expectin' a white child, Mr. Rowen?"

Rowen pushed himself up on his elbows and saw Eden Whitney, dressed exactly as he'd last seen her.

"She's got her suitcase. Looks like she's fixin' to visit a while."

"It's the girl I told you about, the one at the trial."

The giant sunflowers on the dress were now smeared with dirt. The church hat was gone, and her hair hung limp and tangled. The way she stared at him made him realize she'd never seen him at the courthouse.

"If this was the chief witness for the prosecution, I believe Mr. Franklin's gonna go free."

Eden

She looked from one boy to the other. "Where's Miz Adeline?" she blurted.

"Where'd you get that jungle dress?" said Sammy.

"You're a nigger. I don't have to tell you nothin'."

"If you ain't gotta talk to a nigger, what'cha want to see one for?"

"None of your business. Tell her Birch Whitney's daughter is here."

"You ain't got a name?"

Her eyes locked with Sammy's, as if she could stare him into submission.

Rowen sat up.

"What happened to your Uncle Franklin?"

Now that he was at her level, her blue eyes pierced him through. "Nothing. They said it was self-defense, but it wasn't no self-defense 'cause Daddy never done nothin' to him."

"Eden!" Adeline called from the porch, as if she'd been expecting her.

"So that's your name!" Sammy sang out, "The Beautiful Garden of Eden!"

"Sammy Little, the Lord musta left manna in your supper bowl today if all you've got to do is pick on a child. C'mere, Eden." Adeline grabbed the girl's hand and tugged her to the house.

Sammy looked back down at Rowen. "I believe I'm going to hang out on that porch and see what becomes of that girl, since this gate project ain't going anywhere."

"Mind helping me up?"

"Why? Because you're a white boy?"

"No, because I asked."

"You didn't say the magic word."

"Please."

Sammy stuck out his hand and Rowen hesitated. Sure, he'd asked for help, but not in all his eighteen years had he ever touched a Negro man's hand before. If Sammy tuned in on Rowen's thought, he'd back away and the possible loss of fraternity worried Rowen more than breaking custom, so he reached out and Sammy gripped him and yanked him to his feet.

"Thank you."

"See if you can stay upright for a while."

Rowen left Sammy at the door and followed the hubbub to his mama's bedroom where Eden stood next to the bedside while his mama squeezed her hand. Eden fidgeted in her clammy grip. She seemed to know the situation called for her to submit to these attentions from a sick woman even if she didn't care for them.

"Eden," his mama said, "the last time I saw you, you were just a baby and now look how tall and lovely you are. Did you know your daddy and my late husband were second cousins once removed?"

Rowen wondered how come no one had bothered to tell him that he was kin to a murdered man, 'specially after his mother had babbled on about Coman and her husband just days earlier.

"How come you're in bed?" Eden asked. "Are you dyin'?"

"No, no, you shouldn't worry about me." Miz Rita reached over with her other hand and patted Eden's forearm. "I'm just a little under the weather at the moment, that's all. The doctor says I need time and rest, 'specially in this awful heat, but I'll soon be just fine. Why don't you all go in the kitchen? I'm sure Adeline's got tea for you."

Eden

Adeline spoke from the doorway. "Miz Rita, Eden would like to ask you something if you can spare her a moment."

"Yes, Eden?"

Eden rocked back and forth on her heels, as if she was testing the edge of a precipice. "Can I stay with y'all for a while?"

No one said, "Why?" Instead, the women's eyes locked. Rowen had witnessed this ritual between his mama and Adeline for as long as he could remember, where, in pivotal moments, the whole history of White Rock — the long roiling river of its marriages, births and scandals — coursed silently between them until they arrived at some private conclusion about it, not to be shared with him.

At last his mother spoke. "Such awful tragedy to befall the White family, maybe even worse than what's become of us. Adeline, I believe this is a sign. The Lord has brought Eden to us to remind us of the humility and gratitude we should have for still having one another, even if we've lost everything else.

"What have we got in that back room?"

Adeline shrugged. "Nothing much. Your sewing machine is there for when you get better, Mr. Hart's clothes and books, nothing much."

"Will it detain Rowen and — I'm sorry, I believe I heard another boy outside."

"He's Sammy Little, Miz Rita. He come to help Rowen fix the front gate."

"How kind of him."

"Good deeds do till the souls of our young people, removing the tendrils of sin and helping them come up straight."

JAMIE LISA FORBES

Rowen nearly busted out laughing and then covered it with a cough. There were one or two things that Adeline didn't know, such as Sammy wasn't any kind of church boy.

"Do you think it will detain them too much if they clean up that back room?"

Adeline shook her head, "Won't detain 'em at all far as I see, 'cause they done burned up the whole morning and got nothin' to show for it."

His mama turned to him. "Would you, Rowen?"

The back room was sweltering hot and musty. Adeline's "nothing much" was boxes stacked floor to ceiling. Rowen had assumed that Adeline would unpack those boxes and the constellation of objects that had always surrounded him would somehow reappear. Before his father passed, everything had had its place on a polished shelf, or behind a glass door. Staring at the labeled boxes, he felt as if he'd entered a crypt. Nothing of his life would come back to him, not one bit.

He and Sammy hauled boxes out to the porch while Eden poked at a nail hole in the wall.

"All this work's for you, you know," Rowen snapped. "Mind helping us out instead of wrecking our house?"

"Miz Rita told y'all to do it. I don't want to drop any of them boxes and break her things," she answered. She drifted out to the porch and rested her forearms on the railing, looking off down the road as if none of this activity had anything to do with her.

Adeline hustled in and out of the back room, barking commands. When they had it halfway cleared, she ordered Sammy to get a broom and start on the

floor. Rowen moved the sewing machine outside and then noticed that Eden was gone.

He called back into the house. "Adeline, where's Eden?"

Adeline came to the doorway. "You been watching her."

"She was standing right over there, doin' nothing. Now she's gone."

Adeline cupped her hands to her mouth. "Eeeee-dan!"

The collective insect drone—cicadas, flies, crickets—filled the pause around them.

"Eeeee-daaaan!"

Sammy joined them. "She didn't seem like she cared much. Now that we done all this work, maybe she's gone on home, where she belongs."

"Why weren't you watching her?" Adeline snapped.

"Me? I'm not mindin' some lyin' white trash!"

"What makes you so sure she's a liar?"

"Her daddy wasn't nothing but a white trash drunk. Everybody knows that."

"Like you ain't nothing but a nigger? Don't everybody know that too? Birch Whitney went around doing things for folks, white folks, Negro folks, and never looked for anyone's thanks. Next time, you look into what you're talking about before you open your mouth."

Sammy's jaw clamped shut and Adeline turned away. She went back in the house, still calling for the girl. Then she squealed like she'd run into a snake.

Rowen flew through the screen door, thinking that something had happened to his mother, but the commotion was coming from the bathroom.

And there was Eden in front of the bathroom mirror. She'd taken a set of kitchen shears and whacked off chunks of her hair down to the scalp. With her hair gone, her skinny neck jutted out of her collar and her ears were huge, like a clown's.

His mother called out, "What's going on out there?"

"Nothing but a rat's nest, that's what Mama calls it." Eden plucked up another piece and Adeline grabbed her wrist.

"Your mama ain't here," she said quietly as she took the shears from her hand, "and till she gets here, we'll take care of it."

Rowen turned into his mama's room. "That girl's crazy, Mama. She just whacked off all her hair."

"Come here," she said.

Her hair lay loose on the pillow. The color had started to grow out and at least half an inch of gray roots showed. This wasn't his mama. His mama had always been the first to remark how a woman had "let herself go" if her roots were showing.

"No matter how she behaves, be patient with her. Adeline will settle her down."

"Why is she here?"

"She's family to your daddy. Isn't that enough of a reason?"

"You never said anything about that the other day."

"Rowen, I realize you've come of age and you believe you are entitled to know everything simply upon demand, but ill as I am, I am still your mother, and I will reveal what I know when I believe you are ready for it."

Eden

"Whether she's kin to us or not, we're family to Uncle Hugh, and he doesn't keep us up."

"Don't you see she's just a child? Swept up like a sparrow in a hurricane. Surely, we can let her rest here a few days.

"Coman Whitney has lost her husband. She nearly lost her brother, too. Sometimes catastrophe makes people do silly things, cruel things that they'll regret later. In a few days, Coman will miss her child and come get her. Now help her settle in and unpack her things."

Adeline stuck her head in the door. "Miz Rita, Sammy and I are leaving to find the child a bed."

"Leaving?" said Rowen. He glanced to where Eden stood behind her. "What about her?"

"You can't watch a little girl?"

"I just done told Mama. She's out've her mind. I can't take care of her."

"If you think a child's lost her mind for cutting her hair, you best plan on never having children. Remember the College of Life I been telling you 'bout? Today is the child-raising class and Miss Eden, she's your instructor. Now, Sammy and I will be right back. Feed her whatever she wants and don't let her have the shears."

To avoid facing Eden, Rowen followed them to the door. Sammy smirked over his shoulder as the screen door slammed.

Busy. He needed to stay busy so he wouldn't have to talk to this girl. He grabbed a broom and swept up the hair in the bathroom. She followed him and stood in the doorway.

"I don't know why you did this. You looked real pretty that day in the courtroom."

"You were there?"

"You walked right past me. I still got the glove you dropped."

"I didn't see you."

"There were a lot of people there. I guess you couldn't 've seen everyone.

"How come you were dressed in that dress, while your mother was wearing black? How come you didn't have a black dress too?"

"Mama got me one for the funeral, but it was too small, and all the buttons come off. This was the only other dress I had. Mama said she was tired of searching the church basements to find me clothes that I tear up all the time. She says if I can't take care of clothes that she has to scrounge around for, then I can just run around in rags."

He dumped the hair in the garbage pail. She was blocking his exit.

"Guess we'd better find a place for your stuff. What you got in that case anyway?"

"Nothing."

"Nothing? It's so stuffed the hinge is breaking."

He knelt next to the case and looked at her, expecting her to open it. She crossed her arms and stuck out her lip, as if taunting him to open it. He snapped the lock open.

All it contained was a raggedy quilt and, beneath it, the other grimy glove, a sleeveless nightie and underwear.

"This all you got?"

She didn't move. If anything, she stuck out her lip a little farther.

"Seems like if you were running away, you'd 've packed a few things."

"I didn't run away. Mama said I'd lied on her poor brother, who hadn't done anything other

than try to help us when no one else would, and she didn't want to see my lyin' face around the house no more. She said she didn't know why I'd say such lies when I didn't understand nothing about what happened the day Daddy died."

"Are you gonna wear that jungle dress the rest of your life?"

"Adeline said I should come find her if I ever needed help and I didn't have nowhere else to go."

"How do you know Adeline anyway?"

"We've always known Adeline, me and Daddy, that is. You know Adeline ain't got a husband, right?"

"Everybody knows that. He drowned in a hurricane when her daughter was a baby."

"Well, Daddy said he and Adeline became friends when I was a baby. He said he'd heard of some white boys planning to set fire to her house 'cause she caught 'em in her garden and set her hounds on 'em to run them out. So he went and kept watch on her porch every night for a month. He said those boys would call out to him in the dark and holler that he was just a drunk who couldn't do nothing to them, and he'd holler back that if that was what they thought, they oughta try him out and see what happened. But they were just cowards, and when school started up again, they gave up."

Yet more history closeted in secrecy by Adeline and his mama, if what Eden had said had even happened at all. How was a man to feel grounded, looking off from his porch at everything he saw coming, when all the scraps of useful information were squirreled away from him in his own house?

"Because of that, I growed up knowing

Adeline. Daddy took me to stay with her whenever he was playing craps. And sometimes they'd just sit out in her dirt yard and listen to the whippoorwills and visit."

While Rowen struggled with why no one had told him all this before, Uncle Hugh's words welled up in his mind. If he blurted out that they didn't have the money to keep Eden, his mother would hear.

"You hungry?"

"You don't like me. I don't like you either."

"Adeline says I gotta feed you, so whether I like you or not, you might as well eat."

In the kitchen, he slammed a platter of cornbread down on the table and stuck his head in the icebox. He didn't want her to see that he had no notion of what to do. Adeline fixed all the food. He'd never so much as made himself a sandwich.

Eden wolfed a square of cornbread. With her mouth full, she mumbled, "What 're you looking in there for?"

"I don't know what Adeline was going to fix, that's all."

"Ain't you never fixed nothing to eat before?"

"Plenty of times."

"Is there any tea in there?"

He pulled out the tea and a carton of eggs. When he turned, he caught her rummaging through the cupboards.

"Hey, what are you doing?" he snapped.

She turned, holding a tin of tuna. "How about this?"

"Give me that!" He snatched it from her.

Shock at his gesture splashed over her face. Then her eyes hardened as the depth of his

resentment hit home. Without another word, she tore out of the door, and before he'd even reached the steps, she was flying down the road. He ran after her.

"Eden!"

Her legs churned. With every stride, a puff of dirt bounced off the ground. She turned to look over her shoulder, shrieked and ran harder. He caught up with her and grabbed her arm.

"Stop," he said.

"Let me go!" With her other hand, she raked her nails down the length of his forearm. He screamed, and she was running again.

He bent over to catch his breath and the sweat dripped off his forehead. What the hell was he doing? Why not let her go? Come to think of it, he had some secrets too. Adeline didn't know about the money.

What would he say to Adeline? Could he tell her the truth of what had happened with Uncle Hugh? He was afraid to, afraid of that look in her eyes finding him lacking for failing to act as a man should. He burned at the thought. Why should he have to put up with that? None of this was his fault. With his daddy's death, everyone suddenly had a mountain of expectations for him that no one had prepared him for. He wasn't a man, anyway. A man would know what to do.

Even if he let Eden go, Adeline would turn right back around soon as she heard of it and go look for her herself.

When he straightened, there was no sign of her. The sky shimmered white with heat. Going forward or going home, it looked like hell in either direction.

"U-u-hum," he heard. The voice was behind him. He turned and looked back the direction they had come.

"You sure don't know how to find nobody. You ain't never going to be a detective."

Her voice came from a blackberry thicket at the side of the road.

"What are you doing in there?"

She crawled out. Now she was powdered in a fresh layer of dirt. Blackberry scratches covered her arms and legs.

"What'd you do that for, Eden?"

"Were you really in the courtroom?"

"Yes, I was."

"You think I'm a liar?"

Sammy's dismissal of her came to mind. What with blackberry twigs sticking out her patchy hair, she looked worse than she had just an hour before. Maybe she hadn't seen the pipe wrench. Or maybe she had seen it and it didn't matter because it was just a pipe wrench and her daddy was her daddy.

"No. I thought you told the truth. Let's go on home. We'll eat that tuna."

She hung back.

"It's too hot to stay out here."

"Everyone hates me."

That statement wasn't too far from how Rowen felt about himself.

"I don't hate you."

"You do, too, you big fat liar."

"My mama's sick...you seen that."

He longed to blurt it all out, tell her that she needed to leave. But there wasn't any point because he'd still be stuck with Adeline.

"Let's just…go home." He held out his hand.

"I ain't holding your hand. I ain't never holding your hand."

He started back toward the house. He didn't turn around but he could hear her behind him. "You prob'ly don't know how to open that can of tuna."

"You're right, I don't."

"Or how to fix it neither."

"I don't know nothin' about it."

"Are you going to let me do it?"

"I guess I'll have to."

When he opened the screen door, he sensed that something had happened. Maybe it was just his guilt at having left his mother alone, something Adeline never did during the day. He listened. Nothing beyond the steady drone of the window fans. How long had they been gone, anyway?

"Mama?" he called.

He rushed through the kitchen to the hall. His mother was slumped against the wall next to the bathroom. Her eyes, brimming with reproach, pinned him in the doorway. "Where were you? I called and called, Rowen. I had to use the bathroom. And I've just gotten so weak. I have to have help. But I couldn't sit waiting until I wet the bed. I got out of bed and I held on to it until I reached the doorway, but once I got to this hall, I fell. I believe I've twisted my ankle. It might even be broken. And I've been here this whole time staring at these ugly walls. Sea-foam, that must be the color, like that scummy swimming pool at the Sentry Motel when it closed down. They've got to be painted, Rowen."

"Eden ran off."

"Why ever would she do that?"

Rowen looked over his shoulder. Eden watched them from the kitchen doorway. "Don't know, Mama."

"Well come get me up. I believe I'm about to pee all over this floor."

He put his arm around her to heave her up, but she hung against him like a sack of flour. "Mama, can you push up with your good leg?"

"My good leg's gone to sleep waiting all this time."

Eden rushed to her other side, and Miz Rita put her arm over her shoulder.

"Why Eden, what a strong girl you are," she said as she stood up. She leaned on the two of them as she limped to the bathroom. When she reached the sink, she said, "This is fine, children, I believe I can manage from here."

She slowly shut the door in their faces. They stood outside listening as the pee hit the bowl. Eden started to giggle, and Rowen glared at her. The toilet flushed and his mother opened the door. Eden's smirk dropped off her face and she sang out, "I'll help you back to bed, Miz Hart."

"Thank you, Eden. Has Rowen gotten you some lunch yet?"

"No, ma'am. I believe I'll have to make it myself. He don't know how to fix nothin'."

"That's not true. I bet he could do you a nice tuna salad sandwich with tomatoes right out of the garden. Couldn't you, Rowen?"

"Miz Hart, there's nothing I'd like better in the world."

She looked over her shoulder at Rowen and stuck her tongue out.

"Mama, should I go get the doctor?"

"No, I believe I'll be all right with a little ice."

They sat her on the bed, and she eased back into her pillows. "And Rowen, I need some fresh water."

Her ankle was swollen. Rowen propped it up on more pillows and wrapped it in ice. As he was finishing, Eden came in with a glass of water. He reached to take it from her and the glass slipped and shattered on the floor.

"Look what you done now," he snapped.

"I didn't do it. You did!"

"Don't take it out on the child, Rowen."

"Mama...." The words were poised to dive out of his mouth: we can't keep her here, we don't have the money. Then he heard a clatter of household equipment tumbling from the hall closet. Eden hustled back in with a mop and furiously pushed water and glass shards in all directions.

"This all comes," his mother said, "because you've never had to share me with anyone. My love and affection has always been showered on you. Even your father used to complain that I spoiled you. He was jealous of you. And now that you've been part-orphaned, it's only natural that you'd require my attention even more. It's only natural that you'd be jealous of this little child." She patted his hand. "It's only for a brief, brief time, I promise. Now pick up all that glass before she hurts herself."

It was late afternoon and shadows had slipped over the porch by the time Adeline and Sammy returned in a flatbed truck. After Rowen had cleaned up his mother's bedroom, they'd eaten egg salad sandwiches that Eden had fixed. The sandwiches weren't half bad, though Eden had laced the egg salad with allspice, to "give it color," she'd said.

Sammy jumped out of the driver's seat.

"You ain't made it much further with this new gate, Mr. Rowen."

"What do you expect?" Rowen blurted, though by the smirk on Sammy's face, that was just the reaction he'd hoped for. "How was I 'sposed to watch Eden and Mama and go get a drill."

"Miss Eden coulda run to town and picked up a drill. Miss Eden, you ever handled a drill?"

"Sammy," said Adeline, "are you going to unload this bed or stand there and blow more steam outta that mouth?"

Eden crowed from the back of the truck. "Oh Miz Adeline, it's beautiful!"

Rowen looked up at a child's bed the color of Pepto-Bismol.

"Can I keep it?" she asked Adeline.

"It's your own, baby, if we can get these boys to unload it."

In the end, the bed had to be dismantled on the front porch and then reassembled inside. Adeline stood with her arms crossed while Eden jumped up and down on the bed that throbbed pink in the naked room.

"We'll have to fix this with some paint, some curtains...We'll need some drawers. Rowen, give Sammy twenty dollars. We bought the bed at Homer's and borrowed his truck, too. Sammy's got to be taking it back."

"I ain't got twenty dollars."

From her face, Rowen knew Adeline's thoughts were racing back to recollect Uncle Hugh's visit.

"Sammy, go on outside," she said.

"I got to be leaving," he whined. "That truck's got one headlight and I gotta drive it through town. If the sheriff catches me, he's going to lock me up."

"I said, go on outside!"

Rowen's mother called, "Adeline?"

Adeline hadn't taken her eyes off Rowen. "It ain't nothin', Miss Rita. Miss Eden needs a bath, that's all, and Mr. Sammy don't need to be around. I'll be there in a minute."

Eden yelped as Adeline hauled her off the bed and then went limp as a rag doll, nearly pulling Adeline over to the floor.

"I don't need no bath!"

"Mr. Rowen," said Adeline, as she grabbed Eden around the waist and carried her off, "go out and pick some okra for supper, please."

Outside, as Rowen sifted through the plants, he heard the bath water running and then Adeline came out and squatted next to him.

"What did Mr. Grimes say to you last night?"

Rowen took a breath. He'd rehearsed it so much through the day that he thought he could repeat it all, straight out, like any man would do, but instead he blubbered.

"We don't have any money. We don't have enough to live on. We're not even going to be able to pay you anymore."

"What are you talking about? I thought your Uncle Hugh was going to buy out your daddy's share of the business."

"He said Daddy's share of the business didn't come up to as much as he thought."

"What about your education?"

The thought of saying he didn't even want to go shamed him. Wasn't he supposed to be like Chloe, the daughter at Howard University? Adeline's expectations of him were every bit as steep as those for her own child.

It was easier to blurt, "I don't know."

"Did he show you any books, any papers?"

Eden's singing filtered out the bathroom window. "'*Froggy went a courtin' and he did ride, uh HUH...*'"

Rowen wiped his eyes, "No, ma'am."

"You go up there and you ask to see the books of that business, you hear me? You ask him to show you."

"Yes, ma'am."

"Make him prove it to you."

Rowen nodded, but he couldn't conjure the image of walking into Uncle Hugh's office and saying the words that Adeline wanted to plant in his mouth.

"How much did he give you last night?"

"Forty dollars."

"'*Froggy went a courtin' and he did ride, sword and a pistol by his side, uh HUH...*'"

Adeline exhaled a long slow sigh. "Go give Sammy twenty now."

"That's all we got, Adeline, for the whole month."

"You'll talk to your Uncle Hugh tomorra and God'll make him do what's right."

"He's not going to listen to me!"

"David slew Goliath and he wasn't no

bigger than you. And no one's asking you to slay a Phillistine. Your Uncle Hugh's just a man, weak and naked in God's eyes."

"What if he don't give me any more?"

"God'll answer you tomorra. Just give Sammy his money so he can get on out of here."

Rowen handed the okra to Adeline and went inside. He plucked the money from his Sunday shoes and when he brought it back out, Sammy snatched it from his hand.

"If that sheriff catches me, you're gonna be coughin' up your tubakka money for my bail, Mr. Rowen."

"You could just leave the truck here and walk home!"

"You got another twenty dollars to pay rent for that truck tomorra?"

Sammy hopped in the driver's seat and the truck coughed and sputtered. As it rolled into the dark, the sound was soon muffled by the cicada din. Under the porch light mobbed with insects, Eden appeared in one of Rowen's undershirts. "Are you gonna stand there in the road all night?" she called.

Nothing—not death, ignorance, poverty, abandonment—ever seemed to blunt the self-assurance of that girl. Why did it seem like she knew more about what to do and say in the world than he did?

3

"*ROWEN.*" She was shaking his shoulder. "Rowen, wake up." He threw out an arm to swat at her. She pattered out of his room. He listened to the thrum of the fan, waiting for it to numb him back into sleep and in seconds, it did.

Then his eyelids burned, and he woke to a flashlight in his face. "What the hell!"

Eden sprang off his bed to avoid another swing. "You up yet?"

"What are you doing in here? Go on back to bed!"

"I had a bad dream."

"I'm not your mama."

"Adeline's not here and I can't sleep."

"I can't do nothin' about it."

Eden

His mother called from her bedroom, "Rowen?"

"Now see what you done. You woke up Mama."

Rowen switched on the hall light and cracked his mother's door open.

"Is anything the matter?" she asked.

"Eden. She had a bad dream."

"Did she tell you what her dream was about?"

"No."

"Get her a glass of milk. She'll go on back to sleep."

"I don't see her now. Maybe she already has."

"Stop being so hateful, Rowen."

He went back to bed, but no sooner had he drifted back into his own dreams when the flashlight came on again.

"Your mama said to get me a glass of milk. I heard her."

He wanted to choke her, but he couldn't risk waking his mother again.

"All right. Get the flashlight out of my face."

She followed him to the kitchen. He poured a glass and set it on the table. "There. Now I'm going back to bed."

"Come outside with me."

"No."

"I'll tell your mama."

"Whatdoyouwanttogooutsidefor?You'vegot your milk."

"It's cooler. It's too hot in here."

They went out on the porch. Light shown through the underbrush though stars still winked overhead. She was right, it was cool, deliciously so, as if he'd dipped into a pool of water. He sat on the steps and rested his chin in his hands.

"Are you ready to hear my dream?"

"Do I have a choice?"

"I dreamed I was in the courtroom. Uncle Franklin aimed his shotgun right at me. And when I tried to get away, I was strapped in. Just like them electric chairs. And Uncle Franklin, he looked down the sight and squeezed the trigger."

A faint breeze rattled the leaves. Any second now, the first morning cardinal would whistle.

"I don't know what you're worried about. Franklin's not going to bother you."

"How do you know?"

Rowen shrugged. "It doesn't matter to him now. Nothing happened."

"You believed them about Daddy having that pipe wrench, didn't you?"

"It doesn't matter one hoot what I believe."

Eden leapt to her feet. "There wasn't no pipe wrench! You hear me?"

"Okay, Okay."

She kicked him in the ribs. "Say it! There wasn't no pipe wrench!"

He reached for her feet and she jumped away.

"Rowen!" Adeline's voice bellowed from the road. "What are you doing to that child now?"

"She's kicking me!"

"She oughta be kickin' you. You was 'sposed to be up by now to beg Mr. Sawyer for an hour off this morning 'cause you got business with your Uncle Hugh. But here you sit!"

"She's crazy! I don't know why we've got to put up with her when we don't have enough for ourselves."

"Time's come for you to discover there's others in the world besides yourself. Let go what you hold in that clenched-up fist and you find He

give it all back. And more. Now get off that stoop before I kick you myself."

Twenty minutes later he was on the road, strung like a sagging wire between two opposite poles, Adeline on one end and Uncle Hugh on the other. He couldn't accomplish what either one of them wanted him to do, and he hoped a spirit would enter him when he arrived at one place or the other. Like God speaking through Moses.

At the auction yard, men in their overalls leaned against their pickups, jabbering about their tobacco crops and the heat while they waited for the morning hog auction. Rowen skirted around them, hoping no one would notice, and slipped into the office. But there was no escaping Cousin Mabel who greeted everyone from her desk at the door.

"Why, Cousin Rowen!" Mabel said. "What a surprise to see you."

"Hey, Mabel."

Rowen always squirmed at Mabel's enthusiasm to see him. He had a vague recollection of the two of them as toddlers opening Christmas presents when some comment had circulated about them getting married one day. He feared that Mabel remembered it as well and had taken it to heart. Who was going to marry a cripple? He backed up a step or two to prevent her from doing something reckless, like reaching out to touch him. But with distance, he had to admit that she was a pretty girl after all, with a peach-shaped doll face and hair falling in thick curls around her shoulders. He remembered his reaction to her senior picture — a headshot — from a couple of years back. From crown to shoulders, she was unblemished.

"I've been missing you since you left town. There's nothing wrong with your mama, is there?"

"No, Mama's just fine."

"I hope that's true. I've been so worried about her. I've been meaning to come visit ever since you all moved out there. Sundays when I want to come, Daddy has me here working on the books. I do mean to come out some Sunday. Please tell your mama that I mean to."

Her voice plunged to a whisper and she glanced over her shoulder at her father's office. "And Rowen, I need to talk to you."

Before Rowen had an instant to speculate on what she might want to say, Uncle Hugh's door opened, and there he stood in his white shirt and blood-red bow tie appraising Rowen like just another hog.

"I wondered who you was fussing over, Mabel. She doesn't carry on so for regular folk. Nice of you to drop by, Rowen, but we got an auction here today. Your mother all right?"

Rowen hesitated. No chance now to ask Mabel what she had might have wanted and plainly hadn't wanted to say in front of Hugh. Nothing else to do but lurch forward with his mission. "I just want to see you for a moment, Uncle Hugh. It won't take long."

Uncle Hugh grimaced, but gestured toward his office. Once the door had shut, Rowen's gaze pin-balled around the room while he waited for the gumption that Adeline had tried to instill in him. It was useless. As much as he scrambled to conjure up some alternate self, only Rowen inhabited this room.

"Mama's fine, Uncle Hugh. I don't mean to

show you any disrespect, it's just that...we need more money."

"I told you a couple a nights ago. You need to get rid of Adeline. That'd cut your expenses."

Rowen stared at the grime caked in the cracks on the wood floor. "But...Mama wants to know...why..."

There was a knock on the door. It opened, and Eden pushed into the room ahead of Cousin Mabel.

"Daddy, I don't mean to interrupt, but this little girl...she says she's looking for Rowen."

"Ain't this the Whitney child that spoke against her uncle?"

"I don't know. She's asking for Rowen."

Now Uncle Hugh turned, his eyes boring through Rowen's skull. The moment he learned that his mother had taken Eden in, they'd be lucky if they saw another dime.

"Rowen, this girl here's real nice. She says she's your cousin. How come you didn't say nothing about her?"

"This..." Uncle Hugh groped for the right phrase. Eden might be white trash, but even he wouldn't say it to her face. "This...girl's with you?"

Eden stepped right up to Uncle Hugh's desk. "I ain't no kind of liar, if that's what you're thinking. Uncle Franklin shot my daddy. I saw it and I've been telling the truth about it ever since. But Mama didn't believe me, and she threw me out."

Uncle Hugh nodded. "As well she should have."

"You poor thing," said Cousin Mabel, "how awful."

"Mabel, I've told you a thousand times, you needn't be caterwauling to the community about things you don't know nothing about. You don't know what's happened and you wouldn't understand it if you knew. Now get back out there and mind your business."

As Mabel backed her wheelchair out of the office, Rowen said, "Eden didn't have anywhere else to go."

"What'd you say, boy?" Uncle Hugh asked, his head swiveling on his rooster's neck.

"She didn't have a place to go!" Rowen was surprised by how loud his voice sounded.

Beads of sweat glistened on the top of Uncle Hugh's bald head. "Your mama come up with Franklin. I understand that. But I didn't know she had anything to do with Coman," he said. "Or is this Adeline's doing?"

As Rowen fumbled for an answer, he remembered the tried and true chords strung in every White Rock citizen that were plucked as necessary to explain improbable outcomes. "She's kin."

"Kin, you say?"

"Mama says that Eden's daddy and my daddy were second cousins."

"How's that? And how come I don't know of it?"

Rowen shrugged. Boys weren't expected to recite lineages. "I don't know. Daddy didn't talk much about his family, that's what Mama said. But she says it's true."

"I did think it strange that your daddy didn't talk about his family much. Now we know why. Your daddy was kin to a drunkard who got himself

kilt through his own asininity. Makes sense when I recollect all that's occurred."

In the pause that followed, the fan whirred, and beyond it the sounds of men shuffling outside and greeting one another drifted through the open window while Uncle Hugh sat stone-faced, working out how to flush Rowen's request from his mind.

"I hear that phone ringing, Mabel. Are you answering?

"I just told you the other night, boy. Your daddy's share of this business ain't what we thought. It ain't enough to put you through school. It ain't enough to keep Adeline. And it ain't enough to be running no damn orphanage, even if they was kin. If this girl's got kin among your daddy's people, you oughta ferret them out and send her back to them."

"You said the appraiser appraised Daddy's share, but you never told me what it was."

"Let me tell you something, son. First, you're listening to that Negra, then you're taking in this lyin' spawn, who, apparently, you are kin to, and now you disrespect the one man who's trying to steer you right!"

"I'm not a liar!" Eden screamed so loud that Rowen knew her voice must have carried out to the parking lot.

"Mabel!" Hugh shouted, "Get these kids out of here. I got a sale going on today."

Mabel beckoned them out to the foyer, then she pulled a coin purse from a pouch on her wheelchair. "Why don't you kids go out to the concession stand and get you some Cheerwine?" She poured coins into Rowen's palms.

"Before we go, can I try out your wheelchair?" asked Eden.

"No, honey. I need it. I've got to have it."

"How come?"

"When I was a little girl, younger than you are, I got polio. And I can't walk."

"Never, for your whole life?"

"If it's God's will, I will walk one day. Until then, I just have to keep hoping and praying."

Eden took the coins from Rowen and set them back in Mabel's lap.

"Heavens, Miss Eden, why did you do that?" asked Mabel.

"I don't have nothing to give you. Not even a gum ball. The only thing I got is what you give us."

"Bless your soul. You needn't feel sorry for me."

"I just want to help since you meant to help us. Maybe you can take it to church this Sunday. You don't never know. God might look down and see them coins in His box and He'll get to thinking about you above everyone else, and then maybe He'll decide it's your time and you'll rise straight up out of that wheelchair. Then we'd feel real good, better than if we'd had a silly old Cheerwine."

"After that, can I try your wheelchair out?"

"Mabel, are those kids gone yet?" Uncle Hugh hollered.

Rowen grabbed Eden's arm and tugged her to the door.

"You are a sweet girl, Miss Eden," said Mabel. "I'm going to do just what you say. And I'll say a prayer for you. Rowen, be sure and tell your mama I said hello. And come back to see me soon, okay?"

Outside, a hot breeze eddied, carrying the stench of hog waste up Rowen's nostrils.

Eden

He turned to Eden. "What did you come along for?"

"To see what you were doing."

Every second, another truck pulled in cutting off escape routes. He was entrapped in the web of White Rock civilities. As much as those farmers would nod and cluck and ask after his mother, they'd also lump him with this scandalous half-bald child.

Eden bounced up to the men closest to her and sang out, "Hey, Mr. Lunsford, what'cha doing here?"

She did all the talking with Rowen hitched to her side while she blabbed on about how Adeline had brought her to live with him and his mother. Between being miserable and hot and resentful at Adeline, who'd sent him here, and Eden, who wouldn't shut up, Rowen felt ready to explode, and to the one or two listeners who addressed him, he grunted and looked away.

As people peeled off toward the sale barn, he saw his chance and slipped off. He looked over his shoulder. No one was after him and he could give in to the urge to bolt. He broke into a jog. His feet pounding the road one after another brought a wave of relief, though he knew it was illusory. He had passed the lone withering oak tree before he heard the patter of Eden's feet behind him.

"Hey, Rowen, slow down. How come you didn't wait up?"

He slowed but didn't answer.

"Where are we going now?"

"I'm going to Sawyer's. I'll be lucky if he doesn't fire me. I missed half a morning's work as it is."

JAMIE LISA FORBES

"Can I come, too?"

"No."

"I know how to pick tubakka."

He stopped. "If you follow me there, I could lose my job, you know that? You carry on and on, like you're the only one whose daddy's died. My daddy's dead. Did you know that? And my mama's sick. We had to move out here 'cause we didn't have the money to stay in town anymore. And now Uncle Hugh isn't going to give us nothin'. And Mama and Adeline—they say you're staying. So I need you to go on home and leave me alone so I can figure out what's next. I need you to stay the hell at home and shut up!"

Eden's brows scrunched together while he raged.

"I hate you, Rowen!"

"I hate you more than you can ever know!" She tore away from him.

How was it that the heat never dragged her down like it did everyone else? He imagined her bursting through the screen door, hollering for Adeline. He didn't care what Adeline thought now. If she wanted money out of Uncle Hugh, let her go talk to him. He wanted to rip off all these expectations that women had strapped on him. He wanted to go somewhere where he didn't have to think.

At Sawyer's, Sammy and a group of colored boys sat in the shade eating lunch. His friends, Rowen guessed. They seemed like friends, all easy

with one another and laughing among themselves. Sammy looked up at him and smirked. He called out loud enough for everyone to hear. "You slept in again, Mr. Rowen?"

"None of your business."

He regretted his tone, for the boys around Sammy tensed. Seeing the wariness creep over their features, he realized he was his Uncle Hugh to them.

Sammy's tone was chilly. "We're just eating our lunch here, Mr. Rowen. We ain't done nothing to you."

He didn't know how to make them understand. He wanted to settle down with them and joke it all away, but he had just scorched all connections to them, and he didn't know how to make it right. He plopped down at a distance and they soon slipped back into their own conversation. He was thirsty and hadn't stopped anywhere for water. He could smell the juice oozing from their watermelon. If he asked for it, they'd give him some. Not because they wanted to, only because they'd think they had to.

Sawyer and Hester Prynne returned from lunch, and although Sawyer didn't so much as glance at Sammy and his friends, they all rose and scattered among the tobacco rows. No one looked back at Rowen. He rose and tried to sneak past Sawyer.

"I looked for you before now."

"Sorry, Mr. Sawyer."

"How come you and your mama took in that girl?"

The news from the sale barn had outrun him. Rowen shrugged.

"What a fool, boy, to stick your foot in that

snake's nest: Franklin White and his harlot sister and that child whose daddy mighta been Birch Whitney…And she's a damn little apple thief, I'll tell you that. I don't know why you done it. Wasn't nothing for you in it. I hired you 'cause your daddy, he was good to me, and everyone says your mama's sick."

"We had to take Eden in. She's kin."

"Then I'm sorry for ya. If I were you, I'd go pray about it and ask the Lord if you done the right thing. Me, I got to pay off Franklin White at the end of the year. And then, the math's been troublesome…," he gestured back at the ruffling rows of tobacco. "I don't have to pay them as much as you."

Sammy and his friends were moving farther off. He could hear their footsteps, the snapping as leaves broke from the stalks. He was sorry he'd scared them off.

"I'll be going," said Rowen.

Sawyer nodded. "Appreciate it. You tell your mama I hope she gets better."

Rowen crossed back over the bridge, where the same ditch flies swarmed round and round, and back through Sawyer's yard, where the air, trapped under the yellow pines, was dense as sludge, and then back down the road past the dirt yards and empty porches to his own broken gate and porch that was eerily quiet.

The screen door squeaked open, and still there was no sound.

"Adeline?" He felt relieved that she didn't answer. He walked through to his mother's room. She was propped up on her pillows.

"Adeline's taken Eden to find her some clothes. You got mail today, from the University." She held up the envelope.

There it was, the culmination of expectations, the fine paper and raised lettering. It was supposed to bear him out of here, like a magic carpet.

His first urge was to rip it into shreds.

"You're to be there next week."

His hands clenched at his sides. "I'm not going, Mama."

Her chin jerked a little. "Of course, you are. I know you're worried about me. I'll be fine with Adeline. I'll be fine, just imagining how exciting your life will be. Afternoon teas with your professors and football games..." She paused and flashed a flirty little smile, "and the young ladies you'll see every evening."

"Adeline can't stay."

"What are you talking about? Is she unwell? She's said nothing to me about not staying. It's Hugh, isn't it? Well, he's got to see I'm too ill to manage without help. I will talk to him tomorrow."

"Hugh's never coming out here again."

A twist at the corner of her mouth, a scowl. He was almost relieved to see it.

"What's got into you, Rowen? You're talking very strangely. I am aware that as young men get older they speak abruptly to their mothers, but I never imagined such callousness from you."

"The things you rattle on about, Mama, none of them are real! Ever since we moved out here, you go on and on pretending, and I go on pretending with you. Because I wanted you to get better. But it isn't working, and you just go on lying here, and what goes on outside isn't pretend."

Now that she was no longer smiling, he noticed how flaccid the skin was on her jowls, on her arms. Every other second, the current from the fan ruffled the frizzled hair on her forehead.

"I believe the sun's done you in today, Rowen. You're overheated. Go finish the lemonade. Adeline will make some more when she comes back. And when you've cooled down, you can come back and apologize." She closed her eyes. "Now, go away."

Eden

4

RAIN HAMMERED on the tin roof through the night, vibrating through the walls. Rowen smashed the pillow over his head, but it didn't do any good. He felt as if he was trapped inside a drum.

There'd never been a commotion like this back in the house in White Rock. Rain, even hard rain, hurricane rain, had gurgled in the drainpipes, lulled him to sleep. All that time he'd been sheltered, safe and secure, by stout pine beams.

And by illusions with the same heft as beam and brick. He thought of his father coming home on an evening like this one. He'd hear him stomp his feet down below in the hallway. "Terrible evening out, Adeline," he'd say, and Rowen could hear her murmur as she removed his coat. His father would answer, "I'll be driving you home tonight. Don't you even think of sneaking out of that kitchen without telling me you're going home."

When Rowen came down for supper, his father would be sitting before the fire with a tumbler of bourbon on the side table next to him. The tobacco market report droned on the radio. Rowen didn't dare speak when that was on.

"Danville, flyings are up over last week, 68 to 74, Raleigh, 58 to 65, Greenville, 63 to 71, Lugs up, Danville…."

His father would say, without turning his head, "Your homework done, son?"

"Yes, sir."

Still his father wouldn't turn. "Go on, then, get some supper. Adeline's got pork chops and gravy tonight."

Just as termites, unseen, chewed through a foundation, the drain of money had been about to bring his house down. *Money.* Eighteen years without a thought of it, and now it was all Rowen could think of, rolling here in his own sweat.

Rent money was due next week.

And then there was his mama. She wasn't getting better, maybe she never would. If he could get a good job, work hard, save up some money, maybe he could move her back to town. Wouldn't she be happy then? He couldn't hope to put her back in a house like their old one. But he could picture her in a little two-bedroom. Maybe with moss-draped oaks out front. He could imagine surprising her: "Here, Mama, this is for you." Wouldn't that pry her out of that stinky old bedroom?

It would never be possible unless he let

Adeline go. But without Adeline, who would take care of his mother? Somehow, he had to manage. He imagined facing Adeline in the morning, struggling with the words, and all the while, withering under her glare.

The milky grey light in the room startled him. He was surprised to realize he'd fallen asleep after all. All that was left of the rain was a steady dripping from the eaves. The air was cooler but sodden as wet sheets.

Soon Adeline would be here, and he'd have to face her.

He crept into the hall and listened. With his forefinger, he pushed Eden's door open. She lay diagonally on top of her covers with her mouth open and one pale leg hanging off her Pepto-Bismol bed.

They weren't cousins. It was his mother's skill, to look someone straight in the eye and tell the most outrageous lies. He'd watched her do it so many times that he knew he'd absorbed her knack for it. Like every summer when their neighbor, Belinda, brought over a bushel of tomatoes, crawling with mealybugs. His mama would stand right there and sing their praises to the woman's face. Why did she do that? When he'd asked her, she'd just twitter, "Oh Rowen, it doesn't hurt to fluff people up a little."

Fluff them up to where they couldn't see the bugs in their own tomatoes?

But watching Eden, splayed out in her bed, it didn't matter anymore whether she was kin or not. He couldn't turn her out, no matter how the talk flamed against them, no matter if they all ended up living in the road.

He couldn't get the image out of his mind: Eden on the witness stand, the thrust of her chin before that sea of people, all united in resolve to disbelieve her. Eden would tell it like it was. Eden would tell someone if they had mealybugs in their tomatoes.

Rowen looked out the kitchen window and there, in the dawn, a man in overalls tamped dirt around a new gate post. Rowen ducked down behind the sink so he wouldn't be seen. Who the heck was that? Why would a passerby stop dead in the road at the crack of dawn and fool with someone's broken gate post? Rowen listened but all he heard was the sound of his own breathing.

If he went out there, he'd have to explain himself. It wouldn't matter what he'd manage to mumble. All he'd have to do was stick his head out the door and the man would peg him as a sorry-assed kid before he even opened his mouth. Where was Adeline? How long could he stay down here waiting for her? Rowen peeked over the edge of the sink.

The man was still working.

Rowen crawled to the screen door and pushed it open, hoping to see if Adeline was coming, but the door squeaked just loud enough, and the man looked up through glasses thick as Cheerwine bottles.

Nowhere to hide now. Rowen rose and stepped outside.

"I've been driving by here for two weeks looking at this, and it's 'bout got me unhinged," the man shouted. "You all the new tenants out here?"

"Yes, sir, me and my Mama."

"Bert Lowdermilk's your landlord, isn't he? Why didn't he come fix this?"

Rowen shrugged.

The man leaned on his tamping bar. "You didn't figure on asking him?"

"I didn't know I was supposed to. I was going to fix it myself."

"There you go. What were you waiting for?"

Rowen rifled through his responses, wondering what the most acceptable one was.

"I didn't have any tools."

The man turned to a shaggy butter-colored dog in the back of his truck. "He didn't have any tools, Sally." He pulled a handkerchief from his pocket and mopped his forehead. "Sally wants to know if that's the best you can do. With neighbors up and down this road who'd trip over themselves to help out a widow and her boy." The dog stretched over the side and licked his face. "Sally says only a Yankee would come up with some lame excuse like that. Are you a Yankee?"

Yankee. That was even worse than being called a sorry-assed kid.

"No," Rowen answered stiffly, "we're from right here in White Rock. I'm Rowen Hart."

"Your daddy's the auctioneer that's passed."

"Yes, sir."

"You recognize me, don't you?"

"No, sir."

"Colonel Richardson? Devoted husband to Elizabeth in our illustrious annual pageant, *The Flower of Cape Fear?*"

The annual outdoor pageant down at the town park. When he was young, he used to go every summer just to hear them fire the cannons, but the long speeches in between cannon volleys had become so boring that he'd stopped.

He wasn't sure he wanted to say that to this man.

JAMIE LISA FORBES

"Are you sure you're not a Yankee?"

Rowen blurted, "I've seen it! It was just a long time ago. It's just a story anyway."

"Our idle youth," the man sighed, "lacking in industry, untethered from their heritage. There's more here to be repaired than we thought, Sally."

They'd all learned it in grade school: how a plantation wife, Elizabeth Purdie Richardson, persuaded the British general, Cornwallis, to stop at her mansion and then betrayed him. No doubt there'd been a War of Liberation, or so the books said, but who'd slogged through it and what they'd won, or lost, where they'd lived and how they'd spoken, had all been buried deep under for so long that it wasn't of any practical use to anyone. Least of all to Rowen.

"What's the point of it?" he asked, "Those folks were all slaveowners, including Miz Richardson. What kind of heritage is that?"

The old man blinked.

"I didn't count on you being such a shrewd one, Rowen Hart. Although you are quite near useless. Can you tear yourself out of that doorway and help with this gate?"

Rowen shuffled off the porch. From ground level the man shot up tall as a pine. He stuck out a thick calloused hand. "I'm Claude—short for Claudius. I'd have thought an auctioneer's son, near grown, would be working at the auction yard nowadays."

Was Claude taunting him? *How could there be anyone left who hadn't heard what had happened.*

"Hugh Grimes owns it now. He's my uncle. He's not going to offer me a job."

"Hold this gate up, will ya, so I can mark where to drill. There, now…" Claude knelt to mark the holes in the post and then peered up over his glasses at Rowen. "Why wouldn't 'Uncle Hugh' want his kin to work at his business?"

"If you're in the pageant, how come you haven't heard all about this?"

"Well, my acting career is a job like any other. I need to put all my attention to it. But the White Rock gossip stream—it's flowed deep as the Cape Fear River since the first colonists got lost here, and while it keeps my Mary occupied, I find I don't have sufficient mental energy left over to engage with it. So you'll have to catch me up."

"Well, Daddy died owing Uncle Hugh money, and that made him mad, and then Adeline and Mama—they took in that girl that spoke against her uncle, Franklin White."

Claude leaned back on his haunches. "You'll have to pardon me, but I'm having trouble following. All I wanted to know is why you're not working for your kin."

"You didn't hear about the murder trial? Franklin White, the bank vice president accused of murdering his brother-in-law?"

"You didn't murder no one, did you?"

"No!"

"Then what's it got to do with your employment at your daddy's business?"

"'Cause everyone round here owes Franklin White money, everyone. Sawyer, the farmer that lives down the road, and my Uncle Hugh, everyone."

Rowen's grip slipped and the gate dropped.

"Might I suggest to you that in the Lord's Book, the names of all these people of whom you speak are wrote in the tiniest letters, if one could see them at all."

"But Elizabeth Purdie Richardson? Her name's in block letters?"

"We've established that you're not a Yankee, a blessed circumstance, though you are an unmitigated scoffer. Those of us among the faithful believed she saved us from the British so we could enjoy the freedom to enslave others, as you have pointed out. Now, the people you have spoken of may have performed deeds of like merit. It's possible. I don't know them. But you haven't mentioned any that I've heard, and we have yet to resolve the question of why you're not employed. You know how to handle a drill, don't you?"

"No."

"Would you like to learn?"

Rowen shrugged.

"I'll take that as begrudging acceptance. After you're done learning a drill, do you want to crawl back up in that shack and hide behind your kitchen sink, or would you like to learn something about roofing. Lynch & Son Construction is roofing a barn today."

"What would they want with me? You've been saying I'm useless. Isn't that what you're going to tell them?"

"Well I'm the 'Son' in that operation. I see what you're thinking. You're thinking that I no longer look spry enough to be called somebody's 'son.' I assure you that the sweet memories of my daddy are as fresh and dear to me as yours are to you. And when you reach my hoary age, don't you still want to be called his son? Now, to the subject at hand, would you like to learn something about roofing today?"

Eden

"You keep asking me why I'm not employed. I've got to look for work today."

"You can start employment with Lynch & Son Construction right now by fixing your own front gate."

By the time Adeline came down the road, he was helping Claude put his tools away. Adeline paused as she took in the scene, and Rowen watched the suspicions twist in her face. How to deal with this white man—that's what she was thinking.

"What y'all got going on here?"

Claude flipped off his cap, revealing a skull that was shiny bald. "Pleased to make your acquaintance. I'll take it that you are Adeline. I'm Claude Lynch, and allow me to introduce my new employee, a Mister Rowen Hart."

Adeline set her shoulder bag down. "He ain't your new employee for very long. He's a student at the University of North Carolina starting next week!"

Claude stared at him. Sunbeams pierced right through the trees into Rowen's eyes and he broke out in a fresh layer of sweat.

"That's all changed. I'll be going to work for Mr. Lynch."

Adeline's eyes bugged out of her head. "And you've told this to Miz Rita?"

Before Rowen could answer that question, or all the other questions waiting to shoot out of Adeline's mouth, Eden burst out the door.

"Adeline! There's a rat under the kitchen

sink! I got him trapped under a bucket!" She braked in mid-flight to take in her audience and then pointed at Claude. "Who's he?"

Here was a scenario Adeline could tackle without premeditation. "Eden, we need to locate some behavior for you, baby. You don't just sprint out the house pointing fingers at people, like you was firing pistols." She rotated Eden back toward the house. "Now, go back up those steps, walk down — don't run — and say, 'How do you do. I am Eden Whitney, and I am pleased to meet you.'"

Eden took only three steps and whirled back around. She grabbed Claude's huge hand and shook it with both her own. "How'd ya do. I'm Eden Whitney and I'm pleased you get to meet me."

Claude placed his hand on his chest and bowed. "My life was poorer until this very moment. What do you charge for rat catching?"

She squinted up at him for a moment before turning to Rowen.

"What'cha doing out here, Rowen?"

"I'm working with him," Rowen announced with new boldness now that he'd managed to dodge Adeline.

"Adeline, can I...?"

"No. Rowen ain't needing a shadow today. I got plenty for you to do here. You can start by killing that rat. Then I got in mind a pineapple cake you can bake."

Claude offered to kill the rat to spare feminine sensibilities, but Adeline replied that Eden didn't possess any and, in any case, if Eden was unable to finish the task, Adeline herself had dispatched many

a rat with no trouble and Mr. Lynch should be on his way.

Rowen scurried behind Claude to duck any more interference from Adeline, and once he'd slammed the pickup door, he looked with relief in the rearview mirror at Adeline towing Eden toward the house.

"I can see where a man would need respite from vigorous women like those two," said Claude, "though if he had a chance to go to school and escape it entirely, I don't see why he wouldn't take it."

"I don't want to go, and that's all I'm going to say about it."

"Sharp boy like you, I wonder what's left for you here in White Rock. Especially given your opinion on our historical pageant. But the bigger question is, if you're going to forgo the expansion of your horizons, what will you contribute by remaining here?"

How could he be asking that, Rowen wondered. Ever since his daddy had died, everyone except Adeline acted like they didn't owe him anything, so why would he owe anything back? He let the breeze blow the question on out the window. He rested his elbow over the door and let his mind drift with the passing scenery. Houses and fields glided by, and the troubles that had smothered him in the night scattered like birds.

The illusion of release lasted only as long as the trip to the work site. As the truck slowed, the airless heat inflated the cab, while outside the windshield, the crew, colored and white, ogled him.

There was a pause after the cab doors slammed, and Claude spoke up, "Y'all will want to welcome our youngest and newest member, Mr. Rowen Hart."

Not a spark of welcome flickered in any of their faces. Watching one curt nod after another, Rowen wondered which circumstance set their impressions: his age, his ignorance, who he'd been when he'd lived in town, who he was now, or who he'd taken into his house. If he knew, he could try to protect himself against what they might say. As it was, he felt naked. And he resented them for it. Why should they make him feel ashamed when there wasn't one of them without holes in his pants?

Rowen ran up and down the ladders for them, hauling their water jugs, nail buckets and packs of shingles. No one thanked him, or so much as looked at him. Every so often, they leaned back on their heels, dipped snuff and spat it over the side of the barn. He knew he didn't dare say anything about how hot, or tired he was getting, although the heat radiating off the roof could fry eggs.

After they got bored exchanging dirty jokes among themselves, they asked him how come his hands were so soft, like a girl's. They asked him how come he'd shown up to work in Sunday clothes, and they roared when he said he hadn't.

In the afternoon, he was allowed to take a place alongside them. Claude's foreman, Rufus, outfitted him with a greasy apron for his nails. He knelt and tried to align shingles as fast as they did, but at every move he made, Rufus nudged him with corrections. Rowen fought an urge to shove the man away. Rufus' presence was calling attention to all his weaknesses.

At the end of the day, as the men left the roof, Rufus sat down next to him. Rowen braced for

a blast of criticism. Maybe he was about to be fired. Maybe Rufus was just waiting it out until everyone left before doing it.

"You worked hard today, Rowen. We appreciated having you here."

"Do you mean that?"

"I don't know how well you know Mr. Lynch. But we don't spare people's feelings here. Will you be back tomorrow?"

"If Claude will let me."

"Don't take this bunch to heart. They're sorry no-goods. They pretend to be rough, so you'll give 'em the respect they don't deserve. They'll warm up to you in a few days."

Rufus flicked a cigarette out of a pack and offered him one. Rowen shook his head. Rufus smiled as he placed it between his lips and lit it.

"Won't be long before you're as hooked on these as everyone else." He took a long draw and said, "I heard y'all took in Eden Whitney."

Rowen stiffened. "We did."

Rufus took a puff off his cigarette, then gazed out over the treetops.

"It ain't anything you need to be ashamed of. There's folks that thought a lot of her daddy, Birch Whitney. If a poor man needed a roof over his head, white or colored, he'd be the first there with a hammer and nails and the last one to leave."

Rowen couldn't believe what he was hearing. To hear it at the trial, in front of the whole community, Whitney was nothing more than a drunk who was stone drunk on Christmas day, the last day of his life. That's all anybody would remember.

Rufus continued, "White got away with murder, no doubt about it."

"How do you know that?"

"I don't care how drunk he might have been. He would never have raised a hand to any man, much less a pipe wrench. That girl told the truth."

"You weren't there at the trial."

"I didn't need to be."

The clouds on the horizon flamed orange, and the shadows deepened under Rufus' eyes.

"If he could, Birch would thank you."

"I didn't do anything. It's Adeline who takes care of her."

"But it ain't Adeline's house she's living in."

It ain't Adeline's house... Rufus spoke as if Rowen were a man instead of a boy. With his own house. If he had turned into a man, shouldn't he be easy in the world, as all these other men were? Shouldn't the days roll out smooth as a highway without him laying up at nights sweating over them?

"'Night, son," Rufus said, and then he was gone, descending the ladder into the dusk.

Claude shouted up at him, "I'll give you a ride home. Or will you be camping up there tonight?"

Claude offered supper at his house and promised to call Adeline to tell her where he was. Rowen was too tired to do anything but nod in agreement. Now that he was back on the ground, his legs felt like putty. He climbed in the passenger seat and slumped against the door, and he didn't see or hear another thing until they were bouncing down a dirt road toward a house ablaze with lights. Sally barked, and blue hounds bounded from the yard, baying back at her.

Claude shut off the engine. "Don't be rattled

by our welcoming committee. They'll all want a whiff of you to see if you're interesting, and when they see you're not, they'll leave you alone."

Rowen slid out of the seat and the hounds shoved their snouts against his hands. With all the pines around the house, tall and close--he could only glimpse a handful of stars above.Pine needles crunched underneath his feet. He was so tired that the weight of the air alone seemed to pull him down.

He blinked in the kitchen lights and mumbled a "nice to meet you" to Miz Mary Lynch, a woman every bit as tall as Claude. She scolded Claude for "driving this boy to the edge of his death," and sat him down at the table with a glass of tea and a plate of steaming biscuits. By the time he'd wolfed them down, he'd revived enough to hear Miz Lynch introducing him to her niece, Miss Jewell Lynn Nodding.

He recognized her from school, one of the girls in the sophomore class. She'd appeared in his peripheral vison only, never front and center, because she had clung to the fringes of her group, not bold enough to peel away and talk to a boy. Though he himself hadn't launched into easy relations with the other sex. He had always thought that somehow masculine know-how, like what he'd seen in the movies, would tap him like a fairy wand and then the girls would flock to his side. It had to come as a part of growing up, like hair appearing on your cheeks. It just hadn't happened yet. Oh, he'd gone with groups of kids to movies or dances. But the "date" he'd brought along always looked a little restless—chewing her hair or biting her nails—and would bolt from him at the end of the evening.

Like her relatives, Jewell was tall, taller than he was. That might have explained her shyness. She stood stiff as a flagpole, waiting for him to act like a gentleman and stand up. Couldn't she see how beat he was? When he remained seated, she spoke in a rush, as if trying to hurl herself over the awkwardness between them.

"I heard you got into the University of North Carolina."

The force of her effort made him stand at last. She wasn't too much taller, he only had to tilt his chin a degree or two. She seemed so eager to hear his response. He could hardly believe that there was anyone left in White Rock who hadn't heard about all his troubles.

"I'm not going," he said. "I'm going to be working for your Uncle Claude, if he'll let me."

"Oh. I've never heard of a boy not going after he'd been accepted."

He struggled to string words together. "My mama's here...and..."

She nodded. "I understand. You don't want to leave home, that's all. Do you think you'll like working for Uncle Claude?"

"Jewell," said Miz Lynch, "you can see the boy's about to drop. Why don't you get him some more biscuits? She made them, Rowen."

Rowen picked up the prompt. "They're good, I ate 'em all," he said.

Jewell beamed.

He didn't absorb much of the conversation at supper. All he really heard was her tone of voice. She began every sentence in a rush, as if she had no confidence in her own thoughts and needed to

shoo them away before anyone could notice how empty they were. Her long, tapered fingers — that's where her confidence lay. He watched them as she laid out silverware, passed dishes, served him extra helpings. Her hands had performed these tasks with self-assurance for years. He had no like trait. Anyone watching him at the smallest endeavor would see that not only was he clumsy at it, but that he himself harbored no hope of ever performing it.

When he stood up to leave, he said, "You'll be starting school, soon."

"Yes, next week. You're so lucky to be done. I wish I was done and had a job I could go to every day. It'd make me feel like a real person. Same as you."

"I can't cook like you. Eden says I don't even know enough to burn toast."

Jewell twittered. "Eden?"

He cursed himself. He didn't want to have to explain his family's untidiness to Jewell.

"I believe that Rowen's had his fill of feeling like a real person for one day," said Claude. "You ready to go on home, son?"

He looked up at Claude, trying to grasp if Claude had read his thoughts. But he couldn't make out anything behind those bottle-bottom glasses. Whether Claude sensed his discomfort, or his exhaustion, either way, he ought to be grateful for it.

"Yes, I'd appreciate it."

As soon as Claude started the engine, Rowen fell asleep, and it seemed as if only five minutes had passed before Claude shook him awake. Claude nodded to where Adeline and Eden sat under the porch light.

"Your women are waiting for you. Not that you'll be able to keep up with them tonight."

Strains of their clapping game filled the night.

"Miss Suzie had a baby,
She named him Tiny Tim..."

"Pick you up tomorrow?"

"Yes, sir. Please."

Claude shook his head. "Damn shame. Seems I've failed in my efforts of gentle persuasion to get you to leave and pursue that education. And fool that I am, I'm the one making it easy for you to make the wrong choice."

"She put him in the bathtub, tub
To see if he could swim...."

Gentle persuasion, Rowen wondered as he slammed the door. Would he get fired if a few more days of gentle persuasion didn't work?

Eden bounced down the steps and tugged at his hand. "Rowen, guess what, I made the prettiest cake for you."

Adeline brought him a chair. "You don't look so good. Are you all right?"

"I'm all right." It was just that his day had started years ago. It had started with him wondering how he was to go about firing Adeline.

"Guess what kind of cake it is," Eden said. "You won't guess—it's pineapple. I'll get you some right now."

Adeline scooted her chair closer to Rowen's. "You don't have to do this, son. There's other ways. There's folks in town that'll help you with your Uncle Hugh, folks that were friends of your daddy's. You can go to them and they'll talk some sense into that man. They'll make him feel ashamed. You don't have to do this."

Eden

Rowen reached into his pocket and handed her a ten-dollar bill.

"What's this for?"

"What do you mean what's it for? It's part of what we owe you."

She pressed the money back into his hand. "I don't want it, Rowen. You going to that university to make something of yourself — that's all the pay I need. You don't have to worry nothing about it. I'll take care of Miz Rita, no matter what."

Rufus' words drifted back to him. This was his house — Rowen Hart's house.

"I'm working for Claude now and there's plenty of money. You work for us. You take it. It's your wages."

She sat back to consider, but before she could utter a syllable, Eden backed out the door, clutching a plate with a chunk of cake.

"Here you go, Rowen."

"I can't eat all that!"

She took a dramatic step toward him, holding the plate high, and when she had centered it over his lap, she let go and he struggled to catch it.

"Eden! Rowen's worked hard today to put food in your mouth. He don't need to come home to get doused with cake. Quit foolin' with him and get ready for bed."

"Can I bring him some lemonade?"

"You heard me. Get ready for bed and I'll be in in a moment."

Eden looked over her shoulder as she opened the door. "Do you like it, Rowen?"

"How he have a chance to eat it with you peckin' at him?"

Adeline paused after the door slammed,

then leaned into him once more. "What's in your heart, son?"

Beyond the radius of the porch light, the dark squeezed in. He didn't know how to answer. It seemed like his heart should contain some unmalleable core, like the heart of an oak, but all he could focus on was the coming dawn and Claude honking his horn, while the life his mama and Adeline had imagined for him dissipated, as if it had been no more than morning fog.

"Take the money, Adeline. Please."

Her fingers curled slowly around the bill. "I'll pray for you. I'll pray your heart don't wind up twisted and broken."

He looked down at the hunk of cake.

"You got to know, Rowen, to that child, the sun rises and sets with you."

He took a bite and then put the fork back down. Adeline patted his hand. "It's all right. I'll tell her you'll finish it tomorra."

He rose, and Adeline followed him back into the darkened kitchen. The refrigerator door was open and there stood Eden, dressed in only her panties, the light falling on her bony shoulders.

"What in Lord Jesus' name?" cried Adeline.

"I was just going to pour him some lemonade and leave it on the table," Eden cried as she slammed the door and scurried away.

Her bare feet pattered down the hall. Cricket trilling flowed through the open window.

Beside him, Adeline sighed. "I don't know how we'll keep her from getting ate alive."

He was too tired to ask Adeline what she meant. All he could reflect on was the flash of Eden's white thighs as she had fled away.

Eden

5

THE PEA-GREEN STATION WAGON
seemed to roll off Homer's junkyard of its own
accord. Rowen didn't notice it right away as he and
Sammy were taking turns behind the wheel of a black
coupe, wallowing in the splendor of it. It wasn't
until they heard Homer's pumpkins squashing that
Rowen remembered that Eden had come along, but
by then the car was accelerating over the empty
cornfield, flattening the dirt ridges as it traveled.

Sammy was out of the coupe first, his legs
covering a yard with every stride. The wagon was
pointed toward a line of oaks, flaming red in the
distance. Then it hit a ditch and its tail fins upended.

Rowen jogged behind. They'd come out
here so he could buy his first car and instead they

were chasing Eden. *Again.* Claude's work crew had taken their cue from Rufus and had come around to complimenting him for taking in Birch Whitney's girl, a child who was "wide open," the community expression for wild as a hellcat. He was ready to hand her off to any one of them. The one day he'd planned for himself and she'd already ruined it.

Somehow, she had survived because Sammy stood screaming on the ditch bank. "You are the evilest white child that's ever seen the light of day. You know that?"

The DeSoto still purred, its nose snug in the ditch. The driver's door was open and Eden stood ankle deep in mud.

"I was doing just fine. I didn't see this ditch. That's all. It ain't wrecked or nothing. All it needs is to be pulled out."

Rowen turned to look for Homer. Homer stood in the doorway of his office for a moment, straightened his cap and then limped toward them. Old men never hurried, Rowen thought. He'd been in a rush, when he got here, to choose a car, plunk his money down, zoom home and dress up for his first real date with Jewell. But as Homer shuffled along, Rowen realized that for the aged, minutes stretched and pulled like taffy.

Homer even had time to spit and lean on his cane and listen to Sammy and Eden argue before he spoke. He ran his hand over his stubbled face.

"I guess you bought this one," he said.

Moments ago, they'd run their hands over the upholstery in the black coupe. Sammy had nodded knowingly. "This is it, Mr. Rowen, yes, sir," he had said, and in his eyes, Rowen could read the thrills of encounter imagined in those seats. Church-

going white boys weren't supposed to think like that, Rowen knew, but Sammy's thoughts did mirror the ones bubbling in the back of his own mind. He might at least kiss her.

Now, confronted by this old colored man, who had infinite time to consider and decide and speak, Rowen's voice quavered. "I don't need a station wagon," he said.

Two minutes passed — at least — as Homer shifted his weight to his other foot.

"Test driving ain't allowed." He nodded to the car. "You gotta good automatic transmission in that one that shifts real good, real easy for the ladies."

Two and a half hours later, as Rowen stood sweating on Jewell's front porch, he wasn't sure what was more humiliating: the pea green DeSoto or his clothes. His collar was too tight, his sleeves and pant legs were too short. He'd brought her a bouquet of mums, and what with the car behind him, he figured he might be mistaken for a clown.

His self-image was mirrored in Mr. Nodding's face as he looked, first at Rowen, then at the car. "Jewell says you bought that car today."

What to do first? Answer the man's question or shake his hand?

Mr. Nodding shook his hand tepidly.

"I got it today, yes, sir."

"I hope you got a discount for that smashed-in grille."

The house was small, no bigger than his own, and the couches and chairs, plump as market hogs, claimed all the space. The glass coffee table sliced into his shins as he sidestepped along the couch, until he gave up and collapsed so deeply into the cushions that the bowl of Chex mix in front of him was at eye level.

Miz Nodding glanced around from the kitchen and asked him if he wanted a glass of tea. The room smelled of cigarettes and baking ham. His stomach growled and Mr. Nodding glared at him.

"June knows your mama from the beauty parlor," he said. "That's how she talked me into letting Jewell out on this date."

Miz Nodding—June—brought out his tea. She was tall like Jewell and her thin gray hair was coiled on the back of her head.

"Your mother was such a beauty she didn't need the beauty parlor," she said. "You know they miss her very much there. How is she doing? We'd love to see her back in town."

His mama had been propped up on her pillows the last time he'd seen her, lit up by the idea of this date. She'd galvanized Adeline into picking the mums. The delight on her face as he stood at her bedside—stuffed into this monkey suit—was the same as when Adeline had finished dressing the Thanksgiving turkeys before shoving them in the oven. Part of him resisted her fussing, while the other part stubbornly bound him there, in the hope that, in another moment, she'd throw off the covers, stand up and walk him to the door, as she would have done in the life they would have had, but for his daddy wrecking their lives.

"Yes, ma'am, she's much better, thank you."

Jewell swept from the hallway in a flurry of rustling petticoats. "I like your car, Rowen," she

blurted. Her voice was more strained than ever. Still, he swallowed at how lovely she appeared. A white patent leather belt was cinched tight around her waist, and below it the pink skirt flared. A pink ribbon swept her hair away from her face and thick curls cascaded down her back. He leapt to his feet, his shins banging against the coffee table, and stuck the flowers out in front of him.

Jewell and her mother fussed over the mums. Mr. Nodding turned on the TV, plopped back down and lit a cigarette. The calls from a football game blared over the women's voices, and now that everyone's attentions had been deflected, Rowen felt as useless as the discarded tissue paper. The only one still regarding him, with an indifference spilling into contempt, was a white cat on the hearth. Though he itched to grab Jewell and get out of there, he sipped his tea and let the noise swirl around him, waiting for the proper amount of time to pass before Jewell would excuse herself from her mother and reach for her purse.

The evening didn't get any better once they were seated at the restaurant. There were so many obstacles between the two of them: heavy water goblets and menus the size of road signs. Diners in surrounding booths ogled them. Jewell's friends from school popped up to the table to chatter and giggle, each of them carving slices of him that they could parcel amongst themselves come Monday morning. Jewell wallowed in their attentions and he sat back and smiled stiffly because it was what he was supposed to do, but Jewell's distractibility unsettled him. Was she really this excited, or was she avoiding the chore of talking to him?

Afterward, under the car's dome light, she

tugged her sweater around her, settling into her expectations. She expected to go to the movies next. The evening belonged to her—he was supposed to do what she wanted. But he couldn't stand the yoke of this ritual one more minute. Now that she was at last removed from the cluster of family and friends, he thought she'd feel more at ease. He thought she would shift in her seat, their eyes would lock, and in that moment of silence, they'd vault past their blundering onto a magical understanding of one another. Instead, it seemed as if they were in adjacent jail cells, a jail of their own making. They needed to break loose, escape White Rock and all its influences. Or at least get as far away as was possible on one evening's date.

"How about a walk?" he blurted.

She jumped as if he'd pinched her.

"A walk? Where?"

He felt a moment's guilt at her alarm, but he persisted. "Down to Lacy's Creek. There's a trail there through the woods. We don't have to go if you don't want to."

"Oh."

He watched the struggle in her face. *A walk? How would she explain this to her friends on Monday? But it was what her date wanted to do.*

"I guess it would be all right."

Seeing the town lights in his rearview mirror made him press the gas pedal even harder. The air streaming through the open window was moist and warm, but it did nothing to calm Jewell. She sat board-stiff with her hands clenched in her lap, the

nervous chatter all stopped up inside of her. As he turned off the highway and the breeze dropped, he felt her tension swell.

"Haven't you ever been here before?" he asked.

"No. I most certainly haven't. Coloreds live out here, don't they?"

"Some of 'em do. I think Negroes made the trail down the creek, but everyone fishes here. My daddy used to take me fishing here."

The idea that white men fished there didn't bring her any comfort. She just needed to be outside, Rowen thought. She just needed to feel the place for herself, the peace and quiet. He went around to the passenger side and opened her door.

"Don't you have a flashlight, Rowen?"

"No, I didn't bring one."

She rose reluctantly. "It's so dark," she said.

Despite his attempts to ignore it, his guilt at making her do what she didn't want to do was starting to chafe him. He grabbed her hand and squeezed it.

"It's all right. Don't worry. I know the way."

He towed her over a footbridge, her high heels tapping on the planks. Then, they hit the dirt path and he let the downward slope speed his stride. Jewell yanked him back. "You're going too fast," she whined.

"Okay, I'll slow down."

As he eased up, her body pressed against his back. "You're sure no one's going to hurt us out here?"

"I've been here hundreds of times. It's all right."

"What about bears?"

"I've never seen one out here before."

"Well, have you been out here when it's been this dark? It's practically a coal mine out here."

"That's the best time to be here."

"I don't think Mama and Daddy would like this."

"Do you have to tell them?"

She stopped to consider. Whatever her misgivings, she seemed to be finding pleasure in their common adventure. For the first time, a smile — a glowing smile — softened her face.

"I guess I don't."

A few steps on, they ran into a patch of huckleberry and Jewell squealed as her skirt snagged on the shrubs. Rowen knelt in the dirt and worked it free. An updraft from the creek brushed them, carrying the murmur of moving water. One last steep dive down the path and they were on the sand bar.

Next to the creek, it was cooler than it had been in the woods. Jewell shivered against him. They couldn't linger much longer. But he didn't want to let go of the moment either, standing hand in hand along the creek with her pressed beside him. He was afraid that if he moved, he'd lose the first spark of intimacy that they'd ignited.

A canoe with a lantern drifted along the opposite bank.

"What do you think they are doing?" Jewell whispered.

"I don't know. Maybe fishing. Want me to find out?"

She squeezed his forearm. "No, don't do that. Let's guess at who they are. Maybe they're a

girl and boy and her parents don't like him, and they've been forbidden to see each other ever again and they've run away. They're going to float down this creek to the Cape Fear River, and from there, all the way to Wilmington, and when they get to the beach, they'll get married and love each other the rest of their lives."

It was easy to ride the current of her fantasy, to think of floating down the smooth water until the banks split away and the blue sound opened to the sea.

He put his arm around her shoulder. "Maybe that could be us."

She leaned into him and he rested his cheek on her hair, stiff with hair spray. He kissed her forehead.

"What do you think?" he whispered.

She stiffened and pulled away. "We'd better get on back, Rowen."

But once they'd settled back in the DeSoto, she pouted. "It's too early to go home! Let's go somewhere else!"

"Where do you want to go?"

"It's too late for the movie. Unless we go to the late show — and that'll be too late...let's drive to Holly Lake!"

"What do you want to go there for? There won't be anything open."

"Just for the drive. We can walk by the lake anyway."

The resort town along the lake looked like a ghost town as they rolled through the darkened streets. The Ferris wheel was locked down, the popcorn stands shuttered, the scraps of the summer season sodden and rotting among piles of leaves. The only place open was a lone pharmacy with a red Cheerwine sign blinking in the window.

Jewell jumped at it. "Let's get a Cheerwine," she said.

A colored man in a greasy chef's cap leaned in the doorway. "How y'all doing this evening?" he said vacantly, before tossing his cigarette butt in the street.

Lights buzzed overhead, and the counter stools were empty. Rowen preferred the closeness of her beside him in the dark, over the glare of this old man.

"Two Cheerwines," Rowen said, startled by how loud his voice sounded. He noticed a burn scar on the man's face, starting at his cheekbone and spreading all the way down the side of his face and neck. The man gestured to the stools. "Y'all can sit down."

Rowen didn't want to sit down. Without looking at her, he knew Jewell was beginning to feel uneasy, too.

"There's no one here. You must be getting ready to close," she said.

The man plunked straws in their bottles. "Just slow," he said, "with all the summer folks gone. I'd expect to see more kids like you two out on a mild night like this, but...." He gazed out the window as if he could conjure a throng of kids and cars. The knickknacks behind the register were fuzzy with dust.

Rowen paid for the drinks and they hustled out.

"Did you see that awful scar that Negra

had? Why would they let him mind a store looking like that? No wonder they don't have any business. No one's going to go in there," Jewell said.

Nine months ago, before his daddy's death, before the murder trial and Eden, he might have said something like that. He might have even walked out joking about the man. Now he felt like he ought to stand up for him. Twelve years of schooling had left him with the idea that histories were carved in stone. They weren't at all, they were lumps of clay that could be molded over and over by whoever was doing the telling. Someone could tell a story about that old man that wouldn't make it so easy to dismiss him.

But Jewell would not understand such thoughts. He shrugged. "Nothing's going on out here. No one wants to drive out this time of year anyhow."

They crossed the street to a strip of park tacked along the lakeside. A single streetlight lit an empty playground covered in sand. Jewell handed him her drink and sprinted to the swing set. She plopped down in the rubber seat and yanked on the chains. Rowen sat beside her, watching her arc up and down, the breeze from the lake ruffling her skirts and the light skimming over her face, arms and neck. She swung higher, her long legs reaching out and her neck stretching back.

"C'mon Rowen," she called. "It's fun."

When he didn't respond, she drifted back to the ground, letting her heels drag in the sand. She was close enough that he could smell her perfume again. "This isn't any fun for you. I guess I haven't been any fun for you."

"No, that's not it at all." How could he tell

her that the evening, fraught as it had been, was still a release from his sagging house and his mother's illness.

He reached out and her hand slipped into his, and they sat there swinging lazily back and forth, listening to the water lapping the shore and the last crickets quieting. Neither one wanted to break the solidity of their locked hands until Jewell finally murmured, "I'm getting cold," and they dropped hands and stood, and this time their bodies met without any awkwardness.

Children poured out of the school, buoyed by the start of the Thanksgiving break. All around, the last shreds of fall colors blazed, the ember reds and flaming oranges. The flood of children soon siphoned down to a trickle and, still, no sign of Eden. Rowen flicked his cigarette butt out the car window.

Sammy kneed the back of his seat. "Um, um, Mr. Rowen, day before Thanksgiving and I believe your child has to stay after school."

The words fueled Rowen's irritation, as Sammy knew they would. He ought to just stomp on the gas and leave her there. Sammy had to be right: Eden had been near raptured with excitement that morning over their plan to drive to a farm in the afternoon, pick their own turkeys and butcher them for only fifty cents each. She'd refused to budge from the car until he'd agreed that she would be chopping the heads off.

But Rowen was supposed to be at Jewell's by six. He couldn't show up there spattered in turkey guts and feathers.

If she's gotten into trouble again, damn her, it was just too goddamn bad. Let Adeline deal with it, like she always did anyhow.

He jumped out of the car and slammed the door.

Sammy got out, too.

"They're not going to let you in there," Rowen snapped.

Sammy shrugged and leaned back against the car. That grin on his face must have been glued on at birth. No matter how Rowen's days careened off track, Sammy was always grinning.

"I'll be waitin', then. At least leave me your smokes."

The air inside the building smelled sodden and moldy. Sunlight filtered through narrow, dirty windows. He stopped and listened while the last children pushed past him. A sound thrummed through the walls—a moan—no, a child sobbing.

On the day she'd run the DeSoto into the ditch, he'd deliberately lagged behind. He had to admit that he'd been afraid to see her hurt. That was how he felt now. He didn't want to be the witness to her injury. He wanted someone else to do it. He hesitated and thought of going back for Sammy. But bringing Sammy in wasn't going to get Eden out of whatever trouble she'd gotten into. He might as well stir up hornets as bring Sammy in, grin and all.

He had to learn to act like Adeline--take three steps back, measure up the situation and try to bargain a solution.

He followed the sound to the girls' restroom. The door was propped open with a trashcan. He called out. "Eden?"

JAMIE LISA FORBES

"Who's there?" It was Miz Brackett, Eden's teacher.

He edged around the corner. Miz Brackett stood in front of the sinks, her arms crossed over her white cardigan. Eden was on her knees, sobbing in one of the stalls.

"May I ask why you're here? Men aren't allowed in the girls' restrooms." Behind her bat-wing glasses, her eyes glittered hard.

"Rowen!" Eden scrambled to him and threw her arms around his hips.

Rowen gently pushed her arms down. He tried to imagine Adeline here, tried to find her voice.

"I'm Rowen, Rowen Hart. Eden...I guess you know she lives with us. I come to get her. We're picking turkeys this afternoon."

"Eden, Mr. Hart is not here to help you." Miz Brackett sank her claws into Eden's shoulder and pried her away from him.

He looked down and noticed blood caked on Eden's scalp. The sleeves on the blouse Adeline had sewn for her were nearly ripped off.

"Eden, you need to tell Mr. Hart why you're here."

"She's making me clean toilets...with a toothbrush."

"Why?" asked Rowen.

"Biting and scratching her classmates," Miz Brackett answered. "Children only repeat what they've heard, Mr. Hart. They can't be blamed for it. It's unfortunate that Eden was falsely encouraged with all the attention she received at that awful trial. It's natural that put in a spotlight like that, a child will embellish. Dr. Hardigan, our principal, and I have tried to talk to Eden many times. Her uncle

was found not guilty by a jury of his peers. But if she is going to persist with her tales, then the others will make fun of her. There is nothing I can do."

"Who clubbed her in the head?"

"The others were only defending themselves."

But why weren't they cleaning toilets? He swallowed and looked back down at Eden. Her eyes pleaded for him to save her.

He nodded back toward the stall. "Better do as she says. That way we can get on and go pick up those turkeys."

"Rowen...."

"Go on, you heard her."

She shuffled back toward a stall and sank next to the toilet bowl.

"You can wait outside, Mr. Hart."

No sooner had he turned away than he realized what Adeline would do. She would wheedle this woman out of here and clean these toilets herself. He balked at the thought. It wasn't just that it was colored folks' work. Even if no one was watching, even if Sammy wasn't there to snicker, it would mean that he had accepted Eden, same as if she really was his own kin. No more freedom to write her off as the burden Adeline had dumped on him.

In the end, it was Jewell who drove him to it, the image of her waiting at the window, her eyes lighting on every car that turned down the street. Her face would brighten when she yanked the door open, and he could lose himself in her chatter, and then none of this would have ever happened.

"You can go on back to your room, Miz Brackett. I'll watch her, make sure she gets it done."

He waited until he could no longer hear the

teacher's heels tapping down the hall, and then he broke open the paper towel dispenser and grabbed wads of towels to wash Eden's face and head. He snuck out to the janitor's closet for toilet brushes. When he returned, he let Eden shake the Comet can hard until the crystals flew around the bathroom, like snow.

6

"IT'S TIME YOU BROUGHT THAT GIRL
to the house," said Adeline. "Months go by and
it look like you're ashamed of her. Now when do
you plan on doing that?" She opened the oven door
and the smell of cinnamon buns blasted over him.
It was still dark and only she and Rowen were up.

Rowen curled his fingers around his mug. He
tried to imagine Jewell seizing on each detail in the
house, striving to mold it all to fit her world view.
She would be polite and chatty with his mother.
Back home, she'd spill everything to her parents. He
could hear the excuses she would make for him.

"Mama says I don't have to bring her over.
She says she understands how it is."

Adeline snorted. "As old as you are—a
grown working man—she ain't done spoiling you

111

and you ain't done lapping it up!" The baking pan clattered as she dropped it on the stove. "Now wrap your mind around it, you're bringing Miss Jewell over to meet your family."

"What about Eden?"

She crossed her arms. "So it's her you're ashamed of. As if taking in an orphan child is something to be ashamed of.

"Mr. Rowen, let me deliver some mighty big news. Half the white folks in town—including all the folks in Miss Jewell's church and Mr. Claude— they all done told her 'bout Eden. And for all we know, every one of 'em done talked a heap of trash about Eden, but Miss Jewell don't seem dissuaded.

"You think the trouble is what Miss Jewell's going to think. Nope, that ain't it. You've misread it all again. The trouble is how to keep Eden from sinking in the slime of envy the moment she lays eyes on Miss Jewell. That's what I've been praying on. And I got a plan."

"What?"

Adeline set a plate of steaming buns in front of him. "Eden's going to have herself a Christmas party, and she's going to invite all her friends and Mr. Claude and his wife and Miss Jewell and her parents."

"Eden doesn't have any friends."

"This'll allow her to make some. I just want to know one thing—do you love Miss Jewell?"

Rowen squirmed. Why, when they were alone like this, did Adeline always have to poke into where things stood with Jewell? Not just where they were going and what they were doing, but the guts of the matter that, in his mind, a boy shouldn't have to haul out for inspection at breakfast. Or at

any other time. He'd sat captive through more than one breakfast sermon where she'd gone on about him watching himself and behaving like a gentleman and not getting Jewell in trouble. "Even if you was to get lucky and pull out in time," —how could any woman speak those words?—"people find out, people talk, and pretty soon, next time that girl goes to church, there's whispers around her head thick as flies. Nice girl like Jewell don't deserve that."

He was sure that in the half dim kitchen, Adeline had seen him squirm. What was that word "love" anyway? Did it mean you had someone on your mind all the time? He did think of Jewell. Every dawn while he huddled with Claude's crew, waiting for the day's assignment, he would be reliving the feel and smell of her as they had necked the night before. And, yes, he had listened to Adeline's cautions, though it was near painful to do so. That was love, wasn't it?

"I guess so," he said.

"'Guess so?' You better know so. 'Cause you've got a line-up of women whose entire lives stand to be rerouted by your next move. That girl is mighty glued to you. By springtime, she'll be looking for a jewel."

He heard Claude honking—*saved at last.* "Claude's waiting," he said, as he pulled on his jacket and bolted.

Outside, frost plastered the grass to the ground. Claude's pickup chugged softly, the exhaust pluming behind it.

"I hope you brought some for me," said Claude, as he caught a whiff of cinnamon bun. Rowen passed a paper sack over to him.

Claude put the truck in gear. "I've been sitting here nearly ten minutes. You're late because we've been waiting on these, right?"

No way in hell was he going to repeat the whole Jewell discussion with her uncle. He balled his fists into his pockets.

Claude glanced at him thoughtfully as he chewed. "Rufus says you're a heck of a sharp young man. But what I don't understand is, if you're so clever, how come you don't know how to dress yourself. I'm paying you enough to at least afford a coat from the thrift store, aren't I?"

"I don't need a new coat," Rowen muttered.

"That shell you got on is only good for strutting up and down the halls of a high school."

"I'm plenty warm," Rowen muttered.

Claude raised his eyebrows.

"If I may, I don't believe Jewell will be on site checking on how smart you look."

All these adults wanted to talk way more about Jewell than Rowen did. In the front yards they passed, Christmas tinsel glittered in the first sun rays. Dawn was only an illusion of warmth these days. There would be no respite against the cold to be endured until nightfall.

After lunch, filmy clouds unfurled across the sky, then thickened and bloated. Sleet pellets fell, a few at a time, until the clouds opened, and the sleet hurtled down. Icy drops seeped down Rowen's collar. He looked up from the cement floor the men were pouring, hoping to see a break in the clouds, but instead, the white haze was closing around them. The tree line in the distance had vanished.

Eden

"You ladies need to hustle so we can get this cement covered," shouted Rufus. "Soon as we do, you can get out of here."

He'd no sooner spoken than the sleet turned to snow — fat flakes falling slantwise on the wind.

Through the snowfall, a child on a bicycle pedaled up the dirt road. As soon as she stopped and stuck her tongue out to catch the snowflakes, Rowen knew it was Eden. Something's happened. That was his first thought. He dropped his rake and ran out to meet her.

The men behind him hooted. "Jump on her, she might get away!"

"She's got room for him on that bike."

"Does Jewell know?"

Eden's toboggan had slipped so low over her brows that she had to tilt her head back to look up at him.

"What are you doing out here? Is Mama okay?"

"Ain't the snow beautiful? Like angels falling."

Even with the jeers behind him, she stirred his desire to look up into the snow. He glanced back. They were all watching him.

"C'mon Eden, men are working here. Is Mama all right?"

"Yeah, she's fine. Adeline says I can have a Christmas party and we're going to invite Jewell. So she can come meet your mama and me. And we're doing the invitations this afternoon. Adeline's letting me print every one of them out by myself. She says I have to write real slow and careful and not get in a hurry."

"What are you doing out there, then?"

"Your mama told Adeline it was a big to-do and we didn't need no party. But then I wrote an invitation just for her, and she said there wasn't but one choice, and she had to be the first to R-S-V-P and say she was coming. R-S-V-P, I bet you don't even know what that means. It's French talk for you better tell us if you're coming or there might be none left when you get here. And guess what—your mama got up and sat in the living room."

It was some startling good news, worth the trip out here, but not worth another second away from the crew.

"Thanks, Eden, but I got to get back."

"Wait! I have to show you something!" She pulled a package wrapped in tissue paper out of her bike basket.

"Whatever you've got, you're going to mess it up out here in the snow."

"Adeline said I could bring it out to show you. It's going to be my party dress." She lifted a corner of the tissue paper to expose white fabric with large red polka dots. "This is going to be the skirt. And here's the material for the top—see, red velvet. Do you think Jewell will like it?"

The question hung between them, like the vapor from their breath, while snowflakes stuck to her eyelashes. From his first date to this moment, he realized how clogged his thoughts had been with the fear of how Jewell would see Eden and his mama.

"Whatchya standing there for? Aren't ya going to say something?"

What he wanted to say was: I was wrong to ever feel a moment's shame about you. But those words wouldn't come out. The time and place were all wrong, the pressure of the men wanting him to get on with it and get back on the job was too great.

Instead, what he said was, "You're gonna get that ruined out here."

"But what do you think Jewell will say?"

The chill had sunk to his bones and his teeth were beginning to chatter. "I don't know, I'm not a girl. But I'd be real surprised if she didn't like it."

As the light waned, Eden squashed her face against the glass, looking for the first guests.

"Eden, honey, move away from there. You're going to leave a mark after Adeline worked so hard cleaning those windows."

It was a Christmas miracle if there ever was one: his mama dressed in a pearl blue gown with a lace shawl draped around her shoulders. The skirt flounced with her every move. He'd forgotten how pretty that was. He couldn't remember when he'd last heard this tone in her voice, a tone bubbly with anticipation.

"But Miz Rita, why isn't anyone here yet?"

Rowen wondered the same thing. The day had been long, what with Mama's and Adeline's nerves on fire. Every time he came home from town with last minute items they had wanted, he got sent back again. More candles. More ribbon. Not emerald green. Forest green.

Once they'd run out of things to ask for, he'd spent the rest of the afternoon fumbling with the Christmas lights on the porch. It had taken two hours or more to get all the danged bulbs to light up. He'd spent the day half-frozen and now he sat choked in that same suit he'd outgrown.

Adeline had slathered Eden's hair with

what looked like pink lard and then wound it into short little braids, tied off in white ribbons. Eden had fidgeted the whole time, and Rowen thought Adeline would have to pin her down and sit on her to get it done. But once outfitted in her new dress and the patent leather shoes that Adeline picked up from her church's thrift store, she looked like a Christmas doll.

Adeline came in from lighting the luminaries from the porch to the road and Eden ran up to her.

"What if nobody comes?"

"They're coming. Sure as the Wise Men found Lord Jesus, those luminaries will lead your guests here."

And then headlights did appear far down the road.

First came Claude and his wife.

"Rowen, I hope you don't mind. I decided your party needed some live entertainment."

Arlen and Todd, two men from the crew, climbed out of the back seats of the car with a fiddle and banjo. They asked permission from his mama to rearrange the room and, out of courtesy, she gave it, although if they'd attended to the strain in her tone and not the words, they'd have known not to touch anything. She hovered about them, chirping like an unnested bird, about the history and fragility of this or that piece, and reminding them that pieces had to be set down quietly, not merely dropped in place to keep tremors from cracking the century-old china, unpacked especially for the occasion.

Once Arlen and Todd began to play, Rufus and his wife came, followed by two little girls from Eden's school. Adeline had prodded Eden for the names of all her classmates, and whether these

two actually liked Eden or were just consumed with curiosity, no one knew, but after a few shy moments, all the girls were romping through the house. Adeline, in her white apron, served Swedish meatballs while the room warmed with the smells of wool coats and cigarettes and pine needles.

Arlen lowered his fiddle, tapped his foot, and sang, "Hooray Jake, Hooray John, Breakin' up Christmas all night long.... " The girls joined hands and circled to the music. The noise grew so loud that Rowen himself didn't hear Jewell come in until Eden yanked on his arm. "She's here, she's here!"

Jewell was in the living room before he could get to the doorway. The guests parted to let her pass. She went straight to his mama's chair and held out her hand.

"You must be Miz Hart. I'm Jewell Nodding," she said, and then stepped aside, "and these are my parents."

His mama stood, and she gripped Jewell's hand with both her own. "It's wonderful, just wonderful to meet all of you. Wherever did you get that gorgeous dress? That emerald green is stunning on you. Did you buy it in town? I've never seen such quality in our stores. You made it? How talented you are. Your mother must be so proud. I can't think why Rowen has hid you from me all this time. Now why didn't Rowen meet you at the door? He's been taught much better than that, but ever since he joined the company of these laborers, he's lost all his manners. And oh..."

Eden had wedged herself into the huddle. "...this is our guest, Miss Eden Whitney."

Another Christmas miracle. Eden took her

skirts between her fingertips and curtsied. How long had Adeline made her practice that? But it had the right effect.

Jewell bent down slightly and said, "It's lovely to meet you. I've heard so much about you."

From who, Rowen wondered.

Jewell had brought a doll for Eden. And smiles spread around the room when Jewell opened her gift from Eden, another surprise that had been hidden from Rowen. She'd cross-stitched a pair of pillowcases, and these were passed from hand to hand around the room while Eden soaked up the murmurs of admiration.

Claude commented, as he sucked on his pipe, "Miss Eden, I hope all this daintiness you've acquired from Miz Rita and Miz Adeline isn't detracting from your rat-trapping abilities." He took the pipe stem out of his mouth and pointed it at her. "I guarantee, a man would rather know his bed was free of rats than rest his head on some pretty pilla-cases."

"I'll come catch your rats whenever you say," Eden answered.

"In that case, I'll take you home with me tonight, because I don't believe we've ever had as pretty a rat catcher. What do you say?"

"I think," Eden rested her chin in her hand, "you'll have to make an appointment."

"An appointment!"

The room erupted in laughter and Rowen glanced over to Adeline watching from the kitchen doorway. She met his gaze, squared her shoulders and puffed with satisfaction. It dawned on him what her true aim had been all long, as surely as if she'd whispered it in his ear. She'd gone to all this trouble

to draw Eden away from the memory of her father's death one year ago.

He'd stashed away a wad of bills for her Christmas bonus, but how paltry it was. Last Christmas, his father had bought her a black winter coat with a flared skirt and a fur collar. He had made her try it on and then fussed on and on about how she looked just like a city woman, Ethel Waters, maybe. Looking back, giving hadn't been his daddy's true aim. His daddy had spread money around to show everyone how much he had so that he could convince them, and himself most of all, that there would never be an end to it.

Still, more than ever, Rowen wanted to give Adeline something that would flat out astound her, given all that she'd done to save them. No matter what kind of money he had, or would have, whatever he would have to offer her would always fall short.

Come to think of it, he'd never seen her wear that coat.

"Gentlemen," said Claude. "A waltz, please."

Arlen and Todd obliged, and Claude took his mother's hand. "May I have this dance?"

The space limitations forced them to waltz in small steps. His mother danced as she'd been taught, leaning back against Claude's palm. "How old timey they look," whispered Jewell. The notion of waltzing was old-fashioned, evoking dim memories of when he was knee-high. That was the last time he'd seen his parents waltz, his mother leaning back and smiling in the same way.

"Rowen, come dance with me," said Eden.

"I don't know how to waltz."

"It's easy. Just one-two-three."

JAMIE LISA FORBES

He held her hands and tried to follow her steps. They nearly bumped into Claude and his mama. While they clomped around the floor, he felt Jewell's glare burning the back of his neck. She wanted this dance, even though she knew no more about waltzing than he. He quickly backed into his seat and sat down.

"Rowen!" said Eden.

"I don't know how to do it. Go and find somebody else."

Jewell looked away from him. "That was so sweet of you, Rowen," she said flatly, the twitch of her shoulders conveying the opposite meaning. He noticed this habit of hers more and more—her movements contradicted a compliment she'd just uttered. What made her do that? Maybe he didn't say enough, or do enough, to reassure her. He leaned toward her, intending to ask her to dance, but the waltz was ending.

Mr. Nodding looked as if he was ready to leave, but at his wife's coaxing he sat through another tune before saying, "Jewell, you ready to go?"

Eden tugged Jewell's skirt. "I hope you liked our Christmas party."

Jewell put her arm around Eden's shoulder.

"I enjoyed it very much. I'll come see you soon, okay?"

Rowen walked Jewell and her parents to their car, and when he turned around, Claude was waiting on the porch.

"Nice evening. Glad you invited us."

"I didn't have anything to do with it. It was all Adeline and Mama. And you brought the music."

"Todd's got Eden on his lap, plunking on the banjo, while we speak. Maybe we'll build on her talents."

Eden

From the porch, the luminaries still flickered while the stars wheeled above. Claude lit his pipe.

"Her mother never came for her?"

"No, sir, not even a telephone call to ask how she is. Adeline says her mama doesn't deserve to have her back."

"Did you ever consider — maybe that woman wanted to be rid of her husband."

"You're saying she got her brother to shoot him?"

"No. I'm saying the alleys of a human heart have more twists and turns than we know. Or can understand. If I'm called on to come to conclusions about anyone, what I will say is that you've turned out finer than what you admit to. Not every young man raised in our little hamlet would have steered through a reversal of fortune as well as you. And saddled themselves with raising someone else's child on top of it. Yet, I worry about the goodness being wrung from you over time. And our pretty rat catcher has no future here at all.

"Get her out of here, Rowen. It's not too late to get yourself that education. Take Eden with you and don't ever come back."

"What are you talking about? And what about Jewell?"

"We will all survive such yowling as may occur. Jewell most of all. And it would please your mama. She believes manual labor is coarsening you. She's said as much."

"Dang it, Claude, I've finally made it. You've just seen it in there. Mama's doing better. She's not living how she used to, but she's comfortable. You talk about Eden and, thanks to you letting me work for you, we can keep her up. But how do I keep everybody up by going to where I don't know anyone?"

"You all got such big ideas of what you want me to be. Nobody's asking me what I want. And what I want is everything I've got right now. Going away to 'get an education' — that's what Mama and Daddy wanted in that big sham life they were living. How did that all come out? Flat on our backs, that's how that ended. I've given up on everyone's fool dreams. I don't know that they were ever right for me to begin with."

Claude nodded. "From where you stand, it all looks settled. Safe. You've talked yourself into thinking that what's settled is what's right. But you haven't considered time. Time erodes. There is the river we never step in twice. You'll wake one morning and be greeted by your discontent. And by then, it might be too late — for you and Eden. I see by your face that you think I am speaking gibberish."

Rowen was trying to tamp down his impatience. What Claude had said sounded like those speeches in *The Flower of Cape Fear*, all those puffy phrases that had nothing to do with getting out of bed the next morning and counting out his spare change so Eden could have shoes.

"This is the way I see it," said Rowen. "One day Eden's people are going to forgive her or forget the lies they think she told and then, they'll come get her. And I'll be out of it and I won't have anything to do with her anymore. I'll only have to manage for me and Mama."

"Even if you're right, what will become of her?"

"I don't know. She'll grow up and get married like the rest of them, I guess. Isn't that the way it's supposed to be? I mean ...I'm not saying that I'm sorry I took her in, but she isn't one of us."

"Meaning a child with nothing and no education shouldn't expect anything more."

How damn aggravating Claude could be. One minute he would prop a boy up, and the next minute, backhand him.

"I can't change the world to suit her or anyone else."

Claude stared at him while he took another draw on his pipe. "I'll pray that the two of you won't end up ruint."

The tobacco smoke hung in the air. One after another, the luminaries burned out.

JAMIE LISA FORBES

7

The March rain outside reverberated throughout the colored waiting room at the train depot in Fayetteville. Every mutter, every shuffle, every cough was magnified in this draughty room. From his seat, Rowen watched the waitresses ferrying platters with eggs and grits at the diner across the street. His stomach growled.

Sammy heard him. "Mr. Rowen, sir, I don't believe you are going to survive this trip!" He reached into a paper sack and offered his own ham biscuit.

"You're going to need that," Rowen snapped.

Sammy grinned. "You ain't got nothin' but a swallow in the thermos to maintain yourself all the way back to White Rock. That's why the army picked me. 'Cause I got more grit."

Eden

"You volunteered. They're going to take anybody fool enough to sign up."

Sammy waved the ham biscuit under Rowen's nose and Rowen pushed it away. He looked down the row past Sammy's parents to Eden and Adeline at the end. If only they could all walk over and wait in that diner. But it didn't have a colored section. He could go and take Eden with him. Adeline caught his glance and leaned forward.

"You all right?" she asked loudly. Now that grey light filtered through the windows, he noted how weariness had pooled beneath her eyes.

If he asked, she'd say, go on and take Eden with you. But he squelched the thought. It wasn't just that Sammy would snicker at his weakness. It was that Adeline was chilled and as hungry as he was, and yet she settled back in her seat, impervious to need.

For the first time, he'd felt fortunate to have the pea green station wagon, for they'd all managed to squeeze inside. In the rush to leave, he'd barely looked at Mr. and Miz Little, Sammy's parents, except to notice that they were dressed as if they were going to church. He wondered at it—why they'd dress up to ride the forty miles to sit at the bus station. He didn't dare ask. Their faces were as stony as Adeline's, and even Eden, sitting behind the passenger seat, was subdued in the early hour.

If Sammy noticed how grim his parents looked, he didn't pay it any mind. His gaze bounced around the depot, that perpetual half-grin set on his mouth. Had they tried to change his mind? For whatever effort they'd sunk into it, it probably had no more impact than a goat butting an oak.

JAMIE LISA FORBES

Sammy's decision made no sense to Rowen. When Rowen had first heard it a month or so ago, he thought it was one of Sammy's jokes.

"Daylight's thirty minutes old, Mr. Rowen," Sammy had called from the porch, "and you're wasting it. Like always." Rowen had peered out the kitchen window. A white mule, smeared with mud and manure, was tied to the new gate. Rays of sun broke through tree limbs that were still bare, but dotted with buds: pink, ivory, chalk green.

Rowen opened the door and blinked in the bright light.

"Adeline says you're starting your garden today, Mr. Rowen. She told me to bring the mule and run the harrow over here."

Eden shouldered Rowen aside. "A mule — let me see him!" She jumped down the steps, her frame showing through her nightgown. It bothered him. She was old enough to know that she ought to get dressed around men. Over the winter, she'd turned eleven. She'd grown, and the top of her head now reached his collar bone. She ought to be settling down into a young lady. Like Jewell. Even with Adeline's encouragement, the transformation was wildly off course. As she threw a long leg over the mule's withers and hoisted herself on, he concluded that she wasn't cute anymore.

"Eden, go in the house and cover up. Before Adeline catches you like that," Rowen shouted.

Sammy leered. He was seeing exactly what Rowen was seeing through the nightgown.

"You got as much rein on that girl as on a hurricane. And it's only going to get better. I believe I see some buds through that nightgown."

"What she needs is a daddy who will tear up

128

her behind. She won't listen to anyone. Why'd you bring over a mule that's been rolling in mud?"

"Who says you gotta spit-shine an old mule to plow a garden?"

"I don't want crap on me, that's all."

Sammy shrugged. "Eden don't care."

Eden hammered the mule's sides until it broke into a jog. Her thin hair was long now and bounced off her shoulders. There was no point in yelling any more. She'd run into Adeline in a minute or two.

Sammy shaded his eyes to watch her. "Y'all taking her with you after the wedding, or is she staying with your mama?"

"Mama'll be living with us. I keep on hoping Eden's mamma will come get her. But Mama'll never send Eden away."

"Hmm, hmm. You are getting ready to have yourself some kind of household, Mr. Rowen. I'm sorry I won't be around."

Rowen thought he meant the wedding, mainly because he already felt guilty over it. Sammy ought to have been invited. But Rowen didn't have a say — it was all Jewell and her mother and his mother. The affair was the same as the annual historical drama about Elizabeth Purdie Richardson — a pageant scripted and staged wholly by women, and what he was expected to do was play his role and not menace sensibilities with requests to invite his colored friend.

"I've been feeling bad about that, Sammy. I'd like to invite you."

"Don't go flogging yourself. I'm leaving. I joined the Army."

JAMIE LISA FORBES

Warbles and twitters of the spring birds filled the pause that followed when it seemed like there should have been dead silence. Everything and everyone Sammy Little knew was right here. Why would he want to go someplace where he was nobody? Much less be spirited off to some spooky landscape where he'd get shot at.

Sammy took in Rowen's shock. "The world ain't flat, I'm not gonna fall off the edge. I never did see why you didn't leave yourself when you had that chance to go away to school. How could you waste it—that's what I couldn't get."

He looked back down the road after Eden. "There ain't nothing here for me, Mr. Rowen."

Snatches of Adeline's scolding drifted back to them. She had caught the mule's bridle.

"What are you talking about? Your whole life's here."

"That might be true for you. You were lucky on how you got fixed up. You got yourself a nice job, and once you marry that girl, Claude'll set you up right in that construction business. But me? The thought of fields of tubakka now and forever just makes me sick."

"Your mama and daddy aren't going to let you go!"

Adeline had towed the mule all the way back to the gate.

"Rowen, didn't you see this child run out of this house near naked?"

Sammy's mama and daddy were going to let him go after all. Maybe they understood Sammy's choice better than Rowen did, though now that Rowen could study them in this grimy depot, they didn't appear to.

Eden

Travelers stirred all around them. "The bus is here," said Miz Little, flatly.

Sammy bounced to his feet and Eden pressed next to him. "Hey, Sammy, maybe the army could take me."

"Naw, they ain't letting girls into the army, 'specially ones as scary as you."

"When are you gonna come home? Will you have a uniform then?"

Sammy and Eden pushed on through the crowd while everyone else dragged behind. At the bus, the luggage door slid open with a bang and the driver began loading bags. The white passengers boarded, plopped into the front seats and fiddled with their windows.

Miz Little burst into sobs and Adeline gripped her arm. Sammy laughed and threw his arm over her other shoulder.

"Y'all just being silly now, you know that." He stooped a little and pressed his cheek against hers. "Don't be silly, Mama." He shook hands with his father, then boarded the bus and they watched him work his way to a seat in the back. He was squeezed between other passengers, but he leaned forward to smile and wave.

"Everyone's staring at us," Eden said. And it was true. Whites and coloreds, all strangers, turned their heads at Miz Little's sobbing while the bus backed away, filling the air with diesel fumes. Every day of the last year, Rowen had detested that termite-infested weather-beaten shack, but if he could get there in the next blink of his eye, he'd do it rather than endure another moment on display in this crowd. Any face would have been welcome for its familiarity alone, even Uncle Hugh's.

"C'mon Sophie," Adeline murmured, "you got to look up and wave one more time."

Eden's hand slipped into Rowen's. He squeezed it.

"I'm going to miss Sammy," she said. "He was real good to us. But why's Miz Little crying like that? It's not like he's gonna die. He's going to come back to us. It might be a long time, but he'll come back. Right, Rowen?"

"A long time to you is too long for Miz Little."

No one spoke on the drive home. The only sound was Miz Little's sniffles. After he dropped off Adeline and the Littles, the clouds vaporized, leaving behind a sky that was Easter egg blue. Back in his own yard, Jewell was hanging out the laundry. Sheets snapped and billowed and the pear tree next to the clothesline shed petals like snow. The spectacle of Jewell herself drove away all the morning's troubles. Her back narrowed into her shirtwaist and her skirt flapped on her long calves.

"Why's Jewell hanging up them clothes?" asked Eden. "That's my job." She slammed the car door and ran across the yard. "Jew-ellll!"

Rowen willed himself not to run, although he wanted to. He caught snatches of Eden's chatter about their journey. He liked the picture they made together, the tall girl bending down to listen to the younger one. Looking at the two of them, he felt sure matters could come out all right. With Jewell around, Eden would grow up proper. She'd follow Jewell's ways. What was it that Claude had said about time? He couldn't remember the words, but it had all been about taking a longer view. You had to step back to see it.

"Tell you what," Jewell said, "It's such a

beautiful day, let's eat lunch outside on the porch. You go set it up." And Eden bounced off. Once she had gone inside, Jewell took a little hop forward and threw her arms around his neck.

"I'm so glad to see you," he said.

She pecked at his lips. "Sounds awful sitting in the colored section at the bus station all morning. I've made ham and pintos for lunch."

Even at noon, the breeze was still tart. Eden picked daffodils and Jewell set them out in a crystal vase.

His mother shaded her eyes from the bright light on the porch. "Children, why ever are we eating here with that horrible gale blowing? I understand your hunger for fresh air, but we are going to turn into ice right in our chairs!"

"It's shielded from the wind," said Jewell, "and the sun is so lovely today. You can wrap up, can't you?"

"You are becoming part of the family, Jewell, so you may as well be aware of my condition. Dr. Faulk is very encouraged by my progress, but he says I must be mindful of my frailties and not push myself beyond my limits. I know you are about to be married, but you are so young. You won't even have finished high school. Not that you'll be missing anything by skipping your senior year. If you haven't learned what you need to know by your senior year, then another year of Latin is not going to catch you up.

"In any event, your maturation to date has not attuned you to the needs of those who are ill. We will eat in the dining room."

Jewell looked away, smarting at Miz Rita's rebuke, but she and Eden set about moving all the utensils and the daffodils back to the dining room.

"That's our good silver, isn't it?"

"Yes, Miz Hart. Eden and I found it in the back room. We polished it and then it seemed too beautiful to put away. We thought you'd like it if we used it."

"There's occasions for such things. And we will never have such occasions out here in 'terra incognita'. It was very thoughtful for you to care for it and I am grateful. But please put it away."

"Rowen and I are starting a new life together, that's an occasion, isn't it?"

"You will get your own silver for a wedding gift and then you can use it for anything you deem an occasion."

Back went the silver and by the time the table was reset, and everyone seated, the black-eyed peas had turned cold.

"Eden," said Jewell, "it's not polite to have your elbows on the table."

"Look at how yella them daffodils are," said Eden.

"They're yella all right," said Rowen. Jewell frowned at the way Eden had ignored her.

Still Eden didn't notice. "They're not just yella, they're a perfect yella, even more perfect than Crayola yella." She reached out to brush them with her finger and Jewell snapped, "Eden, you're knocking pollen on Miz Rita's table!"

Eden pulled her hand back. "Sorry," she said.

"Jewell, this cornbread is very good although it's a bit dry. You used milk, didn't you? Adeline always uses cream. She has a friend at the creamery who sells her a pint for just a penny. You must try Adeline's recipe. I'm sure she can get some cream for you."

"I've baked this recipe at least a dozen times and never heard anyone say that, Miz Rita. I'll try cream next time. I'm sure we can get it at the grocery store."

"Oh, Jewell, don't take offense. And please don't scowl. Constant scowling will give you heavy jowls as you age. I know you don't want that. My comments are only gentle suggestions intended to make your marriage a long and happy one. And now, talking about your marriage, we must decide how to respond to Hugh's invitation to have a joint wedding reception with Cousin Mabel."

Jewell's scowl, which hadn't eased one bit, swiveled directly to Rowen. She had already told him how much she hated the idea.

By a miracle of biblical proportions, Mabel was getting married. She'd attended a church retreat the previous fall at Holly Lake, the month before Rowen had taken Jewell there on their first date. She'd met a boy who'd come all the way from Bellpointe to visit relatives. His daddy ran a shrimp trawler out there in the sound. Though Cousin Mabel hadn't had so much as one date with anyone in White Rock, somehow, she had swayed this stranger. The story was they'd written each other all winter and maybe it was love and maybe it was escape from Uncle Hugh, but they'd chosen to get married on the same day in the same church as Rowen and Jewell.

"Rowen and I want a reception with our families and friends. We don't want to have to share our special time with these people from Bellpointe who we'll never see again in our lives. What will it be like when we want to show the pictures to our children? 'Who is that?' they'll say. And we'll have to say, 'We don't know. They were what's-his-name's people from the coast.' I don't care what y'all are going to say. It's rude of Uncle Hugh even to think of such a thing."

Rita patted her hand. "It is the most important day of your life, of course. But you're not just getting a husband to have and to hold, you are merging with an entire family, a family that has barely endured grueling tragedy you cannot comprehend. My brother has always been very generous. This may be the way to reunite all of us. Part of becoming adults, my dears, is adjusting one's desires to accommodate the greater need. Think of how much happiness it will bring to poor Mabel."

"If that's what Rowen wants," said Jewell, as she glared at Rowen. It was a clear shove to enlist him in the fray. He wondered why the road from the ring to the marriage bed was so cross-hatched with booby traps.

"Why don't y'all have your party at Mr. Lynch's house?" Eden said. "He's got plenty of room. And it would be real nice there in the woods. And they got that big porch for all the picture-taking. I think it would be real nice."

Jewell would never agree, but at least Eden's idea had given Rowen a detour. "Sounds like a good idea to me," he said, as he stabbed his collards.

Without Rowen to support her, Jewel sighed in defeat. "Well, sharing the reception with Cousin Mabel would save money for everyone. For my daddy, too."

The silence that followed wasn't the silence of contented consumption. Jewell wasn't digesting her defeat over the wedding reception, nor his acquiescence in it, Rowen sensed, and somehow that

disappointment was fueling some new eruption. He wondered if he shouldn't jump up and start clearing the dishes.

"Rowen."

Too late.

"We need to start talking about money. I know how hard you're working, but I don't see how we can keep up Adeline. I know she's been with you since you were a boy and all, but, well, she's getting older, and the thing of it is, you really pay her too much."

Jewell caught her breath and looked over at Rita, but when Rita said nothing to contradict her, she plunged on.

"I can do most of what needs to be done." She paused. "I'm sure I can improve my baking. We don't need to spend our money on help — especially just starting out. Even if we needed the help, we can get a younger girl at half that price."

"No one could take Adeline's place," said Eden. "She's like them yella flowers, she's the perfectest."

Again, Rowen picked up Eden's thread, but this time it was to delay voicing his own shock.

"Who'll help Eden with her homework? Adeline does that in addition to everything else."

"I can take that over, if Eden will let me," Rita said.

"Only Adeline can do it. She does it best," said Eden.

"Silly," said Jewell, "wouldn't you like me to help you?"

"You can help me with reading and Adeline will help me with arithmetic. She draws little pictures so I can understand it."

"Eden, honey," said Rita, "I think you should

start spending more time with Jewell. I understand why you wouldn't want to spend time with an ailing old woman like me. But you're older now, not a child anymore. You're lucky to be getting Jewell as your companion. You want to be just like her, don't you?"

While they spoke, Rowen retreated to the tumult of his own feelings. It had been less than a year ago when Uncle Hugh had confronted him, demanding that he let Adeline go. And he'd known then that he'd never do it. Now, in this new upending of his life that he'd brought on himself by asking Jewell to marry him, could she simply remove Adeline the same way she'd switch out a vase of flowers on a table?

To steady himself, he focused on her, this girl who would be his wife in a few weeks — the long pale hands and the wisps of hair that framed her face. He pictured her in the house they would build one day. She would be out in the front yard, waving to him as he went off to work. And all day long he'd dream of returning home to a kitchen full of supper odors, to a bed, at last, that they would share together.

Jewell was right. Adeline didn't belong in that picture.

Two weeks later, as he and Jewell were out driving through the countryside, he found the land where he wanted to build, a clearing ringed by sycamore trees just off a sharp elbow bend of a dirt road.

They stopped to explore. The grass was ankle-high, and Jewell fretted about snakes. Rowen

Eden

found a set of tire tracks, nearly grown over, that led to an abandoned farmhouse centered among the trees. The trees were so evenly spaced, they must have been planted by those long-ago farmers. The evening sun threw dappled shadows on the grey and white trunks and the new leaves in the crowns quivered in a breeze high above. As he stood holding Jewell's hand, he imagined a new house with a row of azaleas in front.

He liked the way the sycamores divided the parcel from the farmland just beyond. And they were ten miles from town, not too far, but far enough. He didn't ever want to live among White Rock folks again. It was a little oasis here, at least they could make it one.

"What do you think?"

Jewell shrugged. "It's awful quiet. Don't you think it's too quiet? I do like those trees. The bark's so pretty."

He left her sitting on the old cracked stoop while he walked back to the car and got a blanket. They spread it on a bare sandy spot in front of the house and lay down. For an hour, they held hands and watched the colors overhead fade until the stars poked through, and then he rolled over and put his arm under her neck.

She let him go farther than he'd ever gone before. Why not all the way? They were good as married. But when his hand moved between her thighs, she tensed and pushed him away.

"Rowen, stop, we've got to be getting back," she said.

He nuzzled her cheek. "We're engaged, aren't we? What's the difference? Right here is where our house is going to be."

JAMIE LISA FORBES

"That's sweet. But let's not spoil our wedding day. Don't you want that day to be perfect?"

"It would still be perfect, wouldn't it?"

"No, silly, because we haven't been blessed yet." She sat up and began buttoning her blouse. "And we do need our own bedroom. We can't be out in the open like animals."

She jumped to her feet. "Let's get out of here, the mosquitoes are biting."

The memory of that evening played over and over in Rowen's mind as land-buying got piled on to the heap of wedding activities. It ought to have been as simple as pounding on the landowner's door and agreeing to whatever price he asked, but Claude, with a firm shake of his head, terminated that plan and took over the negotiating, which dragged on for weeks until there was a price and papers to sign.

And then followed a question of a mortgage, a bucket of money he'd be paying on for thirty years. Thirty years—the rest of his life. The life he was dreaming of always seemed to lie beyond another slog.

He batted off Jewell's nagging to go to Franklin White. He wouldn't do that, not even if it meant they couldn't have the land. But bank after bank in all the surrounding towns turned them down. Too young, too unknown.

By the Sunday before the wedding, they still didn't have a loan, and it looked as though, after their honeymoon at the beach, they'd be returning to the little tin-roofed shack. He was resigned to putting off the dream. Maybe with a little more money in savings, it was just around the corner.

Jewell fixed Sunday lunch for them after church, and afterwards they'd sat on his porch and

watched the countryside glide into the Sunday afternoon drowse. All the bustle of spring was ending. The trees were done leafing out, the azalea blossoms had browned, and the spring warmth, so welcome in the last weeks, was waxing into the summer heat.

Jewell leaned into him. "Just one week from today, we'll be at the beach. Just one week to go."

Once the "I do's" were finished, he would, at last, be able to think of himself as a man, not a boy. No more wondering about when this transition would happen.

A two-toned green Lincoln nosed down the road almost indistinguishable from the foliage around it until the sun bounced off the hood. Why would someone be driving a car like that down this dusty road? It eased to a stop in front of the house, the engine cut off, and out stepped Franklin White. "Good afternoon," he called, then he went around to the passenger side and opened the door for his sister, Coman.

She emerged dressed in a turquoise suit with white piping. They must have come straight from church. Her platinum blonde hair was tucked into a white hat topped with a turquoise bow. She reached for her purse and then froze against the car door, waiting for her brother to initiate the formalities.

Coman hadn't come to sweep her daughter up and carry her home, Rowen realized. Funny how that awareness pricked him, even after all this time. Though he had to admit he longed to see it, there was no warmth in her powdered face, not even the feigned warmth that White Rock women exuded on Sundays.

Franklin's lips parted, revealing nicotine-stained teeth. "Rowen Hart. It's been a long time. You've turned into a young man since the last time I saw you. I don't believe you've met my sister, Coman. You were just a toddler when she married."

Coman snapped, "It's not necessary to bring my age into it, Franklin."

"Sorry." He shifted toward Jewell. "Is this Miss Nodding? I read about your upcoming wedding in the paper."

Rowen couldn't figure why they were here, but they hadn't been invited and he had no good reason to utter one word to them, though he sensed Jewell's irritation at his ill manners. She stepped off the porch and took Franklin's hand.

"Mr. White. How nice to see you. Yes, we are getting married next Saturday. Miz Whitney, how do you do?"

Coman stepped forward. "It's nice to meet you. I'm getting married myself in a few weeks."

"How wonderful for you. I must have missed it in the paper."

"Birch's death caused so much catastrophe for Franklin, when the world knows he is a man of integrity and honor, that we decided to keep it quiet. I'll be moving away with my husband and all this unpleasantness will be behind us."

"Where will you be going?"

"I am marrying Mr. James Purcell, of Lumberton. He's a lieutenant in the police force."

Franklin turned to Rowen. "Congratulations, although I was surprised to hear you hadn't gone off to college. Your daddy always spoke so highly of you. That's what he wanted for you, God rest his soul."

Rowen felt as if he was being prodded into

this conversation, when all he wanted was for them to leave.

He blurted, "If that's what he wanted, he should never have left Mama. I'd never leave her."

"It was a difficult year. Upheaval for you — and for us, too. How's Rita doing?"

"She's gone in to lay down," said Jewell, "but I'm sure she'd love to see you. I'll get her."

She went inside, stranding Rowen with his unwelcome guests who now crowded him on the porch. Coman reached for a cigarette and Franklin leaned over to light it for her. She inhaled and then her eyes drifted to the mold on the clapboard. "How long have you all been out here?"

"Since Daddy died."

She nodded. "No wonder Rita's missed her club meetings. And you're all she has?"

"Yes, ma'am."

"Hugh wouldn't do nothing for her?"

"No, ma'am."

"Franklin's never let me down, he's always been there for me. I guess some families don't stick together that way."

"Like you've done for Eden?"

Coman absorbed his jab without remark. She took another drag from her cigarette while she glared at him.

Rowen pressed on. "You're taking her with you to Lumberton, right? I mean that's why you all came out, isn't it?"

"Rowen, no one can blame you for your ill feelings," said Franklin, "I know it must be very difficult for you to understand all that's occurred given that you took on such a burden. You see, Coman has suffered terribly. She hadn't even finished school when Birch came along and swept her off her feet. And back then we had such high hopes for Birch which, sadly, weren't realized. Nothing in the way she was brought up prepared her for years of poverty. Which is why I believe my sister deserves the opportunity by herself to start a new life."

His words gave his sister a springboard. "You've got quite the nerve. You're nineteen and you're fed up with the crosses you've had to bear? My guess is you've got running water here, don't you? I didn't. You've never had to haul water from a well twice a day while your baby screams inside the house."

She flicked ash over the porch railing. "And then after all you do for that child, the diapers you scrub in tubs, the scraps you sew together for clothes, the lies you tell to beg milk off the neighbors, after all that, when that man comes in the door after spending all his wages on games and 'shine, your child holds out her arms and cries, 'Daddy.' The love of her life. Isn't that something? And on it goes, year after year.

"Nothing like that's ever happened to you. And yet you stand here, laced up in your haughtiness, your mama's boy."

Not in any corner of White Rock had Rowen ever heard a woman speak this way. What had happened to the "wit that would make a stone laugh" that his mama had gone on about? He couldn't imagine that this stocky, sullen woman had ever been a girl, much less a mama. But if she didn't want to be a mama, why couldn't she just leave them alone? Coman and Franklin were here on a mission—they wanted something.

Jewell stepped out the door with his mother.

"Franklin White—and Coman as well—imagine you two coming all the way out here."

His mother had dressed as if she'd gone to church, though she hadn't. Rowen noticed that she'd pulled out her pearls.

Franklin took her hand. "Rita, how lovely you still are. I'm so sorry I haven't come before now. I've wanted to come for a long time and tell you how sorry I was about—about everything's that happened. But...things got away from me."

"You needn't apologize. You and I go back such a long way. We never expected all the trials we've had to endure. How silly of me, you really did go through a trial. How awful it must have been. With Adeline spiriting us away out here, I escaped all the ugliness."

"Understandable, how you feel. But you've got to be feeling better with Rowen coming up so well and marrying this lovely young girl. All the bad times are bygones now."

"For me, too," said Coman.

"Why, yes, Coman, Jewell has told me. Congratulations. But we are atrocious hosts making you stand outside here in this heat. Do come inside. Adeline's left us a pound cake and Jewell will get you some tea."

"Don't bother, Rita," said Coman. "We're here to pick up Eden and then we'll be on our way."

"She's not here."

Rowen felt relieved to say it. Maybe they'd go on and leave now. "She went off to church with Adeline this morning. She's not back yet."

"You all send her to the Negro church?" asked Coman.

"I'm afraid you misunderstand," his mother

answered. "It's wonderful that the two of you are here now. Not that we've minded keeping Eden. She has always been welcome and has become part of our family. But I'm afraid I haven't regained the strength yet to attend church again. All the...commotion, the throngs with their rat-ta-tat questions, I am not ready."

"Don't trouble yourself. Coman meant nothing by it," said Franklin. "We're obliged to you for taking the child in. As I said, I've meant to come, ever since Coman told me that Eden had run away. We thought it best to wait until passions subsided, knowing how much the trial had upset Eden, and, somehow, the weeks became months, and then we heard the news that Rowen was marrying.

"We can't thank you enough for all you have done for Eden. When you yourselves were under such a strain. It's charity beyond our ability to repay. And Eden didn't know what she saw. Understandable—how she could make a mistake. With Coman remarrying and Eden's hostility towards me, there's only one solution. We've found a girls' school for her in Virginia and I'll be taking her up there."

No, thought Rowen. He wouldn't let them have her.

"I believe we'll keep her," he said, "Mama loves her. Mama needs her."

Jewell touched his arm. "With us starting out and all, they're right. Rowen, honey, we're going to be wanting to have our own family."

"Rowen, I thought you always resented having her here," said his mother.

He shifted to face her, startled by her response, but the look on her face told him she'd

meant what she'd said. No way around it, if she was reminding him of those early feelings from months and months ago, it could only mean that she was willing to give Eden up.

"Mama, you don't want her to go!"

Rita nodded. "I will miss her. But these are her people. Whatever their past...distractions, they have come to do what is best for her now."

Not a wrinkle of doubt creased her powdered face. She didn't see Franklin and Coman the way he did. She had known them all her life and she couldn't, or wouldn't, admit there was any evil in them. Among everyone standing here, he was the only one who believed it possible that Eden might have told the truth.

And Eden was nothing to Jewell. That's who would be his bride in a week. It wasn't like he could haul Eden on his honeymoon. He wouldn't even want to.

And Coman. With Rita's acquiescence, Coman gloated, fully confident that whatever protest he put up would be snuffed out.

They had all made up their minds, and they didn't see him any different than a squawking chicken.

"You just said, Mama. Eden's part of our family now."

"We can't do for her what Franklin can," said his mother. "Think of the things she will have that we can't afford to give her. She'll have an opportunity for a good education, something she's never had." His mother shot a sidelong glance at Coman. "Rowen, you must see this is her one true chance."

"And I did bring some money with me today," Franklin added, "for all your trouble."

"I don't want your money," said Rowen.

"Rowen," said Jewell, "you've kept her for a year and she's not y'all's child. He is just trying to pay you back and we need the money. You want to build us a house on that land, remember?"

"How's Eden going to take it? How is she going to see all this?"

"I know you mean well, son," said Franklin. "I can see how the child has swayed you. But soon you will take vows promising to put your lovely bride here above all other earthly concerns. Let the child go."

The clog in Rowen's throat made him even angrier. "Who is going to tell her?"

"If she's as thick with you all as you say, I don't see anything wrong with you telling her," said Coman.

"Yes," said Franklin, "I hear she looks up to Rowen like a daddy." Franklin pulled five hundred crisp dollars from his billfold. "Now you take this as what I owe you for the last year. And when you get some time, stop by the bank. I know you'll need money for that house you want to build, and I'll make sure you get set up with something you can afford."

Jewell pressed next to Rowen and squeezed his hand. "We will, we sure will."

In the evening, the clematis vine that Adeline had planted at the gatepost opened into plum-colored blossoms. He remembered Eden's phrase

about the daffodils—perfect yellow. These were a perfect purple, the color fluid as blood.

Rowen watched Eden come down the road in the organdy dress Adeline had made for her last fall. Already, the hem was too short, at least an inch over her knees. The lace trim on the new hat he'd bought her for Easter had partially come loose and dangled off the brim. She was barefoot. Adeline must have told her to carry her patent leather shoes so she wouldn't scuff them. And to top it all off, how was it that she was coming from church with knees caked with dirt.

"What you doing out here, Rowen?"

"Nothing."

"Where's Jewell?"

"Gone home."

"Is she coming over for dinner tonight?"

"Don't think so."

"You been out to the garden today?"

"No."

"You're so sorry. Too bad Adeline ain't here to tell you how sorry you are. I'll work on it."

"You better change first. You don't want to mess up that dress. You already got dirt on the hem."

"I ain't stupid, Rowen. Look what I brought you." She offered up a paper sack. "Strawberries."

"You were out picking strawberries in that dress?"

"I know you go crazy for fresh strawberries."

The screen door slammed behind her and the bag sat on his lap, oozing red juice.

When she went to the garden, he watched her from the back door. Marigolds planted at the garden border were already in bloom and Eden was hoeing. And singing.

JAMIE LISA FORBES

"What will you wear, o my dear, o my dear..."
The words came out in puffs of exhalations as she slammed the hoe in the soil. *"What will you wear Jenny Jaynnnn-kins? I'll just go bare with a ribbon in my hair..."*

"Eden," he called. The sunlight was behind her now. All he could make out was that fly-away carrot-colored hair.

"Come out and help me," she shouted.

His feet felt planted on the steps. He didn't want to wrench them from this spot and set the coming moments in motion. He looked down as he shuffled to the row she was working on, until a ridge of dirt spilled over the toes of his shoes.

"Jewell's been showing me pictures in *Ladies Home Journal*. I can have my own bedroom in the new house, she said, and decorate it any way I want. The curtains is going to be pink with lavender ribbons and the walls are gonna be Carolina blue." She stopped and turned to him. "Do you think I can have a canopy bed?"

"Eden, I've got to talk to you."

"What do you look so sick for, Rowen? You look like you're 'bout to heave."

He kicked the dirt off his shoes.

"Ain't Jewell going to marry you no more?"

"Your mama came out here today."

Rowen's heart sank at the hope that brightened her face. "She came to see me?"

"She came out with your Uncle Franklin."

"What did she bring him for?"

"They're coming back. They're going to take you with them. Your mama's getting married again."

"No, she's not."

"Yes, she is."

"Well, who is he? He's not going to be my daddy."

"You're not going to live with them. They found a school for you in Virginia. Your Uncle Franklin's taking you up there."

"I ain't going. I'm staying right here with you."

There was no easy way to do it and he flashed hot with resentment. Just three hours ago, he'd wanted to protect her, but now that she was in front of him—always contrary, always unruly—it only reminded him how much trouble she'd always been.

"Do you ever think about anyone but your damn self? Have you ever thought about how hard I have to work to keep you up? It's not my mamma's fault, nor my fault neither, that your daddy went and got himself shot. And I've been stuck with you all this time. You think I want to be your daddy? I never wanted it. I hate having to haul over to the school every time you get in trouble."

"I ain't goin' to no school in Virginia!"

"Did you ever think just for one moment that you might have been wrong about your uncle Franklin?"

"You can't make me go! You can't make me!" The fury that erupted from her made him step back. Nothing more than a wild white trash child showing her true self after all. Why had he ever bothered to feel guilty about her?

"Jewell won't let you do this."

"You got that wrong. She's already packed your things."

"You're lying, Rowen!"

"Everyone wanted me to tell you before they get back to pick you up."

She fell into the dirt, sobbing.

He knelt by her and gripped her shoulder. "Eden, calm down. It's not the end of the world. You might like it there and you can come visit us."

She slapped his arm away. "None of this would be happening if you weren't getting married."

"What are you talking about?"

"You wouldn't never have listened to them. It's all because of her. And you don't even love her. She don't love you neither."

"You don't know what you're talking about."

"I love you, Rowen. Not her."

She wasn't thinking like a little girl. How long had these thoughts been in her head?

"You and me? You're crazy. You're just a kid!"

"I'll get growed in a couple years."

"That can't ever be, Eden. You've got to give that up."

"Why?" She was staring at him now, tears running down her grimy cheeks.

"Where you grew up, where I grew up, those are places about as far apart as the earth to the moon. We aren't alike. We won't ever be."

"We been in the same house all this time."

"Not because I wanted it. I didn't want any of this."

She jumped to her feet. "I ain't nothin' to you."

"I didn't say that."

She turned and began to walk away. He reached for her arm and she shook him off. "Don't touch me!" she screamed.

"Adeline can't take you in. You don't have no other place to go. Eden, come on. EEEden!"

Eden

She broke into a run. He followed her around the corner of the house, but by the time he'd reached the gate, she was flying down the dirt road. The frogs chirped in the dusk and he couldn't hear her feet any longer. He strained to see her, but the shadows shimmying through the trees swallowed her whole.

JAMIE LISA FORBES

8

NOT EVEN DAWN and his newborn, Marjorie Rose Hart, was already bawling. Rowen groaned and rolled over, hoping to ignore it long enough for Jewell to get up. He knew she'd been up most of the night, so he ought to let her lie there as long as she wanted. But any second that baby would wake up his other daughter, three-year old Lilly, and his mama.

He shook Jewell's shoulder. She hissed, "Can't you at least make the formula?"

He threw off the covers, picked up the baby and carried her to the kitchen. Outside a vireo chirped in the sycamores. The fan on the counter swirled the soggy air back and forth. With one hand, he rummaged through the bottles in the sink. Not one clean.

His mama flipped on the overhead light. "Rowen, what a racket you're making."

"Sorry, I didn't know that no one had washed these bottles last night."

"Our princess, Miss Rose, is going to raise the roof on this house. It must be my fault about the bottles. I'm sure Jewell meant to do them yesterday, but I distracted her. The odors from that diaper pail were so pungent that I was worried for our health. 'Jewell honey,' I said, 'I know you have your hands full, but you must be about to run out of diapers,' and then when she was hanging them on the line, Lilly vomited all over the floor. Haven't you found a bottle there yet? Adeline always kept you so calm when you were an infant, you never made this kind of noise. I think Jewell needs help. You must ask Claude for a raise. He will surely understand. You're related now after all."

Another wail burst from a bedroom. Lilly.

"If Jewell had just asked me, I would have washed those bottles. She must hide the rubber gloves. I never can find them. But just so you know, Rowen, I do offer to help her. I know she tells you otherwise, but I do offer. She always says she doesn't need my help."

Lilly squeezed around his mother's legs. "Daddy," she sobbed.

"Lilly, watch out for Nana Rita."

"Oh, Lilly." Rita tried to reach for her, but she flew to Rowen's thigh. "Pick me up, Daddy."

"Honey, I can't, don't you see I got the baby?"

"Rowen, why is the baby still screaming." Jewell appeared behind his mother. "Miz Rita, let me through."

His mother backed out of the doorway and Jewell lifted Rose out of Rowen's arms.

"Get Lilly some cereal at least, won't you."

He set the cornflakes on the counter and opened the refrigerator door. Then he remembered. Milk. He was supposed to have brought it home last night. Jewell could read his mind when he screwed up and, any second, the powder keg of accusations would explode. He stood with the refrigerator door open, waiting for a solution to come to him. If he handed Lilly a bowl of dry cornflakes, she'd holler and ask where the milk was. Which would give it away.

With Jewell occupied at the sink and the baby on her shoulder, he reached into the cupboard and pulled out a box of Cracker Jacks. He handed the box to Lilly and put his fingers over his lips. "Sssh."

"What's she giggling about?" Jewell asked.

"Nothing."

Best if he got out of the house right away. It was too early to go, but he didn't want to be within a mile's radius when Jewell opened that refrigerator door. The dream house he'd built had become the hen house he fled from every day. Four females all squawking and not one comprehensible to the other.

In five minutes, he was revving up the engine to back out the driveway when Jewell and the baby appeared at the driver's window.

"You're leaving? You didn't get in until eleven last night."

"You're wanting an extra bedroom on the house, right?"

"You know I do! Rose can't keep sleeping with us until she graduates from high school. And

Eden

I've already told you I'd like to get Lilly out of your mother's room."

"Does it look to you like I'm doing nothing? I'm working twelve hours a day or more just to keep straight with the bills. Then, I walk in the door at night and all I hear is, I want, I want, I want."

"You're not the only one working, Rowen." She gestured back to the house. "Does this look like the Holiday Inn? What do you think I do all day? Who do you think is taking care of everyone? And your mother, too. Your mother, Rowen."

"Your mother comes out and helps, doesn't she?"

"That's not the point. The point is when are you going to start acting like a father, a son, and a husband?"

Rowen jumped out of the pickup. "I'm here. I'm all yours. I'll take over here and you go on over to Claude's and go to work."

"Don't act like an idiot. But I might remind you that it was your idea to drag us out to this hinterland miles from town and you're never here."

Rita shouted from the porch, "Jewell, honey, there's Cracker Jacks pieces all over the floor. I can't imagine how they got there."

Jewell turned at his mother's voice. It was like watching a dynamite fuse burn.

Boom!

"You didn't bring the milk back last night. Oh-My-God."

After that, there wasn't anything to do but get back in the truck and slam it into reverse. He didn't have to stoke his imagination much to figure how the rest of the day would unfold: Rita would trail Jewell, yammering about one item of trivia after another until the heat drove her into her room. Lilly would empty the rest of her Cracker Jacks on the living room rug. Rose would burp and go back to sleep, and Jewell would cry into the phone to her mother.

Once the tires bit the asphalt, he paused long enough to light a cigarette before mashing the gas pedal. Wind swooshed the boggy air out the cab, riffled through his hair. Faster, faster. Just a little faster and he just might break through the bonds that held him and shoot...where? Where did you end up when you sped off the edge of the world?

Back when he was a boy in his daddy's house, he'd understood that being a man meant sitting down to dinners that someone else had prepared and then adjourning out to the porch to smoke pipes and play cards with other men long past bedtime. Dishes, glasses, ashtrays were all items for Adeline to clean up. On Sundays, men strolled into church, lacquered in after-shave, families towed behind. They didn't look burdened. They looked buoyed.

But that wasn't his life at all. Forget that a stray unwashed dish was all it took to catapult Jewell into a tirade. The sense of fulfillment that, he thought, came with manhood was sorely missing. With every rotation from sunrise to sunset, a vacuum expanded inside him like a balloon.

He hadn't lied to Jewell about where he was in the evenings. He did work late, long after the rest of the crew had gone home. What he didn't tell her was that he didn't have to.

It had all come about after he'd cheated on her. He'd stopped at the drugstore one evening and run into Maureen, the former senior class secretary, at the cosmetic counter. Back in high school, she had

been one of the girls he'd taken on group dates, one of the many who couldn't find two words to say to him through the evening. Now she remarked on how handsome he was, even in his sweaty work clothes. She spoke as if they'd become bosom buddies during those dates. The way she looked — as if he was in charge, as if he possessed all the answers — propelled him right along to following her home and making love to her there on her sofa, right in front of her TV, which she never turned off the whole time.

It didn't hit him until he'd come home to his sleeping house — his mother snoring in her bedroom, Lilly's chubby arms flung out in her crib and Jewell's pillow over her head — that he'd let them all down. If emptiness was eating him inside out, better to run another form of concrete or nail another row of shingles rather than chase yearnings that dead-ended in a bulls-eye on a TV at midnight.

Today the job was drywall at White Rock's first-ever old-age home. No more carting the old away to hospitals or nursing homes in Fayetteville. White Rock was to have its own home for the aged just as it had gotten its very own Dairy Queen. Progress for all its generations.

Yet, to his horror, Lilly popped up from the truck bed as he stepped out. What a fool he was not to have seen her, and he had been driving so fast!

"Beatrice Lilly Hart, how ever did you sneak in there?"

"You left the tailgate open, Daddy. I wanted to go to work with you."

He picked her up. "Your mama's going to be near hysterical not knowing where you are. You know that?" He hugged her close. "I ought to tear up your behind."

"All Mommy does is fuss all day long. Let me stay with you. Please?"

"Who's going to take care of Nana Rita and Baby Rose if you're not there to help. We all got jobs, and that's yours."

"I never get to be with you."

By now, a few of the crew had spotted him. "Second boss brought his helper to work," that's what they were saying. "Second boss," that's what they called him after Claude had made him foreman.

"I got to take her home," he shouted.

One of them shouted back, "No need. A hard hat to fit her and a hammer and she'll be good to go."

Rowen waved them off and they all laughed. He set Lilly inside the cab.

"Honey, now you're going to make me late for work, taking you home."

"You have to go to the store to pick up the milk. Remember? And when we get to the store, can I pick out some candy? For Baby Rose?"

The sun smoldered midsky by the time he returned to the work site. Claude's truck was there, although he had been hoping, by some miracle, that it wouldn't be. He wouldn't escape Claude's remarks in front of the crew. As it was, they still pulled the age routine on him whenever he tried to assert some supervision, the line about how they'd been there since Lee surrendered at Appomattox, or similar gibberish, and how he didn't know anything.

He even heard it from the coloreds. He was tired of hearing it, tired of being here, bombarded by the constant hammering, drilling, sanding, all interspersed with the endless loop of dirty jokes. Only a quarter of his life gone, and he was already tired of being hot.

"At last Mr. Hart has joined us," Claude sang out, although only a few laughs followed from the few who had heard him. Rowen didn't respond or stop to apologize. He shouldered on past them. If Claude wanted to have it out with him, then Claude could come find him. He could feel their eyes fasten on him as he walked past. *To hell with them.*

By lunchtime, he was in a feud with an older member of the crew over a drywall patch. He'd been doing this work for forty years, the man said, and if Rowen couldn't get his sorry ass to work on time, when the patch was put up, then he didn't have a right to complain about it.

As the machines cut off one by one, their argument echoed through the structure. Then Rowen felt Claude's grip on his shoulder.

Shamed. Again.

Outside, Claude said, "All is not well with the Hart household this morning."

"You know he didn't put that patch in right, Claude. And I'm tired of them thinking they don't have to listen to me. And when I try to show them just how you taught me, you call me out while they stand around and laugh."

"I see."

"To start out with, I did get here on time this morning, but Lilly hid in the back of the truck and I had to take her home. Then Jewell was mad at me for forgetting the milk last night, so I had to stop at the store. By the time I got here, I was too bothered, I guess."

"I need to sit down," said Claude.

The tone in Claude's voice jerked Rowen out of his sulk. Not in all these infernal summers had Claude ever indicated a desire to rest. Claude lifted two crates from his truck and handed one to Rowen.

"Are you all right?" Rowen asked.

"I am as fit as a near decrepit carpenter can be. I did resign from *The Flower of Cape Fear*. The prospect of reliving the Revolution for the twentieth time seemed overwhelming. Sit down, Rowen."

Claude rested his elbows on his knees and gazed down at the dust between his feet. "I am sorry if you have ever felt that I have undermined you here. Nothing could have been further from my intentions. I apologize if I have failed to recognize how prodigiously you have dedicated yourself to Lynch & Son."

"I appreciate hearing that."

"But if you'll excuse an observing eye, you act as if your darling family is nothing more than a burden."

"What's that got to do with the drywall around an electric box?"

"I am more and more consumed by the notion that my intention to benefit you has accomplished nothing other than to stunt you. Before you married, I speculated our community would misshape you in time, but now I see the part I have played in it. Maybe the best way to fix it before it is too late is to fire you."

"Fire me?"

"It's not your lack of ability. It's the utter absence of perspective. Like so many of my grand

schemes, this one's gone wrong. If I cut you loose, you have to venture out in the world and better define yourself. Maybe you'll find that open boy's heart you used to have."

"All right! I'll go back, get down on my knees and beg his pardon if that's what you want."

"What I want? In addition to the rest of your shortcomings, you cling to a fool's assumption that I am going to be planted here every day to steer your life's endeavors."

Fear, as well as the heat, made Rowen sweat. Because he did have that fool assumption. "What's the matter? Are you dying?"

"No, it's Mary who's got cancer."

Rowen pulled a cigarette from his shirt pocket. "Jewell didn't say anything," he said, but come to think of it, he couldn't remember the last time they'd sat down to a meal together. "Can I do anything?"

"You can't do a fool thing. But this is a dreary aside to our subject of the hour, the future and well-being of Rowen Hart. And family."

"What about the future well-being of this job?"

"Too many times I've put that ahead of you."

"If you fire me, I'll lose my house."

"Yet you've never knocked on your Uncle Hugh's door and asked him for your daddy's share."

"We been all over this. He said my daddy spent it all and he didn't owe me anything."

"All this time gone, and you took him at his word."

"He's my mama's brother."

"So he is. It's accorded him great license all these years."

Why wasn't the day already over? It seemed liked he'd lived twenty-four hours up to this point.

"Claude, listen, I know you've done a lot for me. But I've got a family depending on me now. I can't help it if I didn't turn out the way you wanted me to be. Doesn't it happen that way for everyone? You meet your wife, start a family, it's not all pie-in-the-sky anymore. Just let me go on back to work. I'll fix the drywall myself."

Claude pulled his rag from his back pocket and wiped his bald head. "Here's what I want. You'll leave right now and be gone two weeks."

"Who's going to look after this job? Now that you're telling me that Mary's sick."

"I'll take that burden for a while. Your assignment is to assess yourself. Like a construction problem."

"What the heck does that mean?"

Claude shrugged. "For a start, it means going home."

"Now?"

Claude rose stiffly. He put his crate back in the truck.

"Now."

He turned and went inside while Rowen continued to sit there, ripped from his orbit. He listened to the sounds of the job until he couldn't bear the sun beating down on him any longer. He went back to his truck and spun out of the parking lot.

Hearing Uncle Hugh's name reminded him of Adeline. He missed her. He ought to take his daughters and visit her. But Jewell would never allow that. Had Adeline still been in the picture, she would never have let up hammering him

about Uncle Hugh. Uncle Hugh, Cousin Mabel, he hadn't seen them, hadn't given them a thought since she'd married and moved away.

He had run into Sammy almost a year ago at the Fourth of July parade. Among the crowd lining the opposite sidewalk, Sammy had stood out in his uniform. Rowen had waved and waved with no response until he began to wonder whether it was Sammy after all. He couldn't believe that Sammy would deliberately ignore him. Rowen carried Lilly across the street, dodging between the passing floats, and when he was nearly at the curb, he felt relieved to see that familiar grin spread over Sammy's face.

"Mr. Rowen."

"I've been waving at you all this time. Didn't you see me?"

"No, sir. I didn't know who you was until just this second."

Rowen suspected Sammy was lying to him and wondered why he would do that.

As if Sammy had read his thoughts he said, "My daddy's funeral was yesterday. That's why I come home. I'm leaving later today."

Maybe his grief explained his behavior then. Rowen remembered how it was when his own daddy had died—how people and their rote condolences seemed more aggravating than comforting. Rowen glanced at Sammy's mother, who stood next to him, but all he could think to say was a rote condolence. "I'm sorry," he said. "Sorry for your loss."

"Thank you, Rowen," she answered. "So how you been doin'?"

"I got this little one here." He gestured to Lilly. Had her mother been there, Lilly would have been reprimanded, first for rudely staring at folks, and then, for sucking her thumb. "And I got one on the way."

"You've been much occupied, Mr. Rowen."

It was the kind of remark the old Sammy would make, but Rowen didn't feel he was addressing the same old Sammy. It was more than the uniform. Wherever Sammy had been, whatever'd he seen, had changed him to where a distance had opened between him and the people out here in the street who'd known him all his life.

"How've you been, Sammy?"

"I've been promoted. Sergeant First Class."

"I'm glad for you, I can't say I'm surprised."

Sammy's gaze drifted over the crowd. "I'm a teacher now, can you believe that?"

"Yes, I can. I can definitely believe that. What are you teaching?"

"Mechanics, how to fix cars, trucks, tanks."

Within the radius of Sammy's gaze, there was no one who would have ever allowed him to become a teacher. He'd had to go away. And now he no longer belonged among them.

"Nobody could be happier for you than me, Sammy. Will you stop by the house after the parade?"

He'd blurted that invitation before he thought about how he would manage it with Jewell.

Sammy shook his head. "I gotta be headin' out. A colored man in uniform can't be hanging around for too long."

"What are you talkin' about? This is your town."

"You don't remember? That boy in uniform that got shot in Durham?"

"That happened ten years back or more

when we were kids. And that soldier was from out of state and didn't know anyone. There isn't anyone on this street that doesn't know you."

"Beg pardon, Mr. Rowen, they been knowing me — as a tobacco picker. Mama, you seen enough? Parade's winding down, I believe."

Rowen felt stung as Sammy pivoted. He'd hoped that Sammy would see him as different from everyone else. Maybe he shouldn't have expected it.

At the last moment, Sammy shook his hand. "I'm glad you crossed the street, Mr. Rowen. Glad to see you haven't changed."

"Good luck to you, Sammy."

Sammy steered his mother away through the crowd.

"Hey, Sammy, you come back and see me, y'hear?"

Sammy looked back over his shoulder and smiled. At least he'd heard that. And as he watched him walk away, he reflected on Sammy's last comment. No, he hadn't changed though Sammy had. He had no business feeling sorry about it. Wasn't that what he'd chosen after all? To stay rooted where all would always be familiar?

Eden — what had become of her? He'd heard she'd wound up in Lumberton after all with her mother and new daddy. Maybe Coman had come around to acting like a mother. Every time he spotted Franklin White, he wanted to ask about Eden. What had Adeline said about Franklin? "Pure as the driven snow." And she'd been right, one hundred percent. Nobody recalled that he'd shot another man. He was President of the Sons of the Minutemen. He chaired the hospital ball every year. Maybe Rowen could still see that trial clearly, but

JAMIE LISA FORBES

White Rock had slipped back into its channel, the way the river did after a hurricane, to where you'd never know anything had ever happened.

Last thing he wanted was to go home and face those women's dumbfounded expressions. What if he took off for the coast? Sped to the edge of the world? Floored it all the way to Wilmington, spanning bridge after bridge until the salt breeze filled the cab. The last time he'd been there was on his honeymoon. He and Jewell had stayed at a moldy motel where all their romantic anticipations were popped one after another, like balloons— beginning with the drunk couple flailing about in the next room. The fishing trip they'd attempted had soured when Jewell vomited over the side of the boat for hours. They'd come home a day early, sunburned and exhausted, and neither of them had answered his mama who'd twittered, "How was it?"

Still, he remembered how the shore opened up before them and ran on north and south toward piers in the distance and how the surf pulsed against the sand like breathing. He craved the sensation of just breathing.

Could he squeeze in a couple of hours or so there before the sun went down, before he'd have to go home to all those females? The fields rushed by him—tobacco, cotton, peach orchards and the steady tree line marking the Cape Fear River traveling in his same direction.

Unlike the river, Rowen's trajectory was blunted by the highway patrol car in his rearview mirror. Ninety-five degrees, you'd think the trooper wouldn't want to bake too long there on the asphalt, but instead he took his time unfolding from the

car and hitching up his pants. Thirty minutes later, when he handed Rowen his ticket, he said, "Just so you know, your back tire's flat."

"Why didn't you say something earlier? I could have been working on it all this time."

The trooper's jowls twitched. "I hope I didn't hear that attitude, son. Or, do I need to write you a bigger ticket?"

Rowen responded, "No sir, sorry sir," and soon the trooper was nosing his Plymouth out into the traffic lane. Station wagons passed, crammed with road-weary families, near mad-crazy to step out on the shore for the feeling of release—just like him.

An illusion after all.

After he got the spare on, he flipped the truck around. The light radiated differently traveling west—no longer the rising light of anticipation, but the soul draining afternoon blaze.

A pull-out surrounded by a ring of pin oaks came up on his right. The sign at the roadside read *PEACHES*. The "P-E-A" was printed large while the "C-H-E-S" was crammed up against the margin. He slowed. If he couldn't have the ocean, he could have peaches. He pulled in under the shade among the line of vehicles, and for a moment, he watched the customers milling among tables of fruits and vegetables. The girl under the awning at the scales wore a navy bandana and men's overalls. She moved briskly dumping produce into paper sacks. With every customer's departure, her voice rang loud. "Y'all come back."

Those overalls were too big for her. What decent woman wore men's overalls anyway? He couldn't recall a white woman, or a colored woman either, going around like that. A girl dressed that way must not give a hoot what people think of her. What color was her hair? It was all tucked up in the bandana. Her age—he wasn't sure, she could be anywhere from seventeen to thirty. The years of church and school that should have molded this girl hadn't touched her in the slightest. She was too forward, too loud.

He hung on her banter with her customers and his heart started to race. He wanted to shake off the pretense, run up to her, hug her. He had to calm down, get a hold of himself. He took a deep breath. What a fool he was being, getting all worked up over a kid who'd lived in his house for just a year.

He shuffled around the outer tables, pretending to study the okra. When he had worked up some courage, he grabbed three peaches and pushed to the scales, about to explode wondering whether she would recognize him. And if she didn't, would he say anything?

It was her. Those eyes, still piercing blue, gave her away.

"Just three peaches? There's a whole basket out there—fifty cents. Sure your wife don't want to can a bunch?"

"You're right." His hand trembled as he reached across the table to grab a basket.

"How's Miz Rita doing?"

His hand dropped, and he shifted to search her face, hoping to see the same excitement he felt at finding her. But her gaze seemed guarded. It was good that all these people were around to prevent him from hugging her because he could see a hug wouldn't have been returned.

Eden

"Mama's fine. She'd want to see you again. We heard you went to Lumberton with your mama."

"Been right here, working for Miz Aldrick and her son, Fletcher, for a year now." She glanced over her shoulder at a tall boy, also in overalls, unloading a crate of peaches from a truck. "Fletcher, come over here, I want you to meet someone."

Rowen lowered his voice. "So it's all right between you and your mama now?"

She shook her head. "It ain't all right. But things is how Mama wants them to be. We didn't ever talk about what happened to Daddy, if that's what you mean. And because we didn't ever talk about it, she got to hang on to her truth and I got to hang on to mine."

"Where did you go that day you left us?"

Hurt from that day arced in her eyes, as if he'd cut a live wire. How stupid of him to push her like that, but he'd had to find out. He'd wondered about it all these years.

"I went home. Like you said Rowen, there wasn't nowhere else to go. I told Mama I wasn't going nowhere with Uncle Franklin, and she said that'd be all right as long as I didn't cause her no more trouble.

"But once we was in Lumberton, her new husband kept wanting me to treat him like he was my daddy. Like I hadn't ever had a daddy before him. He wasn't my daddy. He couldn't never be. And every time he got to fussin' about something I done, I told him so. He would reach for his belt and I'd hide out in the tobacco fields until he'd leave in his police car. He sure thought he was God Almighty in that thing.

"And then one day when I was running to

get away from him, I looked back and saw Mama standing in the doorway. I slowed down and started to walk to the highway, to see if she would call me back. But she didn't say nothing. She just stood there and watched. She knew I was sixteen and could do what I wanted. And when I got to the highway, I flicked out my thumb and here come Fletcher."

The customers were backing up behind Rowen now. The boy turned and shook his blond bangs from his eyes.

"You all right up there, Eden?"

Rowen hated him the moment he spoke her name.

"Come on up here, there's someone you got to meet."

The boy joined them, taking his time to size up Rowen. He draped an arm over Eden's shoulder.

"Can we help ya?"

"Silly, this here's Rowen Hart. You remember me telling you about how I lived with him and his mama for a year."

"I was just saying 'hello'," said Rowen. "I knew Eden back a long time ago before she was grown."

The boy squeezed her shoulder. "I don't see how that can be. She's been with us far back as I remember."

Rowen wanted to knock his arm off her. Was it jealousy? *No, it was more than that. There was something menacing in the way he hung on her.*

Eden wasn't troubled. She hugged the boy's waist and her eyes flashed hard and proud. Yes, whatever Rowen's feelings, she had known this boy a long time.

Rowen pulled out the cash for his peaches.

"Well, I won't take up any more of your time. Good seeing y'all."

"Y'all come back," said Fletcher, words Rowen knew he didn't mean.

"Say hello to your mama for me," Eden added.

As he walked away, he heard her call, "Hey, Rowen, you ever see Adeline?" He didn't turn. He let the words fall behind him as he slammed the pickup door and mashed the gear into reverse.

Back in his own yard, no one was outside, although Lilly's junk was scattered in a wide arc: tricycle, dolls, plastic dishes, a toy vacuum cleaner. Laundry hung on the line and the only sound was the ever-present insect thrum. Countless miniscule lives, too many to count, unfolded around him—were they as fraught with turmoil as his? The sound never varied. How would one know if they were screaming?

His females were all holed up inside somewhere, napping maybe, as the fans buzzed. He didn't want to face them until he'd found a way to conceal the shock of all that had happened in the last few hours.

He grabbed a hoe and began flailing at morning glories choking the corn. Hoeing, that's what Eden had been doing in the moments before she'd fled his house. It sounded as if she had come out all right, more or less, so why now did he feel guilty that he hadn't stopped her that day? As if it would have made any difference, because he had no idea how he would have prevented Franklin and Coman from taking her away. He hadn't had anything to do with Eden's fate, really.

She'd been born to grow up rough and wild and end up with boys as wild as she was. He couldn't have stopped that outcome any more than he could stop a freight train.

Grains of sandy soil flew up in his face.

Jewell appeared on the back step. "Rowen. You need to come on to the house."

With the sun in his eyes, he couldn't see her face, but that high strain in her voice made him drop the hoe. Something had happened.

He mounted the steps until he stood one step below her.

"How come you're home so early?"

"Claude's told me to take a week off."

"How come?"

He shrugged and looked away to the garden, and out to the sycamores beyond.

"Lost my temper."

"It's good you came home. Your Uncle Hugh's died."

"When? Where?"

"Heart attack at his house, I guess. Your cousin Mabel called. She's on the highway now. She sent the pastor out to pick up your mama. My mama said we could go on and she'd watch the kids."

Rowen slumped against the house. How had so much happened in one day?

"It's not like you were close to him. You haven't spoken to him since our wedding."

"Just surprised…that's all."

She searched his face. *Could she unspool the events wrapped in his head: his thwarted escape, his chance encounter with Eden?*

"I'm sorry for the way I spoke this morning," she said.

"I'm sorry, too."

"Silly, what are you sorry for?"

"I know you're not happy, Jewell. I never wanted you to feel that way."

"It's always hard for married people starting out, that's what Mama says. Mama says if we keep on praying, things'll come out all right."

She put her arms around him. He squeezed her tight and closed his eyes and try as he could, all he could see was Eden under that boy's arm.

JAMIE LISA FORBES

9

ESCAPE TO THE COAST—that's what he
had tried to do on the day that Uncle Hugh died.
Now, eighteen months later, he was on the ocean
and as he watched the fishing boat's wake curl
back over indigo water, he had to admit that the
sense of release he'd sought, both then and now,
had escaped him.

The cabin door opened, and Franklin
White called out, "What are you doing out here
by yourself?"

Rowen straightened. All these threads,
invisible as a spider's web until you run into it, held
him tight. Oh, he had to admit, he'd been scooped
out of misfortune in near biblical fashion. The
surprise inheritance he'd received had ended all the

worry and want and had rocketed him right back
into White Rock's inner circle, back with Franklin
White. No clue in the Bible for how he was supposed
to be at peace with that circumstance. Even after all
this time, he couldn't look at Franklin without Eden
and the trial coming to mind. Not that he could ever
speak those thoughts to anyone.

"Just...watching the waves," Rowen said.

Franklin shuffled over, tentative at the boat's
roll beneath him. In the past year, he'd shriveled
down to a walking skeleton, though he hadn't
complained of being ill. Another swell pitched him
forward and he lunged for the rail, his eyes wild with
panic. It was more than just a fear of falling, Rowen
realized. Fear of his own fraility had burrowed
inside of him.

"You all right?" Rowen asked.

Franklin gripped the rail with one hand and
reached inside his jacket with the other. He seemed
out of breath though he hadn't come more than
six feet.

"I'm fine, fine. No sea legs is all." He pulled
out his cigarettes and his hand shook as he struggled
to light one. Rowen helped him, and once he'd
inhaled, his shoulders relaxed.

"I came out here to check on you. With the
catch you hauled in today, I'm surprised you're not
inside bragging about it with them." He nodded
back to the cabin where the rest of the Sons of
the Minutemen shared fish stories—past, present
and future.

"I'll be in, after a while," Rowen said, as he
eyed the closing distance to shore.

Franklin clapped a hand on his shoulder.
"How'd you enjoy your first ocean fishing?"

"Great."

"Now that you're one of us, there'll be plenty more. Come on back inside."

"Give me a minute. Do you need some help going back?"

"No. I understand. A young man with a family needs a moment of peace and quiet."

Franklin teetered back across the deck and Rowen lit his own cigarette. Below, the water churned brown and the crowd on the pier turned into individuals—eating, drinking, laughing, strolling. The charter boat glided past a small craft thrashing back and forth and sure enough, through the window, Rowen glimpsed naked bodies. Back from sea and sky into the surf of the human world.

On the dock, Rowen helped the charter crew unload the fish. Franklin struggled with his own cooler, so Rowen took it from him while Franklin chuckled at the men's jokes over his weakness. They all lingered on the pier and had another round of beers. One of the men gave the captain a bottle of whiskey. Darkness overtook them and, one by one, they said their goodbyes and started for their cars.

Franklin turned to Rowen. "You ready?"

Smug—that's how the thunk of the door on Franklin's new mahogany Lincoln sounded.

"Look at this," said Franklin, and he flipped a switch. "Air conditioning." Chilled air blasted in Rowen's face. They rolled past a thinning string of beach shops until Franklin hit the gas on the open highway.

"Long day," sighed Franklin. "Long, good day."

Out the window, the countryside was broken only by a yard light here and there, lonely as ships at sea. With nothing to see, the memories of the past

Eden

year and a half ran through Rowen's head, taking him back to how he'd gotten there. Once again, he watched the light stream through the chapel windows onto Uncle Hugh's eyelids. In his coffin, Uncle Hugh had looked like a wax doll caricature of himself and not at all like the flesh and blood son-of-a-bitch who had swooped into Rowen's house month after month to peck at their undoing.

Cousin Mabel, parked by the coffin, had asked him if he remembered that day at the auction house with that little girl—what was her name?—and if he remembered her saying that she had wanted to talk to him. Well, the reason she'd wanted to talk to him was that Uncle Hugh had lied. His daddy hadn't owed Uncle Hugh any money.

She knew how awful it looked, that she hadn't said anything all these years. She knew she should be falling at his feet, begging his forgiveness. But he'd seen what Uncle Hugh was like. Her daddy had watched her every move. She couldn't get away without him knowing about it. He'd raised his hand to her more than once, though—praise Jesus—he'd never hit her. If she didn't keep her mouth shut and do as she was told, he'd said, he'd send her away to a home for drooling retards and cripples. He'd reminded her all the time of how dependent she was on him.

After she'd married, she'd worn herself almost to death thinking about phoning Rowen and telling him the truth. But when she'd reach for that phone, her hand would start to shake. She could hear Uncle Hugh, as clear as if he was in the next room, calling her out, cursing her, threatening her. He might be miles and miles away, but if he found out she'd betrayed him, Lord help her for the vengeance he might take. He'd certainly cut off the money he sent her, maybe he'd even demand back the down payment he'd made on the little bait and tackle store they'd bought. She'd hear him shouting in her head and then it became easy to set that phone back down.

When Rowen's daddy was alive, he never would pay attention to his business, she had said. At the end of the week, he'd as soon as sit down and drink corn liquor with the farmers, rather than stay behind while Mabel worked on the figures. "Mabel honey," he'd said, "I can't keep all those rows straight. You do it." And he'd leave her a little gift, like a bottle of perfume. And then her daddy would come along and tell her to make changes.

Yes, his daddy had asked for advances, and all along her daddy acted like he was lending him the money. But his daddy had never looked behind Uncle Hugh to see if the money he was getting was really his own to begin with.

As she'd spoken, Rowen had glanced back and forth from her to the cadaver. He was disgusted enough with the wasted years to rise to his feet and shout and blame. But Uncle Hugh, cold as granite, had had the last laugh after all. What was the point of a scene in front of his damaged cousin, whose guilt, even if heartfelt, wouldn't repair anything, and the dead man who was past the vanity of blame.

She would make it right with him, she said. And in the meantime, while affairs were being settled, he could live in Uncle Hugh's house in town. And if Miz Rita was owed anything on his daddy's share of the business, she would get paid.

Eden

Hardly five minutes had passed after Rowen had spilled the news to Jewell before she began packing. She tore into house remodeling at Uncle Hugh's like a bear into a honeycomb, snapping at Claude's bug-eyed crew more than he'd ever done. Up went new white pillars on the porch. Up went gallons of yellow paint until the house looked like a chunk of butter.

Before Rowen could chafe at reminders of Uncle Hugh, Jewell had plastered the interior walls with climbing ivy wallpaper. His mama was deposited in a large bedroom downstairs facing the street, which gave her all the opportunity she desired to fret over the clothing or manners of the passersby. She and Jewell didn't trip over one another so much anymore, and that had improved both of them.

He'd zipped over to Claude's, eager for Claude to share in his good fortune, but the old man had let Rowen's words dangle while he gazed up through his pines.

"Claude, you heard what I said?"

"I heard. I'm thinking that when I suggested you re-examine your life's compass, I am not sure that this is what I had in mind."

"What does that mean?"

"You are so exuberant over what has come so conveniently. And yet you had little part in it."

"Last time we talked you were pestering me because I hadn't been to see Uncle Hugh over Daddy's share. Now I'm going to get everything I was owed. And Mama can finally have the life she wants. You've driven me half-crazy all these years because I can't ever figure out what you want from me. You're always acting like....like I've got some kind of mission to perform. What if I don't want it?

I drove out here because I thought you'd be happy for me. You're never happy for me. You always have some lesson to hand out. All I want is to just live my life and be left alone."

The old man's eyes seemed to swim behind his thick lenses.

"Claude, I'm...."

"No, Rowen, you're right. I've run my presumptions out too far. You're a grown man. You've done everything I've ever asked you — and more. I should show you more gratitude. I guess by taking an interest in you, I thought I was."

In the pause, Rowen noticed nests of pine needles on a porch that had always been swept clean. He should have grabbed a broom the moment he stepped foot on it. Now, he knew, Claude wouldn't let him.

"How's Mary doing?"

"Been in the hospital in Fayetteville five days now."

"Why don't you let me clean this porch?"

"Leave it."

"Claude, I'm...."

"I didn't do anything but give a good man a job. There's no exceptional merit in that."

"I want to go back to work."

"At Lynch & Son Construction?"

"You didn't fire me. You told me to go away for a while. I'm ready to have my job back."

Claude spread his hands over his thighs. "You're back here all right, but neither one of us is quite the same as when we last visited. You want your job back?" He gestured vaguely to the equipment in the yard. "Buy it all up. Start the Rowen Hart Construction Business."

Eden

The Rowen Hart Construction Business. Self-doubts burst through Rowen's head like popping corn. He wasn't old enough, he wasn't experienced enough. He was still that kid who felt helpless at a busted gate post.

But later the questions he asked himself turned to "why not?" He had the means. And if his daddy had failed, well, no one would remember that, just as no one remembered Franklin White's crime.

So off to Franklin White for a business loan and now here he was, ferried in Franklin's prized mahogany Lincoln.

Franklin spun the radio dial through boogie-woogie piano plunking until he found Eddie Arnold.

"You want a drink?"

"Sure."

"There's a bottle behind my seat. Reach around there and grab it."

Why not? They still had at least an hour until they reached home, and what more was there to talk about anyway? Rowen took a long swig, then sputtered.

"Whoa, watch yourself. Don't be getting that all over my new car."

Rowen wiped the dash with the back of his sleeve.

"Sorry."

"Haven't you ever drunk liquor before? You don't gulp it down. Here, pass me that." Franklin grabbed it from him and took a quick sip. "There, you see? You don't see me chugging it like a hillbilly."

"Yes, sir."

"Well as much as you just spilled on yourself, Jewell will smell it on you. One thing for you to learn about the Minutemen: they make sure their wives don't know everything that's happened on our trips. Keeps a home at peace."

Rowen stared out the window. *Franklin, of all people, dispensing family advice.*

Franklin shifted toward him and winked. "I'm right, aren't I?"

"Yes, sir."

Franklin settled back into his seat. "What are you going to do with your place in the country? Sell it?"

Speaking of topics for Jewell to fuss over, she had been on him to sell it. After all the work he'd put into it with his own hands and all the moments that they'd filled it with—the ups and downs that added dimension and meaning to a place—turning her back on it didn't disturb her in the slightest. When he'd suggested that they might want to go back once the kids were grown, for the peace and quiet, she'd answered, "You can have all that peace and quiet to yourself, Rowen Hart."

He turned to Franklin. "I believe I'll rent it."

"Good idea. Good investment."

The liquor swirling in Rowen's veins pushed him down channels he wouldn't ordinarily go with Franklin.

"I saw Eden. Over a year ago now."

In the pause that followed, Rowen could almost hear Franklin's good humor drain out of him.

"I didn't realize you knew she was back."

"I didn't, until I ran into her."

"You treated her like one of your own for a good long while and don't you misunderstand me; Coman and I were grateful to you. But time's come for you to take a wide berth around her. She's no good for you or your family. Coman told me they'd

hardly settled down before Eden ran wild on her. Wouldn't stay in school. It pains me to say she might have followed in her mother's footsteps and behaved lewdly.

"Lord knows I love my sister but between Birch's debauchery and the unpleasantness that followed and the trial, where well-meaning but ill-advised people insisted that Eden testify, she never had the upbringing a young girl requires. It's a tragedy, and I am sorry for my part in it, but we must accept that as she is now, she is ruined."

"She was working when I saw her."

"She's marrying that boy. Aldrick. Coman says she has to get married, though whether she's carrying his child or someone else's, at least the child will have a family to call its own.

"I know you might not believe me, but I don't wish her any ill. My deepest hope is that with a husband to guide her and a baby to nurse, she'll settle down. And then the years of disgrace we've suffered will finally be at an end."

"Who's 'we'?"

Franklin glanced over at him. "You might re-think your tone of voice, Rowen. You're sounding harsh. I never wanted Eden to lose her father. I've prayed the Lord for forgiveness every day. But Coman and I—we're not condemned. We don't deserve to be stained for the rest of our lives."

"The day you came out to the house, I thought you cared about her."

"I do care about her. You heard me offer to send her to school. I was willing to do everything in my power to make things right. But God took her fate from my hands. What's come to pass is His plan. We all need to let her go. You, too."

Rowen sagged back into the cushioned seat. Hadn't he also concluded, after he'd last seen Eden, that what had come to pass was her fate? That, by itself, was a way of letting go. And if he and Franklin agreed that Eden's course has been set by some external force, whatever it was called, why cling to the sense of wrong he'd felt on her behalf? No point now. Franklin had escaped punishment and Eden was starting her own family.

Every dawn Rowen had opened his eyes with the expectation that the coming day would be the same as the one before. Now he realized the days had cogged him along to where the landmarks of his life weren't so fixed and unchanging. Like everything else, time had re-molded them.

After the fishing trip, he forgot about Eden until she appeared on a Sunday afternoon in October. Jewell's parents had come over for lunch and, as usual, Sunday lunch on the porch hadn't turned out as perfect as the magazine photos Jewell was always pouring over. Just when Jewell had served coffee in her new china, Lilly plopped her hand in the pie meringue and smeared it all over her church dress. While heads swiveled to watch Jewell clean that up, Baby Rose tumbled off the porch steps and smacked her head against the railing post.

His mama had been the closest to Rose and Rowen had thought she'd grab her, but all she'd done was utter a little squeak.

Jewell, her every last nerve shredded, snapped at Rowen, "Are you just going to sit there?"

Rowen scrambled to pick her up, and as he

straightened, he noticed a pickup rolling to a stop and Eden stepping out in lime-colored high heels. She wore a dress with a crimson sash above her belly, just starting to bulge, and a wide-brimmed hat. And there was the Aldrick boy in a suit and tie.

Eden's eyes widened as she took it all in— Rowen and his screaming child, the Noddings stunned by the eruptions around them, and Lilly blubbering as Jewell scolded her.

A breeze kicked up, nearly uplifting Eden's hat. She mashed it down with one hand as she came up the walk, the high heels clicking unsteadily.

"How you doin', Rowen?"

The brightness in her voice unnerved him. He recognized the tone of a woman who wants something. Yet the same joy he'd felt at seeing her the last time escaped his attempt to suppress it and he took her hand.

"It's good to see you again, Eden."

"Eden!" his mother cried. In spite of Jewell's scowl, his mama rose and hugged Eden tightly. "Oh, my Merciful Lord. What a good blessing to see you again my lovely child. How we've missed you. And look, about to have a baby of your own. How wonderful.

"Rowen, get a chair so she can sit down. I want to hear everything, Eden, just everything. Starting from the day you left us. And who is this handsome young man accompanying you? Your husband? Our Eden, grown and married already. Rowen, where are your manners. Eden shouldn't be standing so long in her condition."

"This is my husband, Miz Rita, Mr. Fletcher Aldrick."

Fletcher took her hand. "Nice to meet you,"

he mumbled, and then he leaned back against the porch pillar and crossed his arms over his chest. The twitch in his shoulders gave away his disdain for them all. Was it because they had more than he had, Rowen wondered, or because they had a claim on Eden that he couldn't share?

"Fletcher, may we call you by your first name?" asked Rita. "Please sit down and join us."

"I don't need to sit, Miz Hart. We just stopped a minute so Eden could say hello to y'all."

Eden sat down in the chair Rowen offered her.

"When did y'all get married?" asked Jewell.

"Just two weeks ago."

Jewell's gaze dropped to Eden's belly. "I imagine the wedding was just lovely."

Rita cut in. "We wish you all the happiness in the world. Now tell me about the baby. Do you have names?"

"If it's a boy, we're going to name him Birch Carver Aldrick. Birch for my daddy and Carver for Fletcher's."

"And what if it's a girl?"

Eden glanced up at Fletcher whose attention had drifted to the carpenter bees buzzing under the eaves.

"We don't have a name for a girl yet. Fletcher's so set on having a boy."

Rita squeezed Eden's hand. "Oh, Eden, I don't believe that at all. Fletcher, as soon as you lay your eyes on that baby, you will adore her no matter who she is."

A shadow of a smirk flickered over Fletcher's face. He hadn't accepted a word of what she'd said.

"Now, where are you living?"

Eden giggled a little and looked up at

Fletcher. Neither one spoke and the pause stretched for nearly a full minute until Eden blurted, "We don't have a place yet. We heard about your house in the country. We wondered if you'd rent it to us. That's what we've come for."

"It's not for rent. It's for sale," Jewell said. "Isn't it, Rowen?"

All heads swiveled to Rowen and, as had become commonplace in his existence, he felt slammed between everyone's colliding expectations. He looked down at Baby Rose's drool staining his shirt. From the odor, she needed changing as well.

No way he'd be able to make Jewell budge from what she wanted. Then, too, he felt Fletcher's gaze burning a hole in his forehead. Fletcher wanted the response addressed to him, not Eden.

But Rowen couldn't stop himself from looking into Eden's eyes. How he wished he could read the thoughts beyond the question she'd come to ask. He wondered if she remembered her words to him all those years ago. If she remembered them, she must understand now that what she'd said she'd felt was just a young girl's crush. She was having this man's child, wasn't she?

He hadn't forgotten the times he'd resented her, the times he'd seen her as nothing more than a stone around his neck. Her low-class manners used to jab him like a devil's poker. But the pleasure he'd felt at finding her again had deflated these old complaints. Face to face with her at the peach stand, he had realized how colorless the world had been without her. Damn what Franklin had said to him a month ago, Eden was family.

Come to think of it, he could use that excuse with Jewell.

He addressed Fletcher. "We were talking about selling it, but it would be all right, renting it to y'all. We'll work out the amount."

Jewell turned away. She was displeased, but she wouldn't make a fuss here, not in front of her parents. Her daddy's attention had returned to his key lime pie.

His mama said, "I think it's wonderful and now, Eden, you must come visit us."

"Yes, Miz Rita."

"Can we move into today?" asked Fletcher.

"It'd be all right." Rowen answered.

Eden stood, and Fletcher put his arm around her.

"It's real kind of you, Rowen. Thank you."

"It's nothing." He glanced at Jewell. "You're family. To Mama."

If the comment meant anything to Eden, she didn't show it. She bent to kiss his mother and they turned to leave.

Rowen said, "Jewell, I think the baby needs changing."

"Seems like you can do it for once, Rowen."

He glanced at the departing couple to see if they had heard her. If Fletcher had, it had rolled off him — he was already starting his truck — but Eden turned and flashed him a wicked little grin. He could almost hear her child's voice: *Told you so, Rowen.*

A week later, he drove out to collect his first month's rent. He owned a new pickup now, a two-tone aqua Ford. He'd deliberately gone on extra errands all over White Rock to show it off. He even drove the block back and forth to the store for cigarettes.

Eden

Now, on his first official trip as a landlord, he remembered how his landlord, Lowdermilk, used to drive out from town in a shiny pickup. Rowen would stand just out of view at the screen door when he heard Lowdermilk's truck rumbling at the gate. Lowdermilk's overalls were pressed. And his boots were polished. Easy to keep his clothes up when all he had to do was drive up and down the countryside collecting money from his peasant shacks.

"Rowen, offer him some tea," his mother would call out. Rowen had ignored her. He'd meet Lowdermilk out on the porch. Lowdermilk had licked his thumb, peeling back each of the bills. He'd slow the counting down, just to savor Rowen's discomfort.

"It's all there," Rowen would say.

Lowdermilk had pushed his bifocals up to his forehead.

"Hart money is too good to count. Is that it?"

And, as usual, Adeline had rushed to the rescue. "Rowen, didn't you hear your mama?" and here she came with sweet tea and cornbread.

He didn't want to be that man for Eden and her new husband, and yet now here he was in a brand new pickup, outfitted in a brand-new suit and tie he'd worn to church.

A storm was blowing in from the coast. Around his house, the sycamore crowns whipped in the wind, their white trunks shiny with rain. The new Aldricks hadn't wasted any time straightening up the place. All the weeds and vines that had grown up in his absence had been cleared and the garden had been tilled. He could imagine Eden out there planting in the spring.

JAMIE LISA FORBES

He ran through the rain up the steps to the porch. Rain thundered on the roof above. There was no vehicle in the yard, and he wasn't sure that anyone was home. He put his ear to the door and listened. How strange it felt to be both owner and intruder. He rapped the door with his knuckles. Then harder.

The lock snapped and there she was.

"Rowen."

"Hi. Came for the rent," he said.

"Fletcher's got it with him, he's just run to his mama's. Come on in."

Rowen froze, tangled by the awkwardness of it all.

"I ain't going to bite you, silly, I used to live with you, didn't I?"

Once over the threshold, the house smelled of fresh-baked biscuits.

"Did your mama have this small room here? Come see, I've been painting it for the baby."

"You're painting it blue. Do you know it's a boy?"

"Fletcher wants a boy."

She seemed much bigger than she had been the week before. She rested her hand on her bulge.

"It's got to be a boy."

"What if it's not?"

"Blue can be a girl's color, too. Put some dotted Swiss curtains on the window and it'll be a girl's room just fine."

"But Fletcher's okay, if it's not a boy?"

"It's just like Miz Rita said. He is going to look at that baby and love it. No matter what."

"And does he love you? No matter what?"

Her eyes chilled. "I don't know what you're saying."

"I'm not saying anything. I just want you to be happy."

"I'm very, very happy. Fletcher treats me like a princess. He treated me that way from the first day I moved into his mama's house. He gave up his own bed so I could have it while he slept on the floor. And he did that for a whole year, Rowen. You want some biscuits? I could heat them up for you."

"No, thanks."

"Tea?"

"I'll take a little."

He followed her to the kitchen.

"Fletcher's the only one who's ever cared for me, ever. Except your mama and Adeline. And I'm going to do everything I can so that all he'll think about every day is coming home to me and our baby." She handed him the glass. "So, now do you believe me?"

"It's not what I believe. It's that... you're special."

"Not special enough for you."

"Eden."

Fletcher burst in the back door and his jaw clenched as he took in the two of them, although they were standing at opposite ends of the kitchen. Then he crossed the room in two big steps, grabbed Eden by her shoulders and kissed her mouth.

"How's my little mama?"

"I'm fine. Rowen's here for the rent."

"Oh, I got that. But first I got this." He pulled her to him again, cupped her ass and squeezed.

Rowen set his glass down. "I've got to be going."

JAMIE LISA FORBES

"Hey, you don't have to go. I didn't mean to embarrass you. It's just that, this is the first time we've had a place by ourselves. First time we haven't had to sneak around and it's...well, it's liberating. I guess you might understand. This is the house you had when you were a newlywed, right?"

Rowen glanced at Eden, flushed from her husband's pawing. "Right."

Fletcher reached for his wallet. "Good thing I got paid yesterday and it's all here." He shoved a wad of cash into Rowen's hand.

Rowen started to peel through the handfull of bills, then caught himself.

"Thanks, I'll be going."

Eden saw him to the door, and he heard it latch and lock behind him. He couldn't count the money on the porch. The wind whipped his pant legs and he felt too open to view, even though they'd forgotten him. He thought he already heard them inside making love. Once he slammed the cab door shut, he opened the bills.

Fifty short.

She was happy, wasn't that enough?

He stuffed the bills in the ashtray and drove away.

Eden

10

"Eden's had her baby, it's a girl."

Rowen was surprised to come home and find his mama alone at the dining room table. Late afternoon sunlight flooded the room. A steaming teapot rested next to the open newspaper.

"Six pounds, twelve ounces, and they've named her Audrey Faye. Lovely name."

If she was sitting here, it could only mean that Jewell was out, because she never left her room when Jewell was in the house.

"Come sit, Rowen, and have some tea. You're standing there shivering. I've heard the wind blow something awful today. It must have run right through you."

Three weeks ago, when he'd gone out to

collect his rent, Fletcher had not been there. He was out visiting friends, Eden said. Rowen hadn't asked why she hadn't gone with him. With her time coming due, he thought maybe the cold and the ice had kept her indoors. In his rearview mirror, he'd watched her wave from the porch, her coat buttons ready to pop over her belly. How would she manage out here alone day by day with no transportation and no neighbors close by? Funny how he considered that now, when Jewell hadn't stopped complaining about how lonely she was when they'd lived there and he'd never paid any attention to her.

"Rowen, by the time you're done filling that cup with sugar, you might as well have tea-flavored syrup! Now listen, there's something else I have to tell you. Adeline's in the hospital."

She pointed to the name under the "Negroes" column.

"I want you to take me to see her. As soon as possible. We should have gone to visit as soon as we'd moved back to town. I've thought of it a hundred times. But you are always up and out the door practically in the middle of the night, and Jewell's face turns horrid if I ask for the slightest thing, even to tell her of a doctor's appointment. I'm reduced to being the family burden, Rowen. Don't look so sorrowful. I must accept God's plan for me and be grateful.

"I can't imagine what's the matter with Adeline. I pray that it's not something awful. She'd been with me — with us — for so many years. I never imagined that I would miss her as much as I do. We must go right away, Rowen."

"Mama, I've tried to do everything to make you happy here. I thought you always wanted to

Eden

move back to town. You got back everything you lost. And I thought you loved to be with Lilly and Rose."

"You're never here. Not that I'm not proud of you. I am. Not that you're not a perfectly wonderful son. You are. But this isn't my house. Jewell makes sure to remind me of that every day." She sniffled and dabbed her eyes with her handkerchief. "And no matter what house I'm in, I absolutely cannot function without Adeline. Now that I think of it, I can't believe you ever let her go. And now, just when I need her the most, something horrible may have happened to her."

Everything he'd done for her had come to nothing at all because Adeline wasn't there to dote on her every minute. The work he'd done, the work Jewell had done, the grandchildren, all of that had not been enough. The notion he'd nursed for years that she would be alright again if he just restored her to where she had been before his daddy had passed — that, as Claude would say, had been a fool assumption. He saw it now as he slurped his syrupy tea, she had never been alright.

The next morning, they were in the hospital hallway, near stifled by air heavy with floor wax and urine. His mother leaned on his arm, and although she hated the odors and noise as much as he did, she stopped to speak with every nurse they saw and ask after her and every member of her family tree. In thirty minutes, they hadn't traveled ten yards.

"Mama, I thought you wanted to see Adeline."

"You can't just barge through and ignore people, Rowen. We must try to rise above our sensory discomforts. At least for Adeline's sake."

"What would Adeline care about Dorothy Clay's aunt's trip to Raleigh?"

"Because Dorothy Clay might know Adeline's nurse, or Adeline's nurse's supervisor, and she might be inclined to see that some favor gets bestowed on this one Negro woman who never spared herself to do for others. Most of all, you."

As if any of these nurses would give them a second thought as soon as they were out of sight.

The closer they got to the Negro wing, the darker it was. Lights flickered or had burned out altogether. He hesitated in the doorway to the women's ward and looked down the rows. Patients who were sitting up stared back at them. At the very end, a woman waved, although he never would have recognized her as Adeline. How foolish it was that he hadn't expected her to look one bit different than the last day he'd seen her, six years ago. Her hair, which had always been in place from the crack of dawn until evening, flew loose about her scalp. And it had turned white.

"Miz Rita and Mr. Rowen, what a happy day to see you all. Get on down here so I can put my arms around you."

His mother didn't let go of his arm until they were at Adeline's bedside. Then she reached for Adeline's hands with both of her own. She was so glued to Adeline's face that she didn't see what startled Rowen. The bedclothes, where Adeline's right leg should have been, were flat.

"Why didn't you write to me when you got sick, Adeline, or send someone to get me?"

"You're a grandmother with two young grandbabies, Miz Rita. I wasn't going to bother you with all this foolishness. Besides, this wasn't any

sickness to speak of. Just a little surgery is all and I'll be on my way the end of next week. So you see, there wasn't any point in worrying you."

"But what kind of surgery?"

Adeline glanced up at Rowen, and it didn't matter that he hadn't seen her in years. He could read her mind loud and clear. Not here, not in this place. She'd do anything, say anything to keep his mama from wailing out loud.

"You haven't even let me speak with Mr. Rowen, yet. Look at how growed up he is. And doing so very well. Got his own company now. Rowen, you sure have made me and your mama proud."

She wanted him to keep up the pretense, but his voice bogged down in his throat.

"Thank you."

"Now I want to hear all about those grandbabies."

"Well," said his mama, "Lilly will be five in May. She is the smartest little thing. She knows her colors and can write her name, and the other night when she was saying her prayers, she prayed 'God bless Mama and Daddy and please give Nana Rita wings.' And when I said to her, 'Wherever did you get such an idea as that,' she said, 'I want you to have wings so that you don't have to wait for Mama to drive you where you want to go. You can fly whenever you want.' Isn't that the cutest thing?

"And Baby Rose is a Fourth of July baby. She will be two. She has the loveliest blonde ringlets and chubby little hands. She is a baby angel. Oh, Adeline, you must come see us."

In her fervor, she leaned forward and set her hand down on what she thought was Adeline's leg.

"Adeline, what has happened?"

Rowen felt the eyes around them—some of sympathy, others of contempt.

Adeline lowered her voice. "I got diabetes, Miz Rita. Couldn't no one help it. But this ain't something you should be troubling over. My wings is clipped, but I am not broken down and I will be walking out of this hospital."

His mother's chin trembled. She thought Adeline was deluding herself. Rowen knew better.

"I'll find someone who will care for you."

"I never needed no one to take care of me. Never will. The One that looks after me is the same that stood by Moses when he parted the waters. Everyone told him he couldn't do it, but when he stepped out on that sea floor, he moseyed along in front of the assembly like he was on a stroll in the country. And that's how I'm going to do."

"What about your daughter, Chloe?" asked Rowen, "Can't you go live with her?"

"Chloe got her Ph.D. and she teaches at Howard University now. She got a husband and two children, and when she gets here to pick me up and take me home, I'm going to say the same thing to her that I just said to you. I got my house and my own garden, and I got no business to go to anywhere else. Couldn't find a better place to grow tomatoes anyhow."

"Adeline," said his mother, "how will you ever manage that garden like this?"

Before she could answer, all heads turned at the sound of rollers squealing around the corner and here came Eden pushing a bassinet, a whoosh of collective astonishment in her wake.

She radiated new-mother pride. "Hi, y'all."

"Eden, how did you know we were here?" asked Rita.

"I didn't. I come as soon as they'd let me so I could see Adeline."

Rowen stepped aside as the women fussed over the baby. Eden was so carried away talking about her delivery and how precious Audrey Faye was that she, too, didn't notice Adeline's missing leg. To hear them chatter on, it was as if they fancied themselves at an ice cream social.

The more Adeline listened to Eden speak of Fletcher, the quieter she got. Fletcher hadn't been back to the hospital since the baby was born. He'd taken a second job, Eden said, as a grease monkey at the Chrysler dealership. No, he hadn't brought up any flowers. He was trying to save up money to buy them a second car, a Sunday car that they could drive to church so Audrey Faye wouldn't have to ride around in his trashy pickup. No, he wouldn't take off a day or two to help her when she went home. That was a silly question—what man did that? All the women in the room turned and looked at Rowen.

"Jewell's mama was around when my girls were born. No one needed me."

One of the other women spoke up from her cot. "I got a cousin that could come stay with you."

"It's all right. We'll be just fine. Here, Adeline, would you like to hold her?"

Adeline leaned forward and took the baby. "Audrey Faye.... Look at those eyes. Cornflower blue. She's going to be tall and wavy as a cornflower in a spring breeze."

As Adeline rocked the baby, Eden noticed.

"What's happened to your leg?"

Adeline spoke right at the baby. "Just a little operation is all. Ain't going to set me back at all, not one little bit."

"But you can't walk."

"Ain't no place in this room for pity, Miss Eden. What you're seeing here is blessing. Blessing that God gives me strength to throw off the fiend of self-pity. There's women in this room that got it worse. You walk down this line and you'll find something to cry about. But don't you shed any tears for me."

Rowen fished for the words that could roll him out of there. He longed to be in his truck with the radio on and a list of jobs to go to, men to talk to, materials to pick up. And then he wouldn't have to think of all this — Adeline trying to walk, or Eden all alone managing with a newborn. And most of all, he wanted to tear free from the eyes of all these women, their judgments massing like hurricane clouds.

He put his hand on his mother's shoulder.

She turned toward him to protest. "Rowen, we've hardly just gotten here."

"I got to get going, Mama."

"Adeline, you wouldn't believe it. Rowen works non-stop. He hardly lays eyes on those beautiful girls."

"He better, 'cause if he don't, morning's bearing down on him when they'll be gone and he'll be all over hisself wondering why he didn't mind them when he had the chance."

"C'mon, Mama. Adeline, you take care. Eden, you tell Fletcher I said hello."

"Oh, Adeline, I'll be back. I promise I will," said his mother.

She grumbled all the way back down the

hospital corridors, and after he'd loaded her in the truck, she said, "We're taking her home with us, Rowen. She's coming to live with us."

"Adeline? Or Eden?"

"Don't be silly. You know exactly what I mean. Of course, I would take Eden home if I could. Appearances being what they are, I'm not sure that husband of hers is up to the task. But it's Adeline I'm talking about."

As if she would get that past Jewell.

"You just heard her. She wants to be in her own home with her own garden. She wouldn't feel comfortable with us, you know that."

"Jewell wouldn't feel comfortable, that's what you mean. Well, maybe it's time for me to find my own house so I can live as I want to and have Adeline there. You needn't worry about us. I'll go look for a place today."

"And who will look after you, Mama? Are you going to expect Adeline to do it now? On one leg?"

"I won't have her tossed aside with no one to care for her. I won't have it."

"We can give her money."

"Promise me, Rowen."

He promised, but this notion wasn't any more workable than bringing Adeline home with them. He imagined Adeline's face as he came to her door with money. He saw her with her arms crossed over her chest and her broad forehead smooth and bulging, solid as Stone Mountain. He'd have to find another way if he wanted to help her, for she'd never take any help if it rammed her head-on.

Lucky for him, he had a business to run.

JAMIE LISA FORBES

He didn't have to keep ping-ponging off the wills of these women. Sure enough, after Adeline went home, the excitement subsided, and he dodged his mother's hounding—and Jewell's—by staying away later and later. Not that he sought out other entertainment. He had an office now, where, at the end of the day, he could smoke in peace and watch the tangerine light drain down the walls until dark.

On a wet March afternoon, while unloading bricks at a site, the drizzle the crew had been working in turned into a torrent, and Rowen had to stop the job. Two men, soaked and mud-spattered, jumped into Rowen's cab, and even with the windshield wipers slapping full speed, Rowen had to inch along the side of the road. A brown-skinned man, Anton, cracked open the little triangle window and rolled his cigarette.

"Wonder your papers is dry," said the man sitting beside him, Gus. Anton smiled and held up a dry packet of wax paper. They chuckled and then quieted. The sound of rain battering the truck unnerved them, and all anyone could think of was being home and dry.

Rowen jumped when Anton spoke. "Mr. Hart, you see that figure on ahead?"

Yes, he could, although just barely through the sheets of rain. He slowed, and Anton rolled down the window.

"Hey, buddy, you need a ride?"

The figure turned, and it wasn't a man at all. Rowen caught the cheekbones and chin.

"Eden?"

Her hood covered her eyes. She pushed it back to look up at them. "Telephone's out."

"But what are you doing out here?"

"There's no food in the house and the phone's out."

"Where's the baby?"

Anton leaned over blocking Rowen's view, "Boss, let her in the truck."

"Then one of us'll have to get out," said Gus.

"There's a gas station just up ahead," said Anton. "I can catch a ride from there."

Before anyone could argue, he jumped out and helped Eden climb in. She pushed her hood off and water streamed off her hair.

"If you'll just drop me off at the grocery store, I'll be fine."

"I thought Fletcher was going to get you a car."

She furiously rolled up the window. "He did."

"What's the matter? It didn't start?"

"Why don't you just drive, Rowen?"

Gus looked at him. He wanted him to drive.

"How are you going to get home from the grocery store?"

"I'll call Fletcher from there."

"I'm still trying to understand why you left a baby alone when you got a car to drive."

Gus spoke up. "We could go out to your place, Miss, and I'll take a look at your car. That way your baby don't have to be alone."

"He don't let me have the keys."

"What?" said Rowen. "I can't hear you with this rain."

"I said, he don't let me have the keys. On weekdays. When he's not home."

Gus stared straight ahead into a windshield clouded with vapor.

Eden said, "If you ain't driving, Rowen, I'm getting out."

Rowen pulled the truck back onto the road.

"You got a wire, I could squeeze it through the window to pop the lock and then jump start the thing," Gus offered.

But Gus wouldn't be around when Fletcher got home, Rowen thought.

"Thank you, I'll be all right," Eden answered.

"But your baby, Miss...."

"She'll be fine, she's going to be just fine."

Rowen blurted, "Who are you trying to convince, him or yourself?"

"Hush up, Rowen."

"Why don't you go to your church pastor and get some help?"

"Pull over, I'm getting out."

"We're all just trying to help you!"

"Y'all have never cared about me. Not one day." She opened the truck door.

"Eden!" Rowen braked. "Get back in!"

"Miss..." said Gus, reaching for his wallet. "You gotta be chilled through. You get yourself a cup of coffee at the gas station up ahead before you go on." He passed her way more bills than she'd need for a cup of coffee.

Her glance at Rowen was a taunt.

"If you won't stay in this truck, there's nothing more I can do for you."

"Don't tear yourself up with guilt, Rowen."

"Don't you imagine that I will. You're the one who's always running away."

Eden

She slammed the door shut. Gus stared at him.

"She'll be all right. She always gets by, somehow."

At home, the power had gone out. His family huddled in blankets in the drafty living room while water dripped from a wet spot on the ceiling.

"Hmm, all that new paint and we didn't think to check the roof," he said drily.

"Is that supposed to be a joke?" Rose yowled while Jewell wiped her runny nose. "The damp and cold are making your children sick and you think it's funny? You could be out there trying to fix it."

"Now?"

"Well, before we drown."

"You know that it's pitch dark out, right?"

"The storm started hours ago. Why weren't you home before now?"

"We left the job hours ago. I could barely see to drive."

"You blare that radio all day long, so you knew it was coming. You could have called off the job this morning. Or have you been holed up with Franklin and his buddies drinking somewhere?"

"Would the two of you please stop, the noise in this cold room is most unpleasant," said his mother.

"You haven't noticed that I'm soaking wet? Do you think if I'd been drinking, I'd do it out of the rain?" Eden's face, framed in the truck window, flashed through his mind. No, he wasn't going to mention that.

Lilly rocked back and forth. "Daddy, I'm cold."

"Come help me build a fire, hon."

It broke the tension—the two of them

gathering kindling and newspaper and lighting a fire. Once the flames crackled and popped, everyone's mood brightened. They warmed cans of soup and even roasted marshmallows until the evening became a camping adventure.

His mother's cheeks turned rosy and she let her blanket slip to her lap. Stray tendrils of white hair stuck to the perspiration on her forehead. He'd been aware that her hair was thinning, but now it struck him that the top of her head was nearly bald.

"This was wonderful, Jewell. What a Girl Scout you have been. You were in the Girl Scouts, weren't you? That explains how you could make everything turn out so delicious. And how cozy we all are. Everything is better even if…well, Jewell dear, you might need to change the bucket catching that leak, it's nearly full." She sighed, "It takes catastrophe to draw all of us together, really together, not just together living separately. It almost makes me want to forget what I am about to say."

"Daddy, can I have another marshmallow?"

"Hush up a sec, hon. What are you talking about, Mama?"

His mother took a deep breath. "I am going to be moving."

Jewell laughed.

"I'm moving in with Adeline."

"That's the silliest idea I've ever heard."

"I know, Jewell, your tolerance for me has been difficult to maintain. We no longer live in the age where families welcome their aging parents into their home. They haven't the time. You have your Rebekah's Hospitality Group at church and DAR and Junior League. It's a wonder with that

phone always ringing that you still have time for the girls. I've sat here like a potted plant long enough."

"I've taken care of you, same as Adeline, Miz Rita. If not better. You don't lift a finger for yourself. You don't even offer to do anything for me or the girls. I take you to the doctor and the hairdresser and the pharmacy. If I don't have time for my own children, it's because of you. How will Adeline change your bed with one leg?"

"Well, if you'd just taken the time to look at her, you'd see she has a very nice wooden leg, and she gets around as well as she did before. I've given up trying to help you. You've always treated my comments as unwelcome. Adeline and I were together before you were born. We will lean on one another. As we always have. No one finds my company helpful here, but Adeline will."

"You're going to lean on one another. Where? In the Negro section of town? Or where is it that you're going to be living together?"

"You know very well I have modest means of my own. Adeline will find us a place, even if it means we are forced to move back to the country."

"What about us?"

"What do you mean?"

"You know exactly what I mean. Or is this why you are doing it, to destroy us."

"What an ungracious comment."

"What are people going to say, Miz Rita? And when they're through talking, what are they going to do? You never give a moment's thought to all the bills we pay for you and the girls. Rowen's got construction loans at the bank. You don't see that you moving in with a colored woman is going to hurt his business? Or have you even thought of that? And Lilly and Rose. Have you thought about what they are going to hear?"

His mother's face sagged. "All I am trying to do is to salvage a few years of peace and companionship. I'd never wish anything but happiness for you and Rowen. I'd never do anything to harm the two of you."

"There, you've said it. You thought nothing about us at all. Rowen, tell her she cannot go live with Adeline."

Rowen grabbed Baby Rose.

"Baby's diaper needs changing. I'll do it."

In the candlelit bathroom, he dropped the dirty diaper in the toilet that he couldn't flush while he tried to swab Rose with a clean diaper. Odd that she didn't wriggle and fuss, as she usually did, and make an even bigger mess. He set her legs down and looked into her eyes. She'd been subdued by the arguing. She didn't know what it was about. All she knew was that with loud voices around her, she should keep very still.

And as she lay cradled between his two hands, he wondered why he'd had children. Not that he didn't love her even when she reeked to high heaven. But the notion taught in Sunday school, that children were open vessels of possibility, wasn't true. They were born shackled to places and times that molded them, twisted them, or crippled them. He couldn't say how the tug of war between his mother and his wife would misshape his daughter. He only knew that it would. And would he have had children if he'd considered all that would bind them as they tried to grow? He hadn't thought of it. People in White Rock didn't think that way.

The women were waiting for him when

Eden

Rose toddled out of the bathroom, pulling him by the hand.

"Jewell's right, Mama," he blurted.

"For Jewell's sake, my sake and your sake, I can't stay here any longer."

"You didn't even talk to Adeline about this, did you?"

"Of course, I did."

"If she said yes, it was just to please you, not because it was what she really wanted."

"She said, 'Tell Rowen it will be all right.'"

"Well, he's not moving you over to her house, I can tell you that. He is not going to load up your things and drive you on over there. So, it's settled. You'll stay here with your grandchildren."

His mother's eyes were the same shade of blue as Baby Rose's, even if they reflected pains his daughter had yet to bear. He remembered those long wordless exchanges between his mother and Adeline, how they seemed able to speak volumes to one another without so much as a whisper heard in the room. He used to envy those moments because he'd felt as if they'd shut him out. Now, looking at the fine lines in Miz Rita's face, he saw that the bond forged between him and his mother over their shared years, that too, allowed for a wordless exchange of all their history: the moments of push and pull, the moments of joy in one another, the moments of standing near while the other fell, and looking away so as to pretend it had never occurred.

"I'll take her," he said.

Jewell snatched up Rose. "You're so useless, Rowen, there's pooey running down her leg."

JAMIE LISA FORBES

11

In the end, he built the two of them a house. Not far from the center of town, the Markel mansion had been collapsing in a thicket of wisteria. Markel had been the county physician a century ago. But when Jefferson Davis's spies discovered that he was helping slaves escape to the Outer Banks, they had shot him, and his family had fled. When Rowen was a boy, his friends used to dare one another to break into the mansion. It had been more than just a fanciful undertaking, because if a boy could endure the blackberry bush thorns, ghosts and copperheads awaited him in the house.

Adeline ran down the whereabouts of the great grandchildren so that Rowen could buy the property. He sold part of the acreage to the Town of White Rock. He demolished what remained

and built a snug two-bedroom house. And cleared enough space for a modest-sized garden. The new house was dwarfed by the size of the remaining lot, and his mother couldn't easily spot the passersby from her porch. She had to whip out a pair of binoculars. But other than that inconvenience, both women seemed content with their new dwelling, accessible to anywhere they wanted to go but, also, a little secluded.

The solution untied the knots in Jewell's thinking. No one could find anything wrong with the family maid living with Rowen's mother in a house he had built. When Jewell was out, she dropped the children off at the house without a murmur.

Rowen took the girls with him when he went over to tend the yard. Released from the confines of their own house, they ran and rioted as much as they liked. No blackberry thorns to scratch them. No snakes to terrorize them. He added a playground with a sandbox and playhouse. It soon became a treat to go to Nana Rita's house.

On Saturdays in the fall, he raked up stacks of leaves and the girls torpedoed into them. He was surprised when his mother didn't raise her eyebrows at the absence of lady-like behavior. Instead, she sat beaming in her lawn chair.

When he had finished, he watched them play from the porch. Bright afternoon light shimmied through the tree branches.

> *Let's get the rhythm of the hands*
> *Let's get the rhythm of the feet,*
> *Let's get the rhythm of the hawt dawg!*

His worst worry these days was Jewell's complaints about the songs Adeline was teaching them.

JAMIE LISA FORBES

Eden had another baby, luckily, a boy this time, Birch Carver Aldrick. Eden settled into his old property, more so than Jewell ever had. When he drove out for the rent, she was outdoors most of the time, hanging laundry or tending her garden. Audrey Faye toddled about the yard, covered in sand. Eden wasn't as fussy as Jewell about girls getting dirty. And Birch Carver lay wrapped snug in a bassinet propped on fruit crates.

He always knew whether or not Eden was alone when he turned into the driveway. If Fletcher was gone, she'd smile and wave as he came up the road. If Fletcher was there, there'd be no sign of her, and Fletcher would meet him before he got out of the truck.

One warm afternoon in early spring, he caught Eden nursing the baby on the front porch. She yanked a cloth diaper over her breast, and Rowen was about to apologize when Fletcher charged up from nowhere.

"Hart, can't you ever call before you come out?"

Rowen glanced at Eden. She looked more fearful than embarrassed. She pulled the baby closer to her body.

"I didn't mean to intrude, Fletcher. But you got to know I'd be coming out. If you don't want me coming out, you could come to the office beforehand and pay your rent."

Fletcher crossed his arms and his eyes narrowed, like a pig's.

"We'll be looking for a new place soon, closer to Mama's, where she can watch the kids and Eden can go back to work."

"Sounds great. Make sure your new landlord is a little soft on the rent."

Eden

"What are you 'sinuating, Hart? You saying we haven't paid what we owe you? 'Cause as far as I know, we have. Unless you've got some other arrangement with her," he nodded back toward Eden.

"When you're not here, Eden's always paid me what you give her. You tell her what to pay, right? If she didn't pay what you tell her to pay, you'd take care of it."

As soon as the words had spilled out, Rowen regretted them. "Taking care of it"—what had he meant by that? Correct her, that's what he thought he had meant. Surely Fletcher didn't beat her. Men beating their wives was something Rowen heard of now and again, but he'd never seen a mark on a woman, not around town, nor in church. Still, Fletcher craved his authority, craved it the way Franklin White craved his Lincolns. If Fletcher had to seize it by raising his hand, in threat, at least, well there was nothing to stop him from doing it.

Threatening to hit her, that wasn't so bad, was it?

Fletcher smirked. "I take care of what I know about. Are you saying she hasn't paid it all, that she's withheld some?"

"No, I believe she's paid every dime you've given her." He put the truck in gear. "Sure hope you find what you're looking for."

As he turned around, he felt as if she was reeling him back. He glanced in his rearview mirror, but her eyes weren't on him, as he'd sensed. She still held the baby close. *Just his imagination.* Once he pulled onto the highway, out of sight of the house, he counted the money Fletcher had given him. Short again.

JAMIE LISA FORBES

He wasn't going back. He'd worry about it next month.

But he saw Eden before the month was out. One afternoon when he went to pick up the girls from his mother's, there she was. Audrey Faye was playing with his girls in the front yard while Eden and his mother watched them from the porch.

His mother called to him, "Rowen, look who's come to visit. And have you seen this baby? Look how he holds himself upright already. He's marvelous."

Rowen was so preoccupied with how he'd last seen Eden that he didn't look at the baby. He searched her face looking for clues as what had happened after he'd driven away. He felt sure that Fletcher had shouted at her for something, whether she'd done anything wrong or not. Lord Jesus, he hoped that shouting was all it had been. Not a sign of any of it lingered in her face, as open as the sky, and she smiled up at him as if everything between old friends was fine, including the matter of the rent. She did look prettier than she had ever been at her house. She was outfitted in a white sweater with a scalloped neckline and her hair had been pulled back into a bun.

"How'd you get into town, Eden?"

"Thank you, Rowen, I'm just fine. How's Jewell?"

He flicked a cockroach off the porch pillar. It always felt awkward when Eden brought up Jewell.

Eden

"Why ever are you asking about how she got here, Rowen? Fletcher bought her a car," his mother said.

Her eyebrows arched for an instant, but she kept on beaming at him, expecting the answer to her question.

"Jewell's out helping put flowers on veterans' graves. You know, with Memorial Day weekend coming up."

"Jewell's panoply of activities continues to expand to where she is simply not home at all," his mother continued. "I used to think she used them as excuses to get away from me when I was living there, but now I wonder if she is trying to escape her family altogether. Just the other night, Rowen had to fix supper."

"What'd you fix, Rowen?" said Eden. "You always were a top dog in the kitchen."

"Eden was just telling us Fletcher got a raise. Now they can start saving to buy some land and a house of their own."

Why would they do that when they have a house they don't pay for now? Before he could fire off that comment, he saw Adeline coming to the door and rushed to open it for her.

"Y'all come get some lemonade," Adeline called. "Mr. Rowen, you see we got company. Eden surprised us and we fixed her hair and we all went to the church store and found her that sweater. Don't she look like a fashion lady from Atlanta?"

That was exactly how she looked. The way her hair was swept up showed off her neck.

"Uh-huh," he said, "Fletcher will be real pleased."

She'd be yanking out that hair and hiding that sweater before he got home.

"Miz Adeline, you take my chair," said Eden. "Rowen, would you?" She rose and held out the baby to him. Rowen cradled the baby close to his chest to cover his surprise at Eden giving up her chair for a colored woman, without even a pause. The baby blinked, trying to focus on his face, as Eden picked up the pitcher and began pouring glasses for the children.

Adeline hadn't moved. "It's all right with you, Mr. Rowen, if I sit down?"

Rowen felt a sudden jab not to be outdone by Eden.

"Go ahead. You sit right there."

Adeline leaned her head back and rubbed her shoulders against the warmth of the chair. "Don't that spring sunshine feel good!"

"Adeline, you want a glass?" asked Eden.

"Y'all making me feel ashamed, waiting on me like the servants of Vashti. You just remember I'm not a cripple and I won't be treated like one."

Upon inspection, Birch Carver had decided Rowen was not to his liking and he began to fuss.

"Well, here's a job to do," said Rowen and he passed the baby to Adeline.

Adeline perched the baby in her lap. "You just don't know what he wants. He wants to watch all these young ladies, that's all he's asking you to do," and the baby's head did turn to follow the girls' voices.

"Such an afternoon here with all of us together again and happy, I'm plenty grateful. Seems like the wrong time to speak of bad news. I decided to wait until we were all together. I didn't

want to have to tell y'all one at a time, especially as we wanted to fuss over Miz Eden and her babies. There's never a good time for bad news. It's always round the bend, bearing down on us. Don't matter whether we're ready or not."

"Daddy," Lilly cried, "Audrey Faye spilled her lemonade all over me."

Eden grabbed a wad of paper napkins and tried to console Lilly while Rowen and his mother sat tense at the edge of their seats. Was Adeline about to lose the other leg?

"Sammy Little been in a bad accident."

With his incoming breath, Rowen felt gratitude, for Adeline, and as he exhaled, fear for his old friend. It had been three years since he'd seen Sammy at the Fourth of July parade. How tall and dignified he'd looked in his crisp uniform. Come to think of it, white boys with that kind of success had their portraits blown up on the front page of the newspaper. No local newsman had sought Sammy out. The Sammy he'd seen that day might not have cared. He'd seemed to have moved past them all. What mattered was that he'd made something of himself. Hadn't he?

"What happened?" Rowen blurted.

"Are you speaking of that young man who used to be Rowen's friend before he entered the army?" Rita asked.

Adeline nodded. "The same one. He's burned so bad they don't know if he's going to make it."

Eden looked up from mopping Lilly.

"I remember that day we drove him to the train. Every once in a while, I've wondered what happened to him and when he'd ever come back. Lilly, don't cry honey, your mama's not going to yell at you. I'll get that stain out of your dress if I have to wash it myself."

"I saw him a few years back when he'd come home for his daddy's funeral. He'd been promoted," said Rowen.

"Promoted? Why wouldn't he want to come back home?" Eden asked.

"I don't know what his plans were," said Adeline, "but honey, he was an officer at a base clear up in Alaska. He sent money home to his mama, and to hear her talk, Sammy rode right next to Elijah in his chariot. She was that proud of him. And now this terrible thing happens. If he survives, he's likely coming home to stay. But what kind of a boy his mama will have back—well, we've got to put it in Jesus' hands. Right now, we got to be praying for him to live."

"Tell us what happened," said his mother.

"He'd become an instructor. He taught the soldiers how to fix their vehicles. He was in the shop with his students while the soldiers was training outside and someone fired a round the wrong way. It hit his shop and blew it up."

"We must go see Miz Little," his mother said.

"Adeline, if he comes home, I want you to tell me so I can go see him," said Eden.

As if she'd ever been friends with him.

"You never had one good word for him when you were living with us," Rowen said.

"That's not true. I always thanked him for being good to me. I remember how he let me ride his white mule."

"Even if he did come home, Fletcher's not going to let you get anywhere near him."

"Who's talking about Fletcher? Nobody's

bringing him up but you. It seems like you're all taken up with him. Maybe you're just jealous."

Just like her to bite the hand that fed her time and time again.

"Have you told Mama and Adeline the truth about Fletcher? Have you told them how you got home the day I tried to …"

Adeline jumped in. "You all ain't acting any better than these young children. Showing no respect when the boy who did for you both is suffering. Miz Eden Aldrick, a married woman with two babies does not go to visit an unmarried man, no matter how burned up he is.

"And don't you stare at me like that. You've got that look on your face—you can't hide it—that look you had as a child when I knew you had it in your head to turn one-eighty degrees and do the exact opposite of what you was told to do. You may be a grown woman with babies, but you are never going to be able clothe yourself in any kind of guile that I can't see through."

Adeline looked down at the baby's head while she massaged his back. "Truth is, the time has arrived for you to set yourself aside and think about your children. They got a daddy, a good daddy, but for their sakes, you got to soak up who he is, and who he is not. Mr. Aldrick and these babies, they're your horizon now. It's got to contain you."

"Miz Adeline, you just said I wasn't showing no respect for Sammy, after all he done for me. Then tell me, what am I supposed to do for him?"

"Go home and pray."

JAMIE LISA FORBES

On Sunday, Franklin White hosted the Minutemen's Memorial Day picnic. Moonbeam jasmine bloomed all around his house and filled the air—cloying and intoxicating at the same time. Couples just out of church clutched paper plates and drinks while their children ran shrieking through the yard, tresses coming loose, shirttails flapping out of trousers. Rowen's girls clung to his pants legs, stunned by the melee around them.

Franklin waylaid guests over at the beverages table. Most men grew bellies as they aged, but not Franklin. He still looked like a skeleton—dressed in a seersucker suit today. He wouldn't be doing business on a Sunday, but it was always about business anyway—the soulful inquiries after family, the flattery of women.

Rowen's mother had settled in a wicker chair on the porch where a knot of her contemporaries encircled her as if she had never been out of their midst, as if the years they'd been out of town had never even happened.

He heard a blast of laughter from Jewell— she must have gotten tipsy from the punch. There she was in front of the jasmine in the new ruby dress she'd made for the occasion, all the rigidity gone from her neck and shoulders. She didn't drink at home. Maybe plying her with booze was the solution to the household tension. Might help them in the bedroom as well.

The exuberance of the gathering started to diminish as the temperature climbed. Eighty-five degrees already in the shade—the peach ice cream melted the moment it was served. Guests retreated to the porch, or under the oaks, and women fidgeted, fretting over how those children would have to be

bathed before supper, but no one would dare depart before Franklin spoke.

Franklin's maid brought him a stool. He slumped down on it and mopped his forehead. The gathering quieted, hoping he was getting ready to speak, but he took his time grinding down his cigarette butt and loosening his tie.

"If you all gather around, I know it's getting a little warm, but I want us to remember why we are here today."

As Franklin praised the boys of the community who, for generations, had heeded the call for freedom, the maid stooped to pluck paper plates and napkins off the lawn.

Clark Raeford limped forward, in his wool uniform, to receive the bank's check for the Minutemen. He owned the hardware store, but it was because of his hip wound that he'd been chosen for this honor. How Clark must have suffered for hours in that wool just for the fleeting moment of shaking Franklin's hand and assuring the crowd that every disabled soldier and his family would receive help from the Minutemen. Everyone clapped, relieved that the afternoon was closing.

The maid, too, straightened and clapped once. Twice.

Deep in the night, Rowen woke to a mockingbird singing. For an hour, he drowsed through the warbles and trills until he sat up. It seemed as if he had been dreaming of Sammy waving goodbye to him from the back of the bus. Leaving for that promised better life, just as everyone had told Rowen to do. *What could be worse, Sammy coming home in a coffin, or Sammy, alive, having to ride the hot, diesel-fumed bus back to this place?*

JAMIE LISA FORBES

After the Minutemen picnic, the furnace of summer ignited, and the only thoughts Rowen had energy for were of his work. No point trying to sleep anymore through the humid, insect-mad nights. Rowen was awake on his front porch, fretting over supplies, schedules, labor shortages when the mockingbird sounded off at midnight. By August, Jewell said that if his only contribution to family life was snapping at everyone in sight, he might as well stay away.

That month he'd started building a rural fire station, and he arrived at the job site before dawn one morning to wait for the truck delivering cinderblock. The sun bulged over the horizon and then shot upward, but though Rowen strained to hear beyond the cicadas, there was no sound of a truck in the distance. He stood fuming on the concrete pad, smoking cigarette after cigarette, while the crew arrived, skirted him, and camped in the shade. The chatter of his crew sounded ever more ridiculous as his temper frayed.

When they started in on whether a "polecat" was a weasel or a skunk, he wheeled around and shouted, "Can't you all just shut up?"

Instead of a truck, here came Eden, barreling down the road in her own vehicle, and his first thought was she'd become awful good at stealing the keys from her husband.

She rolled the car window down.

"Eden, get that car off the concrete, I got a delivery truck coming any minute."

Eden

"There's not even a bicycle behind me, Rowen. Nice to see you, too. I brought someone out here who's asked to see you."

"I can visit after working hours. Go on and move that car."

But Miz Little had already got out. She reached back to help the man inside, and as he unfolded there in the glaring light, it was his height that struck a chord in Rowen. The height, then the grin on the face that was otherwise scarred past recognition.

"Mister Rowen, is that you ordering people around? Just as the Bible says, the stone the builders rejected has become the cornerstone."

Rowen felt as if the wind had been knocked out of him. All these people around him added to his sense of gasping for breath. He hated that they were there to watch his shock — and weakness — overtake him. Including Eden. Most of all Eden.

But Sammy couldn't see how he was feeling, and Rowen scrambled to keep it from him. He stepped forward and gripped Sammy's hand.

"That grip's mighty strong. I'm surprised you are this glad to see me. Sure wish I could see the look on your face. I thought I was going to scare you half to death."

"I wish I'd seen you more often before now."

"Got to be honest with you. I never thought I'd be with you again."

"How are you?"

Sammy chuckled. "What do you think? Don't you think I'd have been better off if I'd passed?"

"Sammy, hush, don't talk like that," his mother said.

If he was in Sammy's shoes, he'd think the same thing, but he wouldn't say that in front of these women.

"No, Sammy," he said, "I'm just glad you're home again."

"You meet me in front of the courthouse where I'll be shining shoes and we can talk about it then."

"You won't be shining no shoes," said Eden. "Your mind ain't burned. I bet you learn to read those words in dots and maybe you could be a teacher again. You're just starting over on something else. That's all."

Sammy's face twisted, as if he was struggling to be grateful while, at the same time, rejecting what she'd said.

"Y'all were good to bring me out here."

Rowen and Eden exchanged glances. Fletcher didn't know about any of this. The way her eyes darted away; he knew Sammy hadn't learned about Fletcher either.

"If I can be happy about anything, I'm happy things turned out so well for you, Mr. Rowen," said Sammy.

"Don't call me 'Mister' anymore. I've always hated that, and you know it." Rowen didn't understand why he was close to breaking down after all these years when he thought he'd learned to master himself. "You've gone farther and done more than I ever will. You had the stuff to be someone outside of this place. I never did. If you could see me, you'd see the same fool you left behind."

Sammy squeezed Rowen's forearm. "If I hadn't gone, maybe I would have been able to see you today."

Eden

"We got to be going," said Eden. "Adeline's got my kids."

Rowen turned to Eden. "One of these days Fletcher's going to catch you, you know that."

He regretted the remark as soon as he'd made it. She'd intended an act of kindness, for both him and Sammy, and he'd ripped it apart.

"What are you talking about?" asked Sammy.

"Nothing," she said, "he ain't talking about nothing. Rowen, your precious truck is coming up the road."

JAMIE LISA FORBES

12

Less than two weeks later, Rowen got the news that Claude was in the hospital. Yet another spectacle that no one could prepare him for. He slumped in the doorway gazing down at the big man shrunk to a husk, legs moving aimlessly under the sheet. The minutes ticked by, measured in machines buzzing, burping or beeping while Rowen wondered how he had been ratcheted into this slot of space. They didn't belong here. They should have been on Claude's porch with the pine woods all around, the hounds splayed out in the yard, and Mary coming out of the screen door with sweet tea and key lime pie. Mary — gone two years or more now.

Even after Claude had sold him the business, he'd still been there — just as he'd fussed about — to

steer Rowen's life endeavors. Despite how Rowen had cursed his life when his daddy had passed, he'd been Jesus' blessed child in having Claude come along and not only fix a gate post, but fill the hole blown open in his life. Back then, he'd learned that catastrophe doesn't bring the end of time. You go on putting one foot in front of the other. Difference was no one would appear outside his window and fill the hole once Claude was gone.

Claude turned his head. "I can see you. I can't see who you are, but I see you."

"It's Rowen."

"You gonna just stand there observing my slow demise?"

"No, sir." Rowen pushed away the table with the morning's plate of uneaten grits. "How are you, Claude?"

"Used up," he said. "I've used up everyone's time and patience. They all want me to die and be done with it. I wish I could be more accommodating."

"Stop that talk."

"You been out to the house?"

"Yes, sir."

"Is everything all right?"

"It's just fine."

"Did you take the girls to *The Flower of Cape Fear* this year?"

"They don't call it that anymore. They decided the title was too old-fashioned. They call it, *The Tide of Freedom.*'"

"Well, did you go see it?"

"The mayor plays Colonel Richardson now and no, he isn't as good as you."

"Not as good looking as me?"

"He's bald like you, but short and fat."

"Hard to project the dignity then."

"Yes, sir."

Claude nodded and looked away from him.

"Take me home, Rowen."

"Take you home? There's no one to look after you there."

"There's no one to look after me here."

At Claude's, their gazes could drift off through the woods during moments of silence, but here the only view outside the grimy window was the parking lot.

"I shot all the dogs after Mary died," said Claude. "I was getting to where I couldn't care for them and they had no place to go."

"I know," said Rowen.

"Whatever happened to that girl who used to live with you and your mama? The one who could catch rats so well?"

"Eden?"

"Eden. Whatever become of her?"

"Same as happens to all of them. She got tangled up with an ex-fruit grower named Fletcher and now they have two kids."

"Good man?"

"No."

"Shame. We destroy our own young, Rowen."

"What do you mean by that?"

"We scrub their imaginations clean of possibility to make sure the concept will never stick there."

"You're talking hogwash. When she ran from us, she could have run as far away as she liked, nothing to stop her."

Claude closed his eyes and sighed deeply. Rowen thought he'd forgotten the conversation

and gone to sleep. But with his eyes closed he said, finally, "By the time she ran from you, it was already too late."

Rowen had intended to visit Sammy, but soon the thought subsided down to the murky bottom of things he'd sworn to do, felt guilty about not doing, but somehow never accomplished. And once it rested on a comfortable plateau of discomfort, without jabbing him daily, he spotted Sammy manning a new food cart in front of the courthouse.

Rowen parked his truck and got in line. Sammy seemed content enough, chatting with his customers, dishing out hot dogs and corn cobs. Louis Armstrong blared from an RCA portable radio. Rowen remembered how Sammy always carried the transistor in his cotton-picking days. Things were back to the same as they were. Except twisted from how they were.

"What will you have?" he said when Rowen reached the head of the line.

"Sammy, it's me, Rowen."

"Mr. Rowen, you coming to court today? I remember you do like a good trial."

"I stopped to see you. And I asked you not to call me that."

"You want a hot dog?"

"What are you doing here?"

"Got a home-made relish to go with it. Eden's been whipping it up and bringing it over. Nice to find out that her time with Adeline paid off after all."

"You don't need to be doing this."

"Beg pardon, but how are you preaching to me about what I need to do? As I told you I celebrate your ascent since I've been gone, but I don't believe that career counseling for blind coloreds is one of your new skills."

"I've been meaning to stop and see you. I just never get the time."

Sammy poking fun at him — that wasn't new, but the snarl of rancor underneath the humor was another grim twist of circumstance. With all Sammy had lost, Rowen expected him to be angry, but didn't they share a history and didn't that history count as something they could hold on to? Not the slightest ripple of warmth from the old days surfaced anywhere in Sammy's scarred face.

"We ain't had anything to do with one another in…. how many years? Don't take this personal, but I wasn't ever planning on coming back here to see you or anyone else. So now that the Lord has set me back to my humble beginnings, I don't need to be your burden. I'm glad I came to see you when I came home. And I am thankful that Miz Eden drove me out there. That little trip got the two of us started on this business venture here. But unless you've come to get some grub, you don't need to traipse over here lugging your pity. Now, how about a hot dog? We got tea, too."

"Why are you acting like this?"

"Rowen, you sound so woeful that I almost feel sorry you can't understand. There ain't a world we can be in together. Unless you want a hot dog, because I got people waiting. Court break is only so long."

"I can't believe that you're going to settle for this."

Eden

"And you think I am going to do...what? Rock in my easy chair and wait for the accolades? And donations? My veteran brothers at the Sons of the Minutemen haven't turned up with any aid. You been out in the sun so long it's boiled your brains." He turned to the next customer.

Rowen glanced down behind the cart. He spotted an open carton of Mason jars filled with pickles and he wondered—would Sammy be fool enough to sell moonshine right in front of the courthouse?

No matter. Sammy had fixed the boundaries between them.

"See you, Sammy."

"Y'all come back."

The food cart was open every day court was in session, summer and winter. Every once in a while, rumors circulated that the customers could also buy moonshine.

In the year following Sammy's return, Adeline's housekeeping declined, and she gave up the garden. Though she had walked out of the hospital, just as she'd said she would, and tried to carry on as if nothing had changed, it seemed to take her more and more effort to move from room to room. Rowen overlooked the dust balls in the corners while the pecan trees in the yard spread wider and wider. One evening when he came to mow the lawn, he realized he could no longer see the house for the trees. Adeline and his mama were ever more insulated from view.

JAMIE LISA FORBES

Fletcher Aldrick's dreams of his own place never seemed to come to pass. He lost his job at the Chrysler dealership. Then he lost another job at a mobile home factory. It was good they had his mama's peach orchard to fall back on, at least in the summers. Eden had another child, a girl, Crystal Grace. Some months there was rent, sometimes not.

Rowen admitted to himself that he drove out once a month, not so much to collect the rent as to see Eden, even if it meant that, from time to time, he had to put up with Fletcher.

One winter afternoon when Fletcher was absent, Eden asked Rowen if he would give him a job. By the look in her eyes, Fletcher had put her up to the request. She didn't believe in it. Rowen paused and listened to the voices of her children inside the house.

It wouldn't work, he'd answered.

She nodded and thanked him. Maybe it was just the muted light at late afternoon, but he could have sworn there was some kind of smudge on her cheekbones.

That same month, Claude passed away. Another funeral, another pageant, no more convincing than *The Flower of Cape Fear*. Where everyone could vault their gaze over the coffin up front and see a stained-glass crucifixion, Rowen saw only a big hole.

Franklin White had a stroke and had to be admitted to the nursing home Claude had built.

One morning, Rowen had to struggle to button his pants.

Eden

Lilly and Rose leapfrogged from toddlers to kindergarten to elementary school. Rowen would wake up in the night waiting for a baby to cry and then remember that it had been years since he'd changed a diaper. *At this rate, they'd be in high school in what would seem like a matter of days. High school!*

Did he even have a say in what would become of them? Neither of them was as contrary as Eden, but that didn't stop the day from coming when they might turn their backsides to him and sprint down the road, fast as they could run, without looking back and heedless as to where they were headed. The desire for motion itself—that might have been what had carried off Eden back in the day. He'd felt it himself a time or two when he'd wanted to forget who he was.

One night while those thoughts cycled through his head, the bedside lamp snapped on.

"Rowen, are you awake."

"Yes, you too, I guess."

"What are you thinking about?"

"Nothing. What are you thinking about?"

"I've been lying awake thinking of us night after night."

"Us?"

"Yes, Rowen. Who are we? We're a married couple, but we're really like two planets in separate orbits that pass each other once in a while. I'm lying next to flesh and blood, but Rowen is not present."

Rowen sat up and leaned on his elbow.

"What do you want, Jewell? Don't you have everything you want? You hated it in the country. So we came here to Uncle Hugh's. Just as you wanted. You redid the house your own way. I never said anything. You and Mama didn't get along. I got

Mama another house. You can't name a time I've ever said no to you. Whether it's house, or the yard or the girls."

"You're not hearing what I'm saying. I don't have you, Rowen. That's what I don't have."

Half her face was in shadow, but he saw the tears. He ran his hand down her thigh. "I'm right here, Jewell. I've always been right here. And baby, look around you. When you look around this town, you've got so much."

Her hand fluttered, as if she was going to push his hand away. But it dropped and she said, "Is there someone else, Rowen?"

He kissed her thigh. "No, there's no one else."

"Have you ever had an affair?"

He removed the covers and looked down at her long shins. He pulled up her nightgown to her hips. Still, she didn't push him away.

"Yes, a long time ago. Before Rose was even born."

"I thought so."

Their eyes met and he realized that she'd known all along.

"You slept with Eden, right?"

"Eden? Why would you think it was her?"

"The way she looked at you that time she came to the house, the way that you looked at her. I hated it that you rented the house to them."

"We took her in when she had nowhere else to go. And it wasn't me, it was Mama and Adeline who did it. I don't have anything for that girl other than feeling sorry for her."

He reached for a pillow and she lifted her hips.

Eden

"She wants you, she still does."

"You haven't seen her in years. She loves Fletcher, they have three children."

"She wants you."

"Jewell, if I had it to do all over again, I'd choose you. Wouldn't even think twice."

"Let's go away."

"Go away? We've already been to the beach with the kids this year."

"Not with the children, I mean something romantic, just the two of us."

"Where do you want to go?"

"The Holiday Inn has a weekend special in Wilmington."

"Sounds all right."

"And Rowen, I want you to do something. When we get back, sell the country house. So you don't have to worry about it anymore."

He broke off his lovemaking and looked at her again. How could he hide it from her, that he didn't want to lose his only tie with Eden.

She rubbed his forearm. "So you're here with us, with me."

He gave her the weekend she wanted, and when they came home, he sold the house like she had asked.

On his last trip out to collect the rent, all Eden said was, "It's okay. You don't have to worry about us or nothing."

"Where will you go?"

In the pause that followed, he expected her to lash out. That's what she'd always done. It had taken him years to realize that her bluster was her way of pretending courage in a world always turning its shoulder to her. Now, no reaction, nothing. Was she sick? He looked out to the garden, the yellow squash in bloom. Her hair was smoothed back into a tight ponytail which made her face look gaunt, but the years hadn't dimmed those sparkly crystals in her eyes.

"Fletcher's got a job in the tobacco fields. We'll have plenty of money this summer, so we should be able to find something. I can always start another garden. We'll manage just fine. You look like you want something, Rowen? Do you want something?"

Rowen rubbed his thumbnail along the door post, knocking off loose chips of paint.

"I don't know when I'm going to see you again, and I just want to know that you'll be all right."

She covered his hand with her own. "You don't owe me nothing. You never did. I know I got you to thinking you did, and I liked the way that felt. But it wasn't right. You can let me go, Rowen.

"Did you count the money I gave you? I know you never count it in front of me. Go ahead and count it out now."

She had given him way more than a month's rent.

"What's all this for, Eden?"

"It's every cent I owe you for the last year."

"I don't need this."

"Now there won't be anything between us. We're free from one another."

"Didn't you know that I don't care about t he money?"

"I know you don't."

There was no more to say, and yet they both stood there as if they had just begun to speak.

"You want some squash out of the garden? You keep looking out that way. Let me go get you some."

He smiled at how she jumped off the steps, how she covered the ground to the garden in three strides, and then whisked up her vegetables. Exactly the way she had moved as a girl. Whatever Eden's cares, she poured all of herself into the moment at hand. He'd never taken the time, until now, to appreciate that about her.

Since she'd lived in this house, weeks had gone by when he hadn't thought of her at all. But that was only because he didn't have to wonder about her. He'd known where she was. She was right here, on his own property, contained by her husband, and by the invisible web that wound through White Rock right up to the *Welcome to White Rock, home of Tar Heel hospitality* sign. After how bitter he'd felt over being pushed out of it, he was now one of the guy lines that held that web fast.

Already she had a carton full to give him.

"I put some okra and cucumbers in there, too."

She placed the carton in his arms and stepped back—beaming, proud.

He thanked her, but he'd never stop feeling sorry that he hadn't coaxed her to sit down on the porch until the passing moments had eased better words, truer words from him.

At that moment, he'd felt impatient to leave. The tasks of the day listed on his notepad in the truck had nudged him along, whatever the heck they had been. By the time of Adeline's phone call months later, he couldn't remember any of them.

Thank you, goodbye, and he set the carton in the pickup bed. They shook hands, and each gripped the other tight, until Rowen let go, and the moments that might have yielded a chance to save her slipped from his grasp.

Eden

13

Adeline's description of the shooting looped over and over in Rowen's head. Eden had cycled up to the abandoned tobacco barn where they were living. They'd lost the car, her car, so she'd gotten a bicycle with a cart mounted in back for Crystal. She'd found seasonal work wrapping Christmas gifts at Woolworth's, so it was dark by the time she got to the house. There was no power at the barn. The two older children were with Fletcher and she had carried Crystal indoors. Fletcher waited until she'd set the child down and while she was still in the doorway, he raised his shotgun and shot her point blank.

The folks who'd rented the tobacco barn to them said the shot hadn't troubled them. Hunters in the tree stands—that's what they'd thought—until they heard the children screaming.

When Adeline telephoned late that night, she'd just said, "Come." A foot of snow blanketed the ground outside, and as Rowen stepped out, fat globs of snow plummeted out of the dark, hissing as they landed.

"Don't you go," Jewell had said. "Whatever it is can wait for tomorrow."

By the tone in Adeline's voice, he knew there was no waiting.

Adeline's eyes were on the door when he walked in, but he was surprised to see his mother up as well. She had been failing for some time now. She'd begin a sentence only to drop off and look around her, as if she didn't recognize anyone, and then repeat what she'd just said. Adeline had pulled him outside a month ago and said, "I don't mean to embarrass you, son, but I got to put diapers on her now."

For all Adeline's bullheadedness, she was hardly any better. If he offered to do a chore for her, she snapped at him, yet she huffed with pain through every motion. One day, watching her in the kitchen as she felt along the counter for a can opener, he'd realized that her sight was nearly gone.

Jewell had been on him to sell their house, move his mother to the nursing home and take Adeline to her daughter's. He'd ignored her, as he ignored most of the things she harped on him about. He wasn't going to upend these women. No, sir. Yes, Jewell was right, something was bound to happen, but that coming day could be plastered over with all the activities of the present.

"Why is Mama still up?"

Eden

His mother wailed. "Eden's gone, Rowen, our Eden."

Was she in her right mind? He looked to Adeline, as he had always done, to frame the world for him so it could be contained and rendered comprehensible. She sat up straight, her hands folded in her lap, disciplined and proud, no different than she'd always been, and the only sign that something monstrous had occurred was her silence.

Rowen sat down.

"Before I tell you what we heard, I'm going to ask for His presence and love in this room."

It was true, then. Rowen took off his hat and knelt on the floor while the women bowed their heads.

"Oh, Jesus," said Adeline, "You came to take Eden today and we know, sure as we know that You'll raise the sun in the morning, that she is next to You now and she will never know no more pain. Her pain is gone forever, hallelujah. But You moved through that portal of death, and because You did, You know our hearts are left torn and bleeding behind in this world. You will choose us in Your own time and until that day, we have to move through the rooms of this world and serve, best as we are able. Thank you for giving us Eden. Thank you for giving us the light of that life that brought joy and knowledge and comfort to our days. In the days to come, we pray that You gather us to You so that every time the lash of this grief smites us, we feel Your comfort, You, who died so that we may be free."

Rowen listened to the women's breathing and beyond, to the steady snowfall outside. Adeline would speak again when she was ready and there was nothing to do but feel the current of the world pulsing on, every second carrying them away from Eden who was left behind forever in that one bloody moment.

It was after midnight when he learned what happened, and the only question he asked was, "Where are her children?"

"Sheriff took 'em is all I know."

The murder was on the front page of the newspaper the next morning. Fletcher Aldrick was in jail awaiting trial. But the rumor that drifted from the jail was that Fletcher told the sheriff he'd shot her because she was running around on him, sleeping with a blind Negro, Sammy Little.

The news surged through the town like floodwaters. There were those that said if that was what she was doing, Fletcher was right to do what he'd done. They weren't afraid to say it.

There were those who said Eden Aldrick wasn't any good. Hadn't she tried to finger poor Franklin White for the murder of her father a while back? Some said that Fletcher had made the whole story up. Every time he lost a job, his drinking had gotten worse. He was a customer of Sammy's, and not for the hot dogs. More than likely, he'd gotten drunk and shot her for no reason at all other than she was bringing home money and he wasn't.

And everywhere Rowen went — the auto shop, the hardware store, the lumber mill, the job sites — everyone approached Rowen to offer up their speculations and solicit his. Hadn't he known the Aldricks better than anyone?

He stopped answering the telephone. He turned around and walked away when he saw people coming. He threatened to fire anyone

on his crew if he heard so much as a murmur about it.

But the talk had knocked him off his feet, too, swept him under in waves of doubts. Had she done what Fletcher said? If she had, she'd misled him too. How long? He thought back to when she'd first brought Sammy to the job site. Had it started then, that day? Had he known, would he have let her keep living at his house? Would he have stopped caring about her? Day by day he was jostled among these thoughts, and all the while he circled around and around the image of her lying there in the doorway of a tobacco barn with no one to offer her the smallest last comfort.

Two weeks later, Sammy was arrested for selling nontax paid liquor.

The next day, when Rowen went to his mother's house, he was surprised to find Adeline sitting on a stool to wash the dishes. He'd never seen her surrender to her own needs before. By itself, that wouldn't have troubled him, except the way her shoulders slumped suggested an even deeper collapse that did scare him.

"Miz Rita is asleep," she said, "She sleeps most of the time these days." Her head wobbled as she turned to him, as if she couldn't pinpoint where he was. "Do you all think you can take her back to your house?"

"What about you?"

"Chloe's been wanting me to come with her long before I lost my leg. You know I've resisted it. I would have felt like an elephant squashing on her family, her marriage. But my grandkids are grown. They got kids of their own now. I am not going to abandon Miz Rita, I'll always be there for her long as she needs me, but I'd like to…I'd like to just sit down, close my eyes and listen to children, Rowen. Just sit and listen to them."

"I'll talk to Jewell. Can it wait until after Christmas?"

"We can hold out till then."

He paused, afraid of what he might hear. "Did you hear about Sammy?"

The water sloshed; the dishes clattered.

"I heard."

"Adeline, tell me…"

"I ain't going to answer you, Rowen."

"Would you let me do those dishes?"

"No. Just the silverware left, and then I'm done."

"Do you think I should put up bail for Sammy?"

"I ain't going to tell you what to do. More than ever you need to heed the Lord's voice about what you should do, not anyone else."

No point in her hearing what he wanted to say, that there wasn't any Lord to heed to. The Lord, if He'd ever been here, was done with White Rock, done and gone, the instant Fletcher aimed at Eden.

He waited in the smoky lobby outside the cells, for hours it seemed, until the deputies brought out a stooped, unshaven man who no longer resembled the boy who could strip a tobacco stalk before you could blink.

Once they released him, he stood, head tilted, as if expecting further instruction, until the deputy said, "You're free to go. I believe Mr. Hart will take you home."

Sammy turned slowly in the room. "Mr. Rowen," he murmured hoarsely.

Rowen sprung from his chair and took his elbow. "Let's get out of here," he said.

He held his questions through the long moments it took to shepherd Sammy down three flights of stairs and then over the ridges of ice on the sidewalks. A woman on the curb rang the Salvation Army bell and Sammy yanked him to a halt.

"I want to drop two-bits in her pail."

"We can come back and do it. You're moving slow enough as it is, you'll freeze to death in those thin pants."

"You seem to be in a mighty hurry. Seems if you was outdoors working, you'd be used to this chill by now. Or, maybe you don't need to get out of your warm truck anymore. It won't take but a second."

Sammy veered toward the bell, then fished for coins while Rowen fumed. He felt along the pail for the hole, but to Rowen's relief, the woman took the coins from him. Sammy smiled at the ring of them dropping in the pail.

"Merry Christmas," he said, as she thanked him. Then he turned to Rowen. "Aren't you going to give her some money?"

"Sure," said Rowen, and he thrust dollar bills in the woman's hand.

"Bless you," she said.

"Do me a favor," said Rowen, "don't say that."

Sammy's jaw dropped, as if he was only now understanding Rowen's mood. He held back a moment, as if he had a response, then he exhaled and let it go. He was limp in Rowen's hands and quiet all the way to the truck until the doors slammed and then he said, "I was going to thank you, but now I gotta know, what did you get me out of there for?"

Rowen pushed the fan all the way to high and let the blasting air fill the pause between them.

"I want to know about Eden."

Sammy snorted. "What if I tell you to go to hell? You going to take me back up there and get your money back?"

"No."

"I was never anything in White Rock until a white woman got killed. Now, I got lots of white friends, Mr. Rowen. Lots of white men want to talk to me. Well, I'm tired. I don't want to talk right now. I want to go home and have a shower. Did you know they let Fletcher have showers?"

"Why are you thinking of me as one of them? Don't we know one another better than that? You know I tried to take care of her. I just want to know what happened."

He put the truck in gear, thinking that if the truck was in motion and Sammy thought he was going home, he might start talking.

"But why do you want to know? That's a situation we've got to understand. 'Cause my hunch is you want someone to lay gentle soft hands on your head and say, 'You're forgiven, son.' Well, you got to buttonhole Jesus for that, not me. Hey, what are we stopping for?"

"I stopped at the diner. I thought you'd want something hot to eat."

"Now you've lost your mind. I can't go in here."

"I thought I'd run in and get you a plate."

"I don't want anything to eat. Give me a cigarette."

Rowen lit one and handed it to him. Sammy cracked the window open.

Eden

"He beat her. You know that, right?"

With the engine off, a chill seeped through the doors.

"No, I didn't."

Sammy laughed. "I wish I was a seeing man right now so I could see the look on your face while you sit there spouting your lies."

"She never said anything to me. I guess she talked to you."

"She didn't have to say anything to me. It is damn funny that a blind man could figure out what a seeing man can't see."

"She was helping you with the food cart. Everyone knew about that. Why'd you let her do it?"

"We were helping each other. Whatever anyone was saying, they lined up around the block for her hush puppies. Sometimes, people seen her there and somebody'd call her a white trash whore and you know how she'd answer? She'd say, 'You go ahead and tell all your friends I'm here and I'm proud to be seen with a man who went out and raised himself up and every one of us along with him while you sat here safe on your sorry ass.'"

"If you knew he was beating her, why didn't you tell somebody? Why didn't you do something?"

"You mean, tell you? Because of all of us sitting here, who could do more than you? I was doing something. She was giving me money to save for her. What she planned to do was run away with the kids, as soon as she could get enough together."

"Were you going to go with her?"

Sammy took another drag and exhaled a cloud of smoke.

"Damn, you're a sad man, Rowen Hart. I

believe you're even sorrier than me. If I'd known what that son-of-a-bitch was planning, I would have taken that bullet myself."

I would have too, thought Rowen, but he was in too big of a hurry to uncover the truth, if he could.

"Did you love her?"

"You don't want to know if I loved her. That ain't what you're asking. You want to know if a colored man fucked the girl you loved."

"All right, goddamnit it. That's what I want to know."

Sammy flicked the butt out of the window. "Now I got a question for you, boy. What difference does it make?"

The week before Christmas, Rowen sat in his office late every night and drank and smoked. Still the holiday he was trying to shut out flashed through the closed blinds in blinking greens and reds.

One night he heard the key turn in the lock, and he knew exactly who it was. He'd known this confrontation was rumbling toward him and he hadn't cared. *Let it come.* And there she was, Jewell, only she'd brought Lilly and Rose with her. All three were dressed in coats, hats, gloves. Jewell was in the middle, holding the girls' hands.

He was sorry the girls were here; sorry they were seeing him this way.

"Rowen, I've tried you on the phone a dozen times. Why aren't you picking up?"

"I didn't want to be disturbed."

"Men are calling the house all the time now

because they can't reach you here. How long is this going to go on?"

"I don't know."

"How much longer can we afford for it to go on?"

"Work's slow right now. Once the holidays are over, I'll get something going."

"We're on our way to the school. It's the school program tonight. The girls are both in it. We thought we'd stop by and get you."

"Thanks, but I can't make it. Y'all go on. I'll see you afterwards."

"This has got to stop. You are ruining their holiday. They don't understand this, Rowen. They don't understand why some woman dying—someone they didn't even know—is taking their father away from them."

"She wasn't just 'some woman' and you know that."

"She wasn't a fairy princess either. I know you and your mama brought her up and you think of her as a little girl. But she made her own choices. All on her own. Without anyone standing in her way. She could have gotten help from her Uncle Franklin. She threw that away. Just as she wanted to. She married the Aldrick boy. No one forced her to, even if she was having his baby. That was her choice, Rowen."

"So it's her own fault she got shot?"

"Well, what was she doing with Sammy? I'm not saying Fletcher's telling the truth, but a white woman in the public company of a colored man, how could she have not known? And what if Fletcher is telling the truth? Is she such a white lamb then?"

"You were always hateful to her, always. Hateful from the very first."

He watched as Jewell's jaw clenched. "I want to know. Did you love her?"

"I never slept with her if that's what you mean."

Jewell slapped her hands over Lilly's ears.

"Rowen Hart, in front of the children. Shame on you! You know what? I am not fooling with this anymore. We are going on to their program. Then we are going home. And whether you are there or not, we're leaving. I am taking the girls and going back to Daddy's. And we are staying there, Rowen, through the holiday and on, until you stop your lusting after a ghost."

Lilly broke away from her mother and threw her arms around his neck.

"Don't let her take us to Pa-Pa's, Daddy. Come home with us, please."

The intensity of her grip stirred Rowen from his stupor. He turned his cheek to hers and stroked her hair.

"It's all right, Lilly, go on with your mother. I'll be along."

"She's always loved you more than anyone. And this is what you do to her."

"I'll be there with you on Christmas day and we'll all open presents together."

Lilly squeezed him tighter.

"C'mon, silly," Jewell urged. "You don't want everyone to see you with a sourpuss face at your program, do you?"

Lilly began to cry.

Sometime in the last year, Rowen had noticed that matters between Lilly and her mother always

funneled down a channel that dead-ended with Lilly in tears and Jewell seething with frustration. The more he'd watched, the more helpless he had felt to derail either of them. But neither did he want to be the cause of their skirmishes.

"Quit this fuss, Lilly. Do as your mother says. You don't want a paddling, do you?" He stood and pulled away from her.

Jewell grabbed her arm.

"Let's go to Pa-Pa's and get your face cleaned up. We'll need to hurry. How are you going to feel if we're late, young lady? Everyone is going to be staring at us. Is that what you want? In front of your friends? At Christmastime?"

Rowen closed the door behind them.

JAMIE LISA FORBES

14

On New Year's Day, following days of icy sleet, the sky cleared and split open icicle blue over the bare tree crowns. A flock of cardinals perched on the branches, their reds cherry bright, like the last remnants of the holiday. They hardly stirred as they soaked up the new sunlight. Melting ice dripped from Rowen's eaves as he sat slumped in his porch rocker.

Smoke curled up over the rooftops; he thought it was odd for someone to be having a bonfire at noon on New Year's Day. He lit one cigarette and then another while the phone rang and rang. It wasn't until sirens broke out all over the sleepy town, like baying hounds, that he decided to pick up the phone.

The caller was from the sheriff's office. The old age home Rowen had built with Claude was burning down. And Franklin White was missing. Would Rowen go look for him?

Rowen growled back, why were they asking him? He hadn't seen Franklin White since Coman had put him in there. Why would anyone think he would know where Franklin had gone to? The old man still had a house, didn't he? Had they checked there?

They had checked there, the caller said. Hadn't he and Franklin been good friends? All those fishing trips they took every fall. That's what folks remembered anyway. And hadn't he let Franklin's niece, what's-her-name, the one who had gotten herself killed, stay at his place?

Eden.

Yeah, that was her. Everyone knew that Rowen had been friendly with her. Maybe her passing had upset the old man somehow.

Rowen asked, were they sure that Franklin wasn't somewhere in the building.

The fire had started in his room, but no he wasn't there. If Rowen didn't want to go out, well they were sorry they'd troubled him.

"I'll go," said Rowen.

First, he drove to the fire. From behind the barricades, he could see that the roof was gone and only the framing remained. The rest of the residents, those who hadn't been picked up by relatives, were wrapped in blankets. The air reeked of char. Nearly everyone Rowen knew, white and colored, had abandoned their New Year's Day festivities and come to watch, the enormity of the fire reflected in their faces. They'd all been drawn here, as to any other White Rock spectacle. Some force was at play that both lured and devoured.

By the time Rowen turned away, the clouds had barreled in again. He drove through the empty downtown streets, past Franklin's old bank, the Sears store and around the courthouse. He wove in and out of the residential streets, past the house where he'd grown up, past his mother's and Adeline's house. He turned onto the main road out of town and drove past the hardware store, the Ford dealership and the new hamburger joint freshly sprouted from its roots in the big cities. His town. He saw these places not as destinations he'd visited a thousand times or more, but as someone passing through would see them: tawdry, grimy, old.

He flipped around and searched the downtown again. This time, he drove down each alley, pausing to look up at each fire escape. Sleet fell. If Franklin was still alive and had any sense left in him, he would have to find shelter. Rowen cursed the man who'd called him. Franklin must have had closer friends who would know better where he might be. And what about Coman anyway? He didn't see her out here driving around. For all Rowen knew, Franklin might not even know his name anymore, much less recognize him. What a fool notion that anyone had thought to connect him with Franklin White.

To hell with it. He decided to go to Jewell's parents and see his daughters. He thought of Jewell opening the door, the usual judgments stamped on her face. Seemed like she should be softening up by now. What was there left to fight about? Everything having to do with Eden had been swept away from them, carried off in a tide. When she opened the

door, he'd ask her to come home before she could say anything.

Just a quick detour home for a shot of whiskey first.

Through the sleet, he saw a figure in front of his house wearing nothing more than a pair of pajamas. Rowen jumped out of his truck. He flinched at the ice pouring down the back of his collar, but it was just as shocking to find the old man, the object of the search, Franklin White, drenched and wretched right there before him.

Rowen realized he hadn't wanted to find him.

"Franklin, what are you doing here? You got everybody torn up wondering where you are."

Franklin's jaw dropped slightly, and it seemed as if bones in his skull were about to break through his skin.

"I don't want anything to do with them."

"Let's get you inside. You're going to freeze in those wet clothes."

Rowen yanked Franklin through the laundry room into the kitchen. He tossed his own wet coat on the floor, stripped Franklin naked and toweled him down.

"I'll call the sheriff and tell him to bring some clothes."

"I don't want anyone coming here. I don't want anyone seeing me."

"What are you talking about? They're out there looking for you."

Steam fogged up Franklin's glasses. "I want you to help me to leave. I've got to go away and never be seen again. I meant to kill myself, Rowen, I tried. But I'm a coward, I couldn't do it."

JAMIE LISA FORBES

"You're ill. Let me get you some coffee."

"That's why I set the room on fire. But then the smoke was choking me. I got scared and ran out."

"You're out of your mind. You probably dropped your cigarette butt on the mattress. It was just a bad accident. Everyone got out all right. No one's been hurt. And you're all right. White Rock just won't have an old aged home anymore. That would make Claude happy. He always said old people need to be set out on their front porches to share their lessons with all the world, they didn't need to be warehoused in glorified crypts. Think about it, you can go home to your own front porch."

Rowen heard the floor creak behind him. He jumped and turned to see Lilly standing in the doorway with water running off her hair. And though she was soaked through, his first thought was that she was staring at a naked man.

He threw a towel around Franklin's waist and shouted, "What are you doing here?"

"What are you doing with that man without any clothes, Daddy?"

"He's sick, that's all. Where's your mama?"

"She's still at Pa-pa's. I told her I was coming home. I didn't want to stay there anymore. I wanted to be here with you."

"She told you not to go out in this, didn't she?"

"I can take care of myself."

"You waited until her back was turned."

"It wasn't like I was going to get lost. I know my way home."

"Go on up to your room and get dry, please."

"Are you going to take the strap to me?"

"No, Lilly, would you please go on upstairs."

"Mama will want you to take the strap to me."

"We'll talk it over in a few minutes."

"You didn't say who that man is."

Franklin's head dropped, and he croaked out sobs that sounded more animal-like than human. "I wanted to kill myself because of what I done to her."

"I am going to take that strap to you, Lilly, if you don't go upstairs right now."

Lilly vanished from the doorway.

Rowen wrapped a fresh towel around Franklin's shoulders and set him down in a chair.

"You're mixed up, Franklin, you got it all wrong. You were in the rest home the whole time. Her husband shot her. He's in jail. You didn't have anything to do with it."

"Listen, Rowen. How it happened was Coman asked me to do it. She told me she wanted him dead. I couldn't say no to my baby sister."

Franklin's towel slipped to the floor. Rowen didn't bend to pick it up.

"Where was the harm if Coman was free to have the life she deserved? She'd made a mistake, but she'd spent years paying for it. Whitney couldn't provide for them. No one would miss him."

"Except his daughter."

"I believed I could give her and her mother a better life."

"What about the pipe wrench?"

"It was on the floor of his car within his reach. I was sure he was going to pick it up and strike me. My heart was pounding so hard, Rowen. I was in fear for my life, but then he looked up and saw her and told her to get back in the house. And the last thing he shouted was that he loved her."

"She didn't hear him because you fired the shot."

Franklin broke into a fresh round of howls. "I meant to save her. How could I know it would all go so horribly wrong?"

"Go horribly wrong? Everyone called her a liar. Because you called her a liar."

"I meant to make it right."

"You weren't ever going to make it right."

Franklin picked the towel off the floor, took a corner of it and wiped his glasses.

"If I went to prison who was going to be there for her and her mother? The fact that no one believed her — it was for her own good, that's what I thought. My whole life was ahead of me."

"You didn't do anything for her. It was Adeline and Mama and me."

"I begged Coman to get the child. The only way I could finally get her to go was to promise that we'd send her away to school. And when they'd moved to Lumberton, I sent money every month. Coman said she couldn't ask her husband to support the child."

Rowen looked out on the darkening street and the houses grown so familiar to him. Tawdry, grimy, old.

"Where are Eden's children?"

"Coman sent them to the orphanage."

He imagined picking the phone up, dialing the sheriff.

"Why me, Franklin?"

"I've always known that you never stopped loving her."

Eden

"It wasn't enough."

"You pitied her, then. Pity me as you pitied her. Say you forgive me."

"Where's the need? You didn't lose anything. You never went through even an hour of suffering. You held the whole town in your hand."

"When she was killed, then I understood. An eye for an eye, Rowen. I meant to close the door and let the smoke do its work."

"You'll get away with that, too, won't you?"

"Haven't I treated you like my own? Haven't I spoken well of you in every corner of this town, in spite of what your daddy did, humiliating your mother? Say you forgive me. I'll go to prison now if you want."

"All those years when you could have spoken out and told the truth. What would that have meant to her?"

"It would have ruined me."

Rowen felt the swell of memories flood the room: his father's funeral and his mother's illness and that sweat box of a tin shack in the country and Eden's Pepto-Bismol colored bed and Claude with his yellow dog at the front gate. And above all— over everything—Eden in her blazing sunflower dress speaking truth to a roomful of people, and it hadn't saved her.

"I don't want that coffee, but would you mind if I had a drink?"

Rowen poured two glasses. What was he doing? What was wrong with him? He ought to heave this man out of his house. Better still, shouldn't he yank his own shotgun out of the shed.

He set Franklin's glass on the table. Then he picked up the phone. After he dialed the first number, he paused. A pool of water spread out from under the dining room table over Jewell's polished floor. He bent down and saw Lilly under the table, huddled and shivering, with her arms wrapped tightly about her knees.

Eden

15

The years that followed Eden's death all revolved around one point — the Saturday afternoon every summer where Rowen dropped his daughters back at Jewell's house after their beach vacation. Beginning in January, he'd anticipate picking the girls up and seeing how they'd changed and grown. Then, when his two weeks arrived at last, the time seemed to pass in seconds, not days. He would find them a house right on the dunes. Day after day, they would haul out beach chairs and umbrellas and camp along the surf until the girls' hair turned white and their skin brown as coffee. Sunset at the end of each day always came as a surprise with the sun dropping like a penny into the waves, splashing colors on the tattered clouds. Then he'd take them to the fish shack and let them eat all the fried flounder and hush puppies they wanted, even if it was ten o'clock at night.

But the year paused while he sat parked in front of his old house in White Rock, long after he'd hugged them goodbye. He was a man split in two in those moments. One half of him could step right out of the car back into the life he'd had in White Rock. He saw himself walking through the front door of the house—his house—where Jewell's voice, even on bad days, was comfortably familiar. He could hear her ask for anything—maybe more shelves for the girls' closets—and he could go to the drawers in the laundry room and find all his tools still there, everything just as he had left it.

Year after year on those hot Saturday afternoons, he sat there measuring the space between the car and the front door—short, yet at the same time infinite.

His second life had begun with the last time he had seen Coman. Two months after Franklin White had died of pneumonia, they had met in a cluttered law office in White Rock. The circumstances that had drawn them together made his head spin. No way that nineteen-year old boy back in his dirt yard could have imagined what would come to pass or what would move him to seek Coman out, as rattled as he had been by her back then.

And how was it that he had ever felt cowed by this hunch-backed old woman sitting across from him?

She reached in her purse for her compact mirror, primped her hair, adjusted her lipstick, all

in a pretense to flaunt her control over him before she said, "Have you been out to the grave?"

She couldn't even guess how little these civilities meant to him now. "Whose?" he barked, "Franklin's?"

She glared at him, the tactic that had succeeded all those years ago.

"Surely you are not toying with me after the lifetime of suffering I've endured. Eden's grave, of course. You must have noticed it's rose granite. Franklin, God rest his soul, told me to get the finest money could buy."

The smugness—how solidly it had borne her through the slop she'd made of her own life and those around her. God, he'd love to see her face if he picked up the phone and, this time, reported everything Franklin had told him, all of it. The satisfaction would be more than he'd ever feel looking at rose granite.

But he wouldn't be the one to upend her and she knew it. She knew he didn't dare risk what he had now staked his whole life to do. What he knew Eden would have wanted him to do.

So on those Saturday afternoons parked in front of his old house, his other self—his newer self—called him back to Bellpointe, where his children waited, children who hadn't been acquired in the normal way. Claude's voice rang in his head, as clear as he'd heard it on that winter evening years ago: *Our pretty rat catcher has no future here at all. Take her out of here, Rowen, get yourself an education and never come back.*

Once again, he could feel his boyhood reaction throb through the veins in his forehead. *The old man doesn't know what he's talking about.*

JAMIE LISA FORBES

What kind of a talk would they have had had the old man lived? At least he'd be able to say that the education he ended up having hadn't been wasted. No question about it, there was no future in the "hamlet," as Claude called it, for Eden's children. Turned out it was easy to discard the comfort he used to feel in knowing the town and everyone in it. Turned out that comfort was just a tattered fancy he'd clung to. *Delusion Claude, all eaten through with rot.*

By now, Eden's children—his children— would be wearing out his Cousin Mabel's last nerve. Some kind of message always came while he was at the beach. Crystal had fallen down the steps and busted her front tooth out. Or Birch hadn't quite caught the baseball thrown at him and had been taken to get stitches in his head. Cousin Mabel always ended these messages with "Don't you worry, we'll be all right," and Rowen was never sure that she wasn't being sarcastic, though once he returned home, she greeted him with the same warmth she'd always shown.

It was a sorry thing, how he'd behaved toward her as a boy, how he'd always been ashamed of her. When he showed up at her front door with three children, she hadn't acted as if she was a bit surprised. She didn't question any of the decisions he had made. She listened, and then helped him with everything to start his new family: a house along the sound, a job at the store she ran with her husband. She found a place for his mother, an old mansion turned into a rest home for elderly women.

Eden

It was as if he had come begging to her as the cripple.

Once settled, he and his new family were no better than strangers at first. The early months had been a dark jungle of tears and tantrums and nightmares. Then one day he'd come in the house to find his framed photograph of Jewell and his girls broken in pieces on the floor. He stared at the mess, not wanting the three of them to see that he was thinking he'd left his children and it was a mistake.

He knelt down and picked up a glass shard.

College of Life. Final exam.

"Who did this?"

The three of them stood wide-eyed and tensed. Not me, everyone had murmured.

One after another he piled the glass shards to the side.

"Y'all get away from this glass before you step on it."

Audrey Faye spoke up.

"It was an accident—Daddy."

One word. No sense in fussing over it when any of them could cut themselves at any second. He wiped his eyes with the back of his hand.

"I know," he said.

On the third summer after he left White Rock, Lilly wouldn't get out of the car when he drove them home.

She watched Rose run inside and then she said, "I want to go with you, Daddy."

He stared at her quietly, while in his head, his separate selves collided head on. Part of his pact with Jewell was never to tell his children of his second family. To Jewell, the thought that he'd take these other children was near blasphemy, she would never accept them. She would never leave White Rock. At the time, it had seemed like such a small thing to agree to everything she had asked when it had been his choice to disrupt their lives. Now, faced with the pleading in his daughter's eyes, all he could think was that everything he had tried to do had ended in wreckage.

There was no turning back now, no way out.

"Why do you say that? You love your mother, you love Rose, don't you?"

"Nothing I do is ever right for Mama."

"That's not true, Lilly. She's very proud of you."

"You say that but you're not here and you don't know. Everything I do is wrong. She hates the music I listen to. She says it's nigger music. She'll tell me to dust her crystal and then she'll come after me and shove the rag in my face and say that I didn't hardly touch it. She says I'm so lazy I'll never amount to anything."

Rowen ran his fingers through her bangs. "I know it's hard." He swallowed. "Everyone's got hard things to do sometimes. I'd like you do something for me, even if it's hard."

She stared at him, not believing him, but wanting to please him at the same time.

"Forget about your own self and think about your mama. When she asks you to do something, she's not being mean. She's not picking on you. She just needs you, and sometimes she doesn't know how to say it. You have to take care of her now."

"Rose will take care of her."

"I can't take you with me, Lilly. I love you, but there's no way I can explain it. You just got to trust me and understand that this is your place here. With your mama."

"Why?"

"Go on, your mother's getting anxious waiting for you."

"But why are you living by yourself and so far away from all of us?"

Jewell was standing at the passenger door. She opened it and glared at Rowen.

"Hey, Jewell," he said.

"What are you sitting there for, Lilly? I'm burning up in this heat waiting for you."

As she yanked Lilly out of the car, he called after her, "Write me, honey."

He sent letters and money in between visits. No one ever answered.

On the fourth summer, as they sat in the car in front of the house, Lilly waited until Rose had gone and then turned to him.

"I found out why you're not coming home, Daddy. You're living with a colored woman."

"Where did you hear that?"

"Mama says it's all over town. You're living with a colored woman and it's sinful."

"I'm sure there's a lot of things you're going to hear about me. And you can always ask me if they're true or not. But I'm not living with a colored woman."

"Can you please stay until tomorrow and go to church with us?"

"Why do you want me to do that?"

"If you'd just sit in church and listen, Jesus might make you see that you should come home to us."

He shifted in his seat and looked over the steering wheel, down the street toward the turn he'd make to leave town.

"It's not that easy, Lilly. Your mama's coming out. You know she hates being out in this heat."

He was not living with a colored woman, but he was seeing one. Whatever Cousin Mabel might have said in passing to someone in White Rock was sure to have been twisted.

The woman was the head chef for one of the restaurants patronized by tourist Yankees, and twice a week she would walk down to the pier to barter for flounder. He'd watch her while smoking outside of Mabel's store. She was taller than he was and carried herself shoulders arched back and proud with her chin up-tilted to the sun. Like Cleopatra would have done. Cleopatra—that's what he began to call her.

One morning she pivoted and started toward him. He thought of ducking back in the store, but he'd been caught. It was clear that she knew she'd been watched. He ground out his cigarette.

"Why do you always stare at me and never speak?"

"I didn't mean anything by it. I'll stop."

"Aren't you going to speak to me?"

No woman where he was from ever stood this close to a man she didn't know or spoke so directly.

"No. I'm old enough to be your daddy."

"Why does that matter?"

She was awful forward all right, but there

was that warmth in her eyes, a burnish in her skin. He felt a need to shield himself, deflect her from the orbit of his two families and the two women he had lost.

"You don't want to mess with me. You don't want anything to do with me."

"Because you are old?"

"It's more than that."

"When you change your mind, my name is Mona."

"Hey, I don't mean to be rude. I'm Rowen, Rowen Hart. I work for Mabel here at the store. She's my cousin."

"I look forward to seeing you again, Rowen Hart."

She tipped that sharp little chin and wheeled in the direction she had come. With every stride, he longed for her to at least glance back his way. He looked down at his work boots and his daddy came to mind. His daddy and his mama both. Funny how the image of them singing in church, shoulder to shoulder, popped up in his head. He heard their harmony as clear as if he'd heard it yesterday.

> *When we reach that shining city,*
> *our race on earth is done,*
> *We'll all shout loud Hosanna.*
> *Deliverance has come.*

His daddy had a bass voice that resonated to the farthest corners of the church. And after the service, he'd linger in the foyer and grasp every man's hand. No one, except maybe Jesus gazing down from the windows, had guessed what was in his heart.

What would Daddy say as Rowen stood here fretting over whether he should follow a colored woman? As if he should even care. He'd despised that man for years. Every memory was tagged with the reminder of how he'd ruined their lives.

Or had he? His daddy's death had opened the door to things that might never have happened. It had brought Eden to him. Eden hoeing and singing in her garden. If his daddy hadn't killed himself, Rowen might have gone to college, but any instruction would have been prattle when set up against all he'd learned from Adeline. To think that Adeline wouldn't be allowed in the hallowed halls of higher education when there'd never be a finer teacher anywhere.

If his daddy hadn't killed himself, he would not, just now, be putting one foot in front of the other to follow that young woman and listen to what she had to say. It would never have been possible. Whatever Rowen would have been, wherever he would have gone, he wouldn't be taking these steps just now. *Goodbye, Daddy.*

He followed Mona all the way to her fancy restaurant where she served him low country boil, grits and tea. And days later, she came home to meet his children. Once she crossed his threshold, memories of both Jewell and Eden began to settle in his mind. Not unmourned. Not forgotten. Just no longer present in the air around him.

The year Lilly turned fifteen, she wouldn't come out to the car when he went to pick them up for their beach vacation. Rose came. He hugged her and then she settled in the back. Their small talk dwindled as the heat in the car grew stifling.

Jewell opened the car door and sat in the passenger seat.

"Lilly says she's not coming. She says she doesn't want to go."

"Why?"

Jewell shrugged. "She says last year she was away from her friends and she didn't have any fun. Rowen, you need to know, I can't handle her these days. I think she wants to chase after some boy."

Rowen looked back toward the house. "She's watching us from the window."

"She's behaving shamefully. This spring, I found out she was stealing my makeup and taking it to school. I sent her to speak with the pastor—she doesn't listen to me anymore—and she came home sobbing as if someone had died and saying how sorry she was and how she finally understood her sin and she didn't want to burn in hell for eternity away from me and Rose and she was going to turn herself around. She dropped at my feet and began to pray right there. We prayed together. But the very next week she stole the makeup again. And put it on at school."

"You think I should go talk to her?"

"She doesn't want to talk to you. She doesn't want to see you."

"If Lilly's not going, I ain't going neither," said Rose, and she got out of the car.

Jewell stayed in her seat and watched Rose run to the front door. "I was sorry to hear about your mother, Rowen. Was she living with you?"

"No, Mabel found her a nice place where they cared for her very well. I think she was happy there. The last couple of years she hasn't recognized me."

"Poor Rita. All the shocks she had throughout her life. She probably didn't want to remember anymore."

Rowen didn't respond. If Jewell wasn't yet implying that he was to blame for his mother's decline, she was about to start down that path. Maybe she was right. Maybe that was another crime he should accept as his. It wouldn't help anything if he told her that before Rita's mind failed, she had approved of his plan to take Eden's children. If he added that detail, Jewell would flare up like a lit match thrown on gasoline.

"I heard you're engaged," he said.

"And I hear you're living with a colored woman," she snapped. "There's no end to it, Rowen, no end to the scandal you've brought down on your children. Look what it's doing to your daughter. She's turning into a harlot, just like your precious Eden."

"How can what I'm doing have anything to do with what she's doing when I've done just like you wanted and not told them anything? We've kept it all from them. Maybe Lilly would be better off if she knew the truth."

"She doesn't want truth. She wants her daddy."

"She has me. She's always had me. And Rose too."

Jewell was crying now. "The lies you tell yourself, Rowen," she said, before getting out of the car and slamming the door.

He hadn't been able to prevent her flaring up after all.

Eden

He forgot all about his faulty lungs, jumped down the ladder and met them before they reached the gate. He swept Lilly off her feet. She hugged him back for a moment and then pushed away. Up close, he saw her clothes were rumpled, as if she'd slept in them. She looked at Audrey, then at him, and without one word, began to blubber.

He gripped her shoulder. "Are you all right? How did you get here?"

Audrey spoke up. "She just walked right into the store, Daddy. She told Cousin Mabel that she was Lilly Hart and she'd been traveling for two days to find her daddy. Cousin Mabel asked her if her mama knew where she was and she said no, she didn't. Mabel says the worry is gonna kill her poor mama. She told me to take her on up to the house. On the way here, I told her that my name is Audrey Faye Hart and that I'm her sister and she said that couldn't be, that she only had one sister back in White Rock."

"Daddy," said Lilly between sobs, "you didn't really adopt three children, did you?"

Rowen took his handkerchief and wiped her face. "Let's start with how you got here. Since your mother doesn't know."

Lilly sniffled and glanced at Audrey. "I got a boy to drive me, but his car broke down, so I left him and hitched the rest of the way."

"You left him? Why? Who was this boy?"

Lilly looked away. "Nobody, just a boy I know from school. He was a senior, so he had a car."

Rowen let her response hang in the air. Daughter and stranger at the same time. She hadn't traveled overnight with a boy who was nobody.

And then there were her clothes and hair. She stared back at him, the tears streaming down her face. She knew what he was thinking.

"Are you all right?" he asked again.

She nodded toward Audrey. "Does she have to hear?"

"Audrey, go in the house and tell Mona that Lilly's here all the way from White Rock." After the door had closed behind Audrey, he said, "Now, tell me about this boy."

"His name's Bentsen. I've been seeing him since last fall. Mama wouldn't let me go. She said I'm not old enough to ride in boys' cars. So I would tell her lies about where I was and who I was with. No one else liked him. No other girls would go out with him. I didn't really like him either. I pretended to like him because he had a car and he'd take me where I wanted to go. It was easy to make him do what I wanted, because no one else would look at him. Right after his graduation party ended, I told him to take me here. We left last night, and the car broke down early this morning."

"But you didn't want to bring him here?"

She shook her head.

"Kind of harsh, isn't it, Lilly?"

"I told you. He ain't nothing to me."

Rowen paused. "Did anything happen between the two of you?"

He watched her smooth her hair with her hands while she reckoned with whether to pitch more lies. The young woman emerging in her face, he could tell, was ready to shed the lies.

"I wanted something to happen, but nothing did. I'm sad about it, and glad at the same time because I didn't want to fake something that's

supposed to matter. I could see that wouldn't do me any good. I'm telling you the truth, Daddy."

"I never said you weren't. I'm trying to figure things out here."

"Bentsen doesn't matter. Coming here wasn't about him. It was about you."

She still hadn't answered the question of whether she was all right. But whatever had happened physically seemed beside the point. She had been maturing for a long time without him. And whatever had happened with this Bentsen character, she had left him behind and passed into womanhood. He took her cue and let it drop.

"Let's go into the house," he said.

The children and Mona all crowded awestruck in the entryway.

"You've met Audrey. This is Crystal and Birch and Mona."

He watched the thoughts fly right off Lilly's face. *This is the colored woman he's been living with.*

Mona held out her hand. "Pleased to meet you, Lilly."

He should have remembered Mona's boldness. She never paid any mind to the subtleties of racial decorum. She'd made a name for herself here, and she didn't have to. Still, she'd heard enough of White Rock to know that Lilly hadn't shaken a colored woman's hand in all her life. He remembered his own mingling of revulsion and guilt the first time he'd touched Sammy's hand.

Lilly barely brushed Mona's fingertips, and then her hand dropped to her skirt where she tried to wipe it without anyone's notice.

When she saw that Mona had seen what she'd done, she said, "I didn't mean anything disrespectful."

Mona's gaze lifted from Lilly's hand to her face.

"You are a brave girl to have struck out on your own. Now that you are here, I hope what you see will change you forever. Whatever your feelings about me, us, you are welcome here. Your father has missed you and your sister for a long time."

Lilly turned to Rowen. "Are these her children?"

"Lilly," said Rowen, "I have to call your mother first thing. Go out on the deck and wait for me."

When he got off the phone, he found Audrey blocking his path to the back door. "I asked Lilly if she would go out with us to hunt oysters tomorrow. She said she ain't never done anything like that before. She can borrow Mona's waders."

"She'll have to do it some other time. Her mama's starting out from White Rock tonight. I expect she'll be here in the morning."

"What if Lilly doesn't want to go? You want her here with us, don't you?"

Jewell had been so distraught on the telephone that he'd felt that he had no right to suggest that Lilly stay. Hadn't he gambled his family, and lost? It had been enough just to know that Lilly had come all this way to see him.

"If it was up to me, she could stay as long as she liked. But her mama needs her."

"It was Lilly's decision to make this trip," said Mona. "Has anyone asked her what she needs?"

"All right, everybody," said Rowen, "why don't y'all go eat dinner and let us be for a while."

Outside, he was surprised to find a thumbnail moon already brightening in the dusk.

Eden

Fireflies pulsed high in the trees. Boat lights bobbed on the water. All these points of light traveling their destined paths—that was a comfort, at least, in the murk of his own self-doubts. He sat down next to his daughter, and glanced back to make sure Mona wasn't watching, then pulled out his cigarette pack. His lighter illumined her face.

"I thought you didn't want to be around me anymore," he said. "Remember, when you didn't want to go to the beach?"

"I just didn't want to go the beach anymore. That's all."

"If you wanted to see me, why didn't you call?"

"Because then Mama would have said when I could come and if I could come and for how long. I wanted to see for myself what had happened. You've told lies, just like me. You said you weren't living with a colored woman."

"I wasn't living with her back when you asked. That came afterwards."

"You gave us up for her and these kids."

"These kids aren't Mona's. They're Eden's."

Their eyes locked for several moments until he saw that she remembered.

"That old man said they'd been sent to the orphanage. That naked old man in the kitchen."

"After that, I went and got them."

"That was the last night you were at our house."

"Yes."

"Mama's never stopped saying that Eden was white trash who got murdered by her husband, and that she had it coming."

"Is that what you still think, after what you heard that night?"

"I didn't know what to think. You wouldn't give me any other way to think. I just wanted all this to be over. And to have our family back."

"All right. I'll tell you now. I knew Eden from the time she was a little girl and none of those things you've heard about her are true."

His cigarette had burned out and he could no longer see Lilly's face. Above them, a veil of mist drifted over the moon, lingered and then tore away.

"You loved her? More than Mama? More than us?"

"No, Lilly. I couldn't ever love Eden as much as I loved your mama and you and Rose. I was your age when I met Eden, and she changed my life to where it couldn't ever be the way it was before. She was like those fireflies out there. You can't take your eyes off them. They draw your soul with them as they rise higher and higher. I'm telling you the truth like you told me the truth. I couldn't take my eyes off Eden. But she wasn't your mama.

"Your mama dropped out of high school so we could get married. We loved each other very much. We were hopeful, and you and Rose made us want to try hard to make the world right for you.

"I know I gave up the right a long time ago to ask you to forgive me. You can't hold on to anything, Lilly, the years just spill by, and Eden's dying became just another thing that happened, another thing that's covered over in all the living we're doing for today. But on that night you were hiding under the table, hearing all kinds of ugliness I wish you hadn't heard, all I could see in front of

me, the only thing I could see at all, was a choice of crimes and a choice of punishments.

"I never stopped loving you and Rose..." and then he began to cough.

"Daddy, are you all right?"

The screen door banged, and Audrey came out carrying a platter. "Mona says to bring y'all some nutrition. We got fried oysters and coleslaw. I fixed the coleslaw myself. Daddy, I smell smoke out here. Mona said to tell you she's going to shred your clothes so you can't hide those cigarettes anymore."

Rowen stood up. "I'm fine. Pollen's got me, that's all. I just need a drink. Y'all go ahead and eat."

Lilly and Audrey exchanged glances.

"Hand 'em over, Daddy," said Lilly.

He placed the pack of cigarettes in her palm and Audrey said, "What will you pay us not to tell?"

"A couple of Cheerwines at the store?"

"That," said Lilly, "and a dozen moon pies."

"You can eat that many?"

"No." She nodded toward Audrey. "Half are for her."

"All right, y'all eat, and we'll go."

He watched them from the kitchen while he ran himself a glass of water. Audrey pulled out a transistor radio and a tinny-sounding Buddy Holly played over the girls' voices and the rippling water.

Mona put her arm though Rowen's and leaned against him. There wasn't any heft to her, but it felt as if she was holding him up. He patted her hand.

"Will you marry me, Mona?"

"Useless question. You know it's illegal."

"There's someplace out there that'll give us a marriage license. Maybe Las Vegas."

Mona shook her head. "A waste of money. What difference does it make?"

"Because when I'm gone, I want someone to be able to point to a day that I did something right."

"You're always talking about being as old as my father."

"I am."

"Then I will have to think about it."

"Don't wait too long."

"Lilly has had a long day and has a long trip tomorrow. You should make your daughters go to bed."

"First we have to make a trip to the store."

"Why?"

"A man can have a few moon pies with his daughters, can't he?"

"And you're not going to take everybody?"

"You're right. Everyone will go."

He should hustle, the store would be closing soon. But Rowen lingered, feeling the rise and fall of Mona's ribs while the moon wove in and out of the mists.

In the morning, the coffee had just begun to perk when Jewell came. Lilly had slept in Audrey's room, and they were still sleeping when he heard the car. He watched as Jewell stepped out in a shirtwaist dress, heels and a pillbox hat. It made him smile, the thought that she had dressed up to drive all through the night.

When he met her at the door and asked if

she'd like coffee, she answered, "No, thank you. If you'll just get Lilly, we'll be on our way."

Lilly came downstairs. Mona had washed and ironed the blouse she'd worn, and Lilly had swept up her hair in a ponytail, so while there was a wariness between mother and daughter, they both looked handsome, striking.

"Oh, Lilly," Jewell cried, "I'm so glad you're all right. Anything could have happened, just anything."

Lilly hesitated on the stair landing. "I'm sorry, Mama."

Audrey had followed Lilly down the stairs. "Are you Miz Hart?" She walked past Lilly and held out her hand. "I'm Audrey Faye Hart. Lilly and I are sisters."

Jewell touched Audrey's hand briefly. "I'm Miz Coble now. And Lilly is not your sister. She has a sister at home."

Audrey paused, but plunged on. "Miz Coble, we'd like it if you'd let Lilly stay. Just for the summer."

"I can assure you, young lady, Lilly will not be staying here. It's not her home. Rowen...."

Lilly stepped down next to Jewell.

"I'm ready to go, Mama."

Jewell strode ahead to the car, her skirt swishing. Lilly followed. Rowen, with Mona and Audrey, watched them from the front porch.

At the car door, Lilly turned. Audrey raised her hand and waved. Tears started to burn Rowen's eyelids. Maybe he'd never see her again. He gripped the porch railing. It wouldn't be right to call her to come back. A choice of crimes, a choice of punishments, all of it done, set in stone.

Lilly turned and began to come back. Jewell

called her name over and over, each call more frantic than the last.

When Lilly reached the porch, Rowen's voice crackled. "Don't worry. You don't have to do anything for me."

"I'm not doing what I have to do," she answered.

She climbed the porch stairs and placed her hand on top of Rowen's. She looked back at Jewell, frozen next to the car. With her other hand, she squeezed Audrey's.

"This is my sister, Mama."

Jewell looked up and down the street. Rowen knew she was worried people might hear. She came halfway back up the walk.

"Rowen, take her to the car, please."

Rowen met her. He looked down into her eyes for the first time in years and saw there the girl he had known ages ago.

"I want to let go, Jewell," he said gently "Don't you?"

Tears ran from her eyes, matching Rowen's own.

"I don't know if I can, Rowen."

"It's what Lilly wants. You always were a good mother."

She opened her purse, took out her handkerchief and wiped her eyes.

"We'll see." She glanced up and down the street again. "In the meantime, you take care of her, you hear?"

"We'll have her home for school."

Jewell reached down and took his hand. He could hear his waking children call for Mona, who turned and went inside. The sun rose

Eden

ever higher. All around them, bacon fried, boats pushed away from their slips, cicadas whirred, the air warmed.

Still Rowen and Jewell stood hand in hand, as if they were anchoring the world.

JAMIE LISA FORBES

Eden

Acknowledgements

First, thank you to the individuals who contributed to the editing and revisions of this story: Annette Chaudet, Celia Urion and Trish Nelson.

Many thanks to Angela Liverman for her family stories about eastern North Carolina.

I am grateful for the feedback and encouragement from: Letty Coykendall, Lauren Emily Sarraf, Beth Smith, Janet Lane, Jack A. Williams, Susan Eastman and Julee Fortune Marshall. It is thanks to Julee that I have been able to discover the rich heritage of North Carolina.

During the years I worked on this novel, several people passed who had supported and encouraged me and who inspired my work. May their memories be for a blessing: Beverly Swerling, Ruth Ortega Arthur and Debi Bird O'Donnell.

JAMIE LISA FORBES

Eden

About the Author

Jamie Lisa Forbes was raised on a ranch along the Little Laramie River near Laramie, Wyoming. She attended the University of Colorado where she obtained degrees in English and philosophy. After fourteen months living in Israel, she returned to her family's ranch where she lived for another fifteen years.

In 1994, she moved to Greensboro, North Carolina. In 2001, she graduated from the University of North Carolina School of Law and began her North Carolina law practice.

Her first novel, Unbroken, won the WILLA Literary Award for Contemporary Fiction in 2011. Her collection of short stories, The Widow Smalls and Other Stories, won the High Plains Book Awards for a short story collection in 2015.

Her law practice gave her the opportunity to travel many of the back roads of North Carolina and meet the unique and diverse individuals who inspired *Eden*.

CPSIA information can be obtained
at www.ICGtesting.com
Printed in the USA
BVHW041535290720
584765BV00003B/11